Be the first to learn about Raina Joy Wilder's upcoming releases by joining her newsletter!

make me a double

AN ENEMIES-TO-LOVERS ROMANTIC COMEDY

RAINA JOY WILDER

MIRROR HOUSE PRESS

For my mom,
who encouraged me to just write
a happy love story for once.

isadora

LET me tell you what it is I plan to do with my one wild and precious life: read, write, and get a lot of joyful strangers drunk.

Welcome to Gertrude's.

At present, it doesn't look like much—a gutted building that was formerly a Thai restaurant, now heaped with rubble, framed by drywall, and riddled with exposed wires. But consider this a first draft. With some sweat and revision, it will be a masterpiece.

Since my first year studying 20th century literature at Santa Caterina University, I've been dreaming of opening my own literary bar. An elegant retro dive with artisanal drinks named after famous writers from years past, with old-school typewriters on writing desks, decorated with bookshelves and home to weekly open mic nights for local poets. And now, a year after graduation, it's finally happening.

But I'll tell you what I never planned on doing with my

one wild and precious life: ripping out moldy carpeting that is probably older than I am.

Gag. Literally and figuratively. This N-95 mask does nothing.

"You still sure you don't want to hire someone to do this crap?" Zofie asks me, arms crossed, eyeing me and then the carpet and then me again.

I stand up. "What, pay someone thousands of dollars to do something I'm perfectly capable of doing myself?"

"'Capable?' You're about to hurl."

"I need a moment is all."

I step away to the open front doorway and move my mask to the side for a moment to breathe fresh air. Outside, women in sundresses bounce by with shopping bags on the sidewalk and a double-decker with tourists passes by on Riviera Avenue. Those lucky people are probably headed for a day of swimming, sunbathing, and whale watching. When I turn back, Zofie is on the floor in her overalls, tearing the carpet and grunting. Of course she is. Zofie is not only an incredible actress and cute as a button, she's strong as hell. Her dad is a general contractor and quite honestly, I couldn't have done all this without her.

And I don't know what I'm going to do when she moves to LA next month.

"This is how you have to do it," Zofie says, throwing an enormous piece of carpeting on the pile. "Breathe through your mouth if the smell's getting to you. Channel your rage at the carpet. Think about how strong your biceps are gonna be after this."

"You should be a life coach."

"I *am* your life coach. Pro bono, babe."

I get down on my knees next to her, breathe through my mouth, and do what the woman says. I think about things that provoke anger within me. Like people who don't use their turn signals. Or that pretentious guy (named, of all things, Guy) in my poetry workshop senior year who declared the sonnets I wrote were "antiquated and contrived." I start to think about my mom being killed by a drunk driving teenager back in Brockman, but that's too much. The rage, the sadness there, are wells best left untapped, even though it's been almost nine years since it happened. By the time I stand up and assess the damage we've done/progress we've made, there's a mountain of what was once carpeting and my eyes have filled with sweat or tears or a brackish mix of both.

"See?" Zofie says, slapping my arm lovingly with a plastic-gloved hand. "And that's how you do it, you badass bitch. Now buy me a sammich."

"You and your love affair with sandwiches."

"Don't forget beer. Buy me a beer, too."

A prime selling point of this location, besides the fact we're a half-mile from the beach and on the main downtown drag, of course, is the proximity to Gio's. Gio's is the Italian deli on the corner of Riviera and Palmera and you can smell the glorious hot pastrami from half a block away. Gertrude's is a half block up, so lately I eat here often. I would venture to say my affection for their hot pastrami sandwiches edges on an addiction at this point. And Zofie's my enabler.

Gio's is everything you'd imagine an Italian deli to be: long glass case of gleaming deli meats, an assembly line of messy-aproned sandwich-makers, and Gio's son Luca manning the cash register, answering the phone, and shouting orders across the room. There's a cornucopia of Italian canned goods and shelved specialty items in the middle. And in the back, a spread of tables with red-and-white checkered tablecloths where Zofie and I split a hot pastrami and drink tall cans of beer.

"On one hand, I can't wait to get to LA and become this generation's Meryl Streep," Zofie says through a mouthful. "On the other, I could just stay here and marry Luca and eat like a queen."

Luca has asked Zofie out, in a half-joking way that means he's also half-serious, pretty much every single time we've come here. Can't blame the dude; Zofie is gorgeous, with slanted, Slovakian eyes, skin tan as wet sand, and bleached blond hair to her waist. If she wasn't five feet tall, she could probably be a supermodel. That said, what makes Zofie absolute perfection is the fact she wears jogging pants most of the time and keeps her hair in a messy bun on top of her head with a Dodgers cap. Basically, she dresses like a celebrity in hiding and she hasn't even moved to LA to become a star yet. It's still not enough to keep guys from swarming around her like flies.

Like right now for example, the ginger-haired gentleman standing next to the gleaming refrigerated drinks. In addition to a Metallica shirt, board shorts, and checkered Vans, he's got a staring problem and a crooked grin.

"Lookin' good over there," he says.

"Who asked you, perv?" Zofie says, and shows him the chewed-up food inside her mouth.

Even I wince.

"Gross," he says. "I was talking about the sandwich. But thanks, I've lost my appetite now."

"And after seeing you, I've lost my sex drive," she says.

"Christ on a cracker," he mutters, and walks away, shaking his head.

I'm laughing so hard beer comes through my nostrils. The burn!

"Bit much, Zof," I tell her.

"Listen, I'm beyond over these entitled assholes who feel like they can say whatever's on their mind."

"What if he *was* talking about the sandwich?"

She gives me an are-you-kidding-me look.

"You'd better learn to bite your tongue before you start auditioning," I tell her, raising one eyebrow—one of my greatest talents. "You're going to have to regularly deal with some creeps."

"I'd like to see someone try to Harvey Weinstein my ass. I've got a black belt in Judo."

"Yes, I know. You've only mentioned it about every five minutes since we met." I finish my beer in a swig and put it on the table. Maybe it's how fast I downed it or the fact it was an IPA, but a wave of emotion washes over me and I find myself tearing up looking at her—my co-worker at the bar Study Hall where we met, my lover for a fleeting and wild July, my housemate for the last two years, the best friend I've ever had. "I'm going to miss you."

Zofie balls up her sandwich wrapper and tosses it into a garbage can with the grace of a basketball player. "I'm moving ninety miles away and not leaving for two weeks, no need to have an emotional breakdown in a deli." She leans across the table and puts a hand to my face. "You're gonna be just fine. You've got a lot of college buddies here."

"Like who? Most of them moved after graduating."

"Hey, I offered to bring you to LA with me and you said it was—and I quote—'the land of soulless sycophants.'"

"Sorry I said that."

"No, it's why I love you: even your insults are eloquent."

We get up, throw the rest of our trash away, and exit out the back door.

Zofie takes my arm. "We're pursuing our dreams. Both of us. We love it, right?"

"Yes," I agree.

And we do. I just wish our dreams were in the same vicinity. But I adore Santa Caterina, and she can't become the next Meryl Streep unless she moves to Hollywood. So I've got to let her go.

But first, we've got a whole lot of nasty carpet we need to scrap. Tomorrow the flooring company comes in to lay out the white oak floors that cost about as much as a year of my college education. The day after, the electricians are rewiring and installing the new lighting. Then the carpenter comes in to build custom shelving and the stunning bar and after that, my furniture's getting set up and the booze is getting delivered. And in under a month from now? Doors open. I'll officially be a business owner.

Back at Gertrude's, I'm opening the front door while Zofie goes to feed her parking meter when I feel a tap on my shoulder. Turning around, I'm baffled at the sight of the man Zofie had the rude encounter with at the deli. My stomach does an ugly flutter—yikes, did he follow us? Is he stalking us, enraged about how she spoke to him before? But he doesn't appear enraged; he still has that crooked grin on his face. And he's holding a pile of envelopes.

"This your place?" he asks.

"Yeah," I say. "What's up?"

"I believe I got your mail." He looks down at the pile in his arms. "Gertrude?"

"Isadora," I say, puzzled, taking the pile from his hands. "Gertrude's is the name of the bar."

"A bar," he repeats.

I look down at the mail, trying to understand how he had it in the first place. "I'm sorry—who are you?"

"Chuck," he says. "I own the place next door."

"The bead store?" I ask, even more confused. On one side, there's a bead store owned by a hippie woman. On the other, an empty storefront that used to be a diner.

"Do I look like a man who would own a bead store?" he asks, pointing to his Metallica shirt.

"I don't know, I'm not one to stereotype," I say, but no, no he does not look like a man who would own a bead store. Or any store, for that matter. He looks more like someone who is one backwards baseball cap away from belonging at a frat party.

"Your other next door," he says.

"Ahh, you're in the restaurant space."

"Correct."

"Well, this is awkward," I say. "After what my friend said to you in the deli."

"Yeah, that was fun."

"Wasn't it?" I offer a grimacing grin. "So what kind of restaurant are you opening?"

"Not exactly a restaurant," he says, his blue eyes twinkling. "A bar, actually."

I become, in one instant, a woman plummeting toward the center of the earth. This is the *last* thing I expected or wanted to hear. "You're kidding."

"Nope. Brady's. A sports bar."

I sigh in relief. "A *sports* bar," I clarify. "Okay. Well, that's good at least. I'm opening a literary bar, so … pretty different."

"What the hell is a literary bar?" he asks. "A bar where people sit around reading books?"

"No, a bar that celebrates famous writers and the readers who love them." It's my tagline. I know it like I know my own name now.

"And this is a thing people want?" he asks, snickering. "Seriously? Are you being serious?"

"Yes," I say, my cheeks burning.

"So, a nerd bar."

"Better than a jock bar," I can't help myself from replying.

"This should be interesting," he says, smiling wider. He backs away, walking backward toward his storefront. "Well, best of luck to you."

"You too, *Chuck*."

And he's gone. Gone into the store next door. And I'm left with a queasy stomach and a mind racing with about a hundred things I should have said to him but didn't. A nerd bar?! Excuse me?

Zofie approaches with an inquisitive expression on her exquisite face and two iced lattes in hand, the cherub. "Was that the guy from the deli you were just talking to?"

"Yeah, and you're right," I say. "He's a total asshole."

I go inside and try to focus on getting this place ready for the flooring folks, but as I huff and puff and fill up a dumpster, I can't deny the doom that has passed over me and my beloved bar like a dark cloud. There has to be enough business on this block for two bars, right? Because otherwise what I've chosen to do with my wild and precious life might be a wild and precious disaster.

chuck

WHAT A DISASTER OF A BUSINESS VENTURE.

Not mine. I'm talking about Gertrude, Ida, whatever the girl next door's name is—the one who thought it would be a wise idea to launch a business that pairs books with alcohol.

Has she ever tried to read after a few?

I mean, I did acid once and read two pages of *Lord of the Rings* and it was transcendent, but beer? Beer and a *book*?

There was a panicky sec there when she said the word "bar." Then she kept explaining and I realized I was going to ruin her. And I almost felt bad. Almost.

Imagine what my dad would say if I was run out of business by a bar for book nerds. There'd go my inheritance! This area's a tourist trap and a haven for thirsty college bros. Opening a sports bar on this block of Riviera should be about as easy as a taco truck circling the Donner party. Not that I'm worried or anything.

Which is why I don't even mention it to my dad when I

get inside after delivering the mail to what's-her-face. Why throw that into the mix when he already seems prepared for me to fail?

"There you are," Dad says. "I texted you three times. I thought you'd disappeared."

"Told you I was getting lunch."

"What, you go eat a five-course meal?"

No, Dad. I went down the street, moved my car again, grabbed a burger from Char Man's, ate it on the lawn in front of the *Santa Caterina News* building while scrolling Reddit and laughing at some stupid memes, stopped by the deli, saw they were out of my favorite coconut water, walked two blocks up to the health food store, lingered to survey the surfboards in Thruster's window, picked up our mail and talked to Gertrude about the bar next door. God forbid I have an actual lunch break where I enjoy my life.

"Sorry," I tell him, popping the coconut water can open.

Sorry's currency with me and Dad, easy as hello or goodbye. Well, to be fair, it's currency that goes one way and one way only. I'm the chump, he's the bank. If I had a buck for every time I uttered the word, I'd be as rich as he is.

Dad sits at the mighty wood desk he's parked into the office behind the bar. He's got reading glasses perched on his nose and some dust goggles ready on his forehead. The book he's reading is called *Bartending for Dummies*. Let's be blunt, the only reading my old man does is *For Dummies*. He dabbles. He's a dabbler. After his stint as a pro football player, he retired at thirty-five. Since then, it's been a string of failed hobbies/investment opportunities: the sauna suit pyramid scheme. Cruises for dogs. That makeup subscription company my mom tried to launch last year that my dad funded. And the exclusive fantasy football club that was such an embarrassing bust it was covered in *Sports Illustrated*.

Now it's Brady's. And even though it seems like the biggest no-brainer—sports bar in a buzzy downtown area crawling with thirsty clientele—you have to understand why I'm not a hundred percent confident in all this. Let's be real, my dad has terrible taste in business investments. And now he's investing in me and my future.

Thank god he's a multimillionaire.

And that's far from the first time I've said that in my life.

"Seth called and said there's some mold issue," Dad says, licking a finger, putting finger to page, flipping the page. My dad's what some call *intimidating*, an ex-quarterback for the Grizzlies and 250 pounds of pure muscle. The man spends his me-time pounding protein shakes while lifting barbells and catching up on ESPN. For fun, he watches documentaries about American wars. I can confirm he *is* intimidating. It's not much better being his son. The closest I've been to the man was in high school when I was named a "promising pick" for college football teams on a state sports blog. But I ruined my knee three weeks into fall semester senior year and, well, me and the old man have had little to talk about ever since.

Until recently when he bought me this bar.

"Shit," I say, putting the mail down on the edge of his desk, into the wire basket he bought for exactly that. "Near the bathroom?"

"The wall behind the bar, actually."

"Great," I say, taking out my phone. "Guess I'll have to figure out who to call."

"I called a mold remediation company already for an assessment," Dad says, not looking up from his book. "This afternoon, four p.m."

"You know I've got practice at three."

"Well, might be time to think about freeing up your afternoons. You going to be a business owner or a babysitter?"

"Coaching football isn't babysitting."

"When they're six years old it is."

They're not six. My team's made up of nine to eleven-year-olds. Dad knows this. He probably even knew I had practice at the time he scheduled the mold remediation company to show up and booked it anyway, knowing it means I'd have to choose.

"I can't back out of practice this late," I say. "They're counting on me."

He doesn't respond. He ignores me, like I'm nothing, like I'm air. He turns a page and lets out a sigh. It's funny because my dad has a professional reputation for being a hothead—back when he played quarterback for the Green City Grizzlies, he famously cussed his offensive line out for a playoff loss that made every newspaper's sports section across the country. At home, though, he's irritatingly level-headed, and when he gets pissed, he ghosts.

Guess what, though? I can, too.

I put my phone back in my pocket and go out to the bar.

A whole crew has dropcloths on the floors and talk to each other in Spanish as they paint. A plumber in the main bathroom is installing new toilets. A contractor's on the floor in the back with a sander and earmuffs on. Me? I don't know what I'm doing here. I don't even have to pee, but I make my way to the back bathroom, just to try to squeeze out a piss and kill some time.

It's an employees-only bathroom, which is about as charming as a cell in solitary confinement. The walls are boards barely painted over with in white, exposing the nails. The high, tiny window is broken, spiderwebbed. One toilet, one sink, grime everywhere. As I unzip my fly I can hear a conversation through the wall, the wall on the side of the nerd bar.

"It's incredible," a woman's voice is saying. "The location, everything. Restaurants and boutiques and … and the only other bar nearby's a *sports* bar. There's such an opportunity here for something innovative, cultural, something artsy. I can't wait for you to see it, Daddy."

I scoff while I pee. On her side, I hear a flush, and then the fall of her voice as she leaves. I zip up and wash my hands, unreasonably annoyed with her. I know it's the girl I met outside. The girl with the narcissistic friend. The fuck was that, by the way? I was talking about how delicious her sandwich looks and she assumes I want to play hide the hoagie? Way to flatter herself. She's a far throw from my type.

What is it that annoyed me about that through-the-bathroom-wall conversation, then?

I sit on a stool at the bar and get on my laptop to work on our social media pages, the one thing I seem to know how to handle that no one else does. Is it the fact she's opening the bar next door? Or is it the fact it sounds like she has an actual relationship with her father and a life worth sharing with him from afar, and here I am sitting in silence with my own dad a room away?

Oh well. Bar won't market itself. I spend an hour making square social-friendly fliers for our opening in a month and researching ad spends for small businesses. Then I get restless after hearing my dad in there clearing his throat for an hour and I tell him I'm going to move my car again.

"Again?" he asks.

Yeah, again. I could have gotten better parking. But then I'd have no excuse to get up and go somewhere every ninety minutes.

Outside our glass doors, I step into the salty air. There's a refreshing parade of lovely women, happy families, and skateboarders. Man, I'm so glad to be out here and not inside. And I think something I've never thought before in my life: *thank God for meter maids.*

When I attended Oceano Valley Junior High, I walked a thousand miles on this campus. Past classrooms strip-mall style painted a putrid olive green, connected by unsexy steel beams, wide sidewalks, and potted plants. It all led toward a recessed plaza of social doom in the middle of campus right next to the cafeteria that was eighty-eight percent pizza. Behind that, though, there was an earthly sea of possibility: the wide, green field where I spent my afternoons running. The perimeter was a perfect mile. I could observe the soccer players, the football players, the sprinters with their hurdles set up, but from my slow pace outside it all. In seventh and eighth grade, I had this blissful feeling that I existed just outside real-world expectations. But then my dad came in, and my mom provided her solid role as backup.

"You're built for football," my dad said, clapping my shoulder. "It's in your genes."

Was it *really*? Picture me at age thirteen: a ginger kid who weighed about seventy pounds and wrote Mario Brothers fanfiction in his spare time. A kid whose only advantage was, I could outrun any bully in pursuit of giving me a wedgie.

"Running on its own isn't a sport," Mom said, tousling my hair. "In real life, running's what people do when they're too scared to fight."

"Give it a year," Dad said. "Give football a year and see how you feel."

So freshman year I signed up to shut them up. Growth spurt hit that year and I bulked up and hit six foot two. The truth was, as much as I wanted to find my own way, I did begrudgingly like football. I liked the team spirit, the unique nature of each player, the quick intelligence it took to make a decent play. It was strength and speed combined in impossible ways. I made friends in ninth grade I'd never dreamed of. I wore those shoulder pads and that jersey and it symbolized that I was part of something.

For the first time in my life, I kind of understood my father.

Then, senior year, I sprained my median collateral ligament and my football career was over. And Dad and I have had a hard time finding common ground ever since.

You'd think we wouldn't. I mean, I still love watching sports. Is there anything greater than sitting in a soft easy chair abusing my body with cheese puffs and beer while judging the acumen of professional athletes? And I coach pee-wee football because I've always loved kids. But that's not the same in Dad's eyes. That's weak shit, actually. In his eyes, I was supposed to be on the field doing more than coaching a preteen O-line.

And you know, I do wonder what pipsqueak Chuck would've thought about me now: back on the field of Oceano Valley Junior High voluntarily, whistle around my neck, setting up cones for today's drills. Smile on my face because this is where I love to be, even if it pays barely more than minimum wage.

I blow the whistle.

"All right, team. Line up. Five-ten-fives," I say.

Fifteen kids showed up to practice today and only six of them remembered their shoulder pads. This nine to eleven age group's a doozy—you've got a couple squirts who look like they just graduated kindergarten and a couple who hit their growth spurts early and could be in high school. Aiden's the oldest and probably weighs close to what I do. Even though he's got a face like a grumpy Persian cat and a low threshold for failure, I've got a soft spot for him. He's the only kid whose dad shows up to practice every day and paces the touchline like a gorilla in a cage. His dad wears a visor and writes notes down on a yellow legal pad about Aiden's performance. Even now he's taking notes, when all Aiden's doing is waiting on the end of the line for his turn to run back and forth touching cones for an agility drill.

"That's it!" I clap as each kid runs through the drill, touching the first cone, doubling back, touching the second. "Pick it up, pick it up."

My phone buzzes in my pocket. I give it a glance and see my dad's name and put it back in my pocket without reading. Really, Dad, you can't wait two hours? It keeps buzzing all throughout the first round. Afterward, I gather the kids and give the team a few pointers, clap a few high fives, and take another look at my phone, where there are now twelve messages from Dad, the last one visible and reading CALL ME NOW.

"Wait here," I tell the team. "Be right back."

I can feel Aiden's dad's eyes on my back as I jog over to Tyrus, head coach who's setting up the line blocking drills at the thirty-yard line. Tyrus is the coach I wish I'd had as a teen. He builds the kids up without screaming at them. He emphasizes the fact that the game doesn't care how long you've played or how you're built; it's about putting in the work and the passion to become a team player. Tyrus has also mentored me for a year now, telling me he thinks I'd make a good head coach someday. He's given me a lot of space to run drills and coach the O-line. I try to tell myself his kindness has nothing to do with the fact that my dad is Cory McCaffrey, but when you're a Grizzlies star quarterback's son, you've always got to wonder. Especially since Tyrus is currently wearing a Grizzlies beanie over his locs.

"What's up, man?" Tyrus asks as I come over.

"I'm sorry, I've got to peel off for a few to make a call. You mind taking over the drills? Just finished the three cones, they're ready for four."

"We're good, I'll start the blocking drills. Everything okay?"

"Yeah, I'm sure everything's fine. Just need a minute."

"Take your time, I got you."

I jog off the field to the opposite end of the touchline, away from the burning gaze of Aiden's father who apparently has no life of his own. Pacing the line, I call my dad back.

"What, you have your ringer off?" he asks when he picks up.

Not a hello or goodbye man, my father.

"Give me a break here, practice just started," I tell him. "What's going on? This can't wait ninety minutes until I'm back at the bar?"

"You didn't read my texts?"

"I saw 'call me now'; I called you now."

"Well, we've got a serious mold problem on our hands," he says. "The whole back wall behind the bar's gotta go. Which means we likely need to rewire it. So that's probably going to set us back at least a week."

"Okay."

I wait for something that needed to be said so urgently that practice was interrupted.

"'Okay?'" he asks. "That's your response?"

"What are you expecting me to say?" I ask. "So we'll bust up the wall and hire an electrician."

"I'm feeling like your head's not in the game here."

"My head is in the game. It's literally in a game right now; I'm at practice."

"Not pee-wee football, Charles. This bar is supposed to be your future."

I hate it when he calls me Charles. Up above my head, the sun brightens the clouds and glows up the purple mountains that run up against Santa Caterina. It's perfect here. I've got a life other people dream about—a quasi-famous dad, a fat inheritance that means I hardly need to work. I just need to do what he says. Run a sports bar. End of story! Doesn't even require any knowledge or talent on my part. I just need to hire the right people, bust out my dad's checkbook to foot any bills that come my way. It should be so easy, the easiest thing in the world. So why is my chest tightening?

"Charles, you there?" Dad asks.

"Still here."

"You're at a crossroads here. If you're serious about running this bar, show me you're serious. Pick up the damn phone when I call. Pee-wee football's not an excuse to run off in the middle of a work day. You know, I'm about to leave town for a week and I need to know you can handle the bar without me. You've gotta make a decision here about what your priorities are."

In high school, I used to have this feeling sometimes when he talked to me. When he tried to pump me up before games or give me advice about girls. I'd feel the Chuck evaporate out of me and I'd become someone else: I'd become Charles. I'd go blank, like I didn't know who I was. It's happening again now.

"You know this bar's my first priority," I say with my eyes shut.

"Then prove it to me," he says, and hangs up.

Across the field, the boys are working on drills. Tyrus holds up a blocking pad as Aiden methodically shoves the pad, giving it his all as his dad shouts "Go! Go! Go!" from the sidelines. What a jerkoff.

My legs feel like lead and my chest's still tight. Because I'm about to head back toward Tyrus and the team. And I really don't want to disappoint them—but I absolutely can't disappoint my dad.

I'm standing here at a fork in a road I never asked to walk in the first place.

I CHOSE the road less traveled, but right now, I'm questioning that choice.

It's seven AM. I snoozed through my alarm, am still donning pajama bottoms, and haven't even brushed my teeth. No time for a cappuccino by the time I get to the bar so I will not have the energy to be faking any smiles this morning.

I've just gotten done greeting the flooring crew (three gentlemen and a whole lot of long planks of white oak) when someone starts knocking on the locked front doors. This happens at least once or twice every day, usually around lunch and dinner time, when former patrons of the Thai restaurant come here and feel the need to express their disappointment to me, a stranger now occupying the space, that their beloved eatery is gone. But seven in the morning is a new record, and when the knocking continues and gets louder, so does my rage.

"Excuse me," I tell the crew, leaving them to unpack and begin their work.

The glass door's covered in butcher paper so passersby can't peek at our under-construction mess, which also means I can't see out. I unlock the door and open it. I'm ready to, as politely as possible, tell someone off. But then I see it's just that asshole Chuck from next door and realize I don't need any pretext of politeness.

"What do *you* want?" I ask.

"Well, good morning to you as well, you little ray of sunshine," he says.

Chuck is obnoxiously chipper. He's got the showered, caffeinated energy of someone who's already had a morning run and breakfast, which further confirms my deep dislike of him. His hair is combed and he's wearing a sweatshirt with a football on it that says Sea Lions. Football. Of course, football. The sport of toxic machismo and chronic traumatic encephalopathy. Explains this guy's deal pretty well.

"I'm about to shut the door in your face," I tell him. "I'm really not in the mood for this right now."

"This being what?"

I gesture toward him. "You. The sight of you. Your existence."

"Look, I didn't mean to get off on the wrong foot yesterday, sorry about that."

"You *laughed* at me and called this a bar for *nerds*."

He breaks into a smile. A smile that may look charming, but it's not. It's a bully's smile. "I mean, you have to admit that part is true. It's a nerd bar, just own it."

I shut the door, but he catches it with his hand and pulls it open again. "Come on, Gertrude. Don't be like this."

"My name is Isadora, you oaf. Gertrude's is the name of the bar."

"And a beautiful name it is."

I know this guy's kind: they "joke" constantly, always at someone else's expense. Women are interchangeable to them—Isadora, Gertrude, what's the difference? They mock female intelligence and ambition. They salivate over human Barbie dolls and cheerleaders. So I must deeply offend him, standing here in pajama bottoms with an explosion of unbrushed, curly brown hair, thick glasses, and a big nose. ("It's a beautiful *Italian* nose," my father likes to remind me. "Don't ever be embarrassed of your heritage.")

I glare at Chuck. "I have an idea: you let me have my *nerd* bar, and you have your *jock* bar, and the two of us move forward in mutual, blissful ignorance and pretend each other don't exist."

"Honestly, that sounds great," he says.

"Fabulous."

I start to pull the door shut, but again, he pulls it back open on his end with his freckled and obnoxiously strong hand.

"There's just one problem," he tells me.

"You?" I ask.

"No, you alluring little fire poker. The wall between the front rooms. The one behind the bar on my side?"

I stare at him, not understanding where this is headed

or why on earth he called me an *alluring little fire poker*. And for the first time, that stupid grin leaves his face—leaves it looking tired, serious, and entirely transformed.

"We have to tear it down," he says.

By the time Zofie arrives at Gertrude's with lattes and breakfast sandwiches an hour later, I've already stress-cried privately in the bathroom and washed my face and patted it dry to hide the stress-cry. I greet her with a cheerful smile but she sees through it right away.

"You're not crying about the wall, are you?" she says, sitting with me in my back office. In here we've got no windows, but we do have towers of cardboard boxes labeled BOOKS, a table with two folding chairs, and some pictures of other literary bars and breathtaking libraries I taped to the walls as inspiration. My gaze lingers on these pictures longingly—far cries from the catastrophic state this bar is in right now.

"No," I say, because technically, it's true. Was I previously crying about the wall? Indeed. Am I currently crying? No.

"You are a very bad liar and also you have a booger hanging out of your nose."

I sigh and go to the bathroom, where there is, in fact, a gargantuan booger that I remove with a tissue. Back in my office, I sit down as Zofie and I unwrap our sandwiches. Yes, more sandwiches. Zofina Vidmar eats sandwiches for breakfast, lunch, and dinner.

"That booger was probably there the entire time Chuck was talking to me," I tell her.

"Probably. Which just shows you what a prick he is. Only cowardly pricks don't tell people when they have a booger in their nose or something in their teeth."

Which is true: a test of character. Like whether or not someone uses their turn signal.

I must look like I'm about to cry again, because Zofie reaches out and puts her hand on my wrist.

"You're going to be okay," she says. "It's a wall. You can tear a wall down and build it back up in a day."

"This is bigger than the wall," I say. "It's got a cascading effect. The wiring's going to need replacing. Who knows what's next."

"Another few hours. Seriously, this will be resolved by the end of the week."

"I'm supposed to open in thirteen days."

"And you will! It's not going to set you back in any major way. The other contractors can easily work around it."

"It's not just that," I say, staring at my sandwich, unable to muster an appetite. "He's opening a *sports bar.*"

"Yeah, I know. Brady's. So what?"

"So, two bars right next door to each other? You don't think that's a problem?" I pause and then add, "Wait, it's called Brady's? How do *you* know that?"

"There was an article about it on that lil blog, what's it called—the Santa Caterina Wire?"

"About the bar next door? And you didn't *tell* me?" I push my food away. An appetite is now fully out of the question. Not only is the sports bar competition, now I find out they're getting press already.

"I didn't know it was next door to you when I read it," she says. "I didn't even fully read the article. I scanned it. Last week. Before all this."

"And?"

"All it said was Cory McCaffrey was opening a sports bar called Brady's. Yesterday after you met the Ginger Asshole who said he was opening a sports bar, I put two and two together. The Ginger Asshole is Cory McCaffrey's son."

"Who the hell is Cory McCaffrey?" I ask, feeling like an idiot who is ten steps behind on news that very much affects my future.

"You know, Cory McCaffrey. QB for the Grizzlies."

Whatever she just said, all I can think about are grizzly bears, and now I'm even more confused.

"QB?" I ask.

"Oh my *God*, girl. How can you graduate magna cum laude, be a literary genius, and still be this dense?" She puts her sandwich down and explains the following to me like I'm in kindergarten. "I'm talking about football. American football. Cory McCaffrey. Former quarterback of the Green City Grizzlies. Kind of a big deal."

"It's *his* bar next door?" I put my head in my hands. "Why didn't you tell me you figured this out *the moment* you figured this out?"

"Because I knew you'd get like this. Let it get to your head. You need to stop. You're being ridiculous. No one who wants to go to a literary bar is going to be attracted to a sports bar, and vice versa. The clientele is completely different."

I remove my hands from my face and take a deep breath. She does have a point.

"Also, Cory McCaffrey is kind of famous for being a horrible businessman," she goes on. "Like, it's a joke among football fans. So he's probably going to fail epically for reasons having nothing to do with you."

"Really?" I ask, brightening. Schadenfreude, sure, I'll take any form of joy I can muster at this point. "That bad?"

Zofie dated a sports broadcaster last year for a few months and got all sorts of inside info into the local sports world. She's a reliable source on this.

"Yeah," she says through a mouthful. "So let it go. Can you do that for me?"

"I'll do my best."

"Truth? I'm a little worried about how high-strung you're going to be without me here to talk you down. Might be time to make friends with my favorite palindrome: Xanax."

"That palindrome and I are already well acquainted," I say, drinking my latte. "And I can live without you, Zof."

But when I say it out loud, doubt blooms. Zofie's become something akin to a sister. Not a lover (not since that summer), but more than a friend. I don't think I've gone a week without seeing her in five years.

"Have you talked to your landlord about the wall situation?" she asks before shoving the rest of the breakfast sandwich in her mouth. Truly amazing how someone so flawless can be such a pig. It's mesmerizing, really.

"Chuck said he already spoke to him," I say, folding my sandwich back up and storing it my purse for later. The nerves of uncertainty have wrecked my stomach this morning. "He's supposed to talk to him again today and said he'd update me."

"How cute," she says with a full mouth. "You exchange numbers?"

"Don't. You know how much I hate this."

"Just think, when that wall goes down, you can just look up and gaze at his big toe face anytime."

"Big toe face?"

"Don't you think his face is kind of shaped like a big toe?"

"You see the weirdest things in people. Remember how you almost dated the girl who you thought looked like a spork?"

"Chelsea. With the spiked hair. She absolutely *did* look like a spork. And that was a dealbreaker."

"You are so judgy. No wonder you haven't found anyone."

"Look who's talking," she says. "You're basically a nun."

"Except for the religion part."

"Eh, minor detail."

I stand up and act fake-excited. "Thanks for reminding me about my nonexistent love life. I'm sure going to miss these pick-me-ups!"

Zofie gets up too and gives me a wink. She's basically the only person in the twenty-first century who can successfully pull off a wink. Or those cargo pants and combat boots she's wearing. We walk into the main room where the flooring team is working. The corner area they've completed looks promising. I can just imagine wood tables under there, some hanging Tiffany-style lamps, a row of bookshelves with antique hardbacks I've been collecting over the years. And there in the front, next to the window, we'll build a little stage for open mic nights.

"It's going to be amazing in here, babe," Zofie says, putting her arm around me and admiring the view, as if together we see the gleaming potential, as if we've entered the same lucid dream.

"I hope we can get this taken care of in the next couple of days and it won't affect our opening," I say, fighting a whine in my voice. "I mean, it's the wall *right* behind the bar where all the shelving is supposed to get put in."

"Forget about that. Carpenters are professionals. They can work around anything. You know who was a carpenter?"

I break the embrace so she can see me roll my eyes. "Jesus."

"No! Not Jesus." She squeezes my arm and her green eyes light up. "Much sexier: a young Harrison Ford."

"Great."

"What do you want to work on today?" she asks. "Maybe best to get out of the way for the flooring installers. How about we do something fun. Go shopping? Décor?"

"That does sound more enjoyable than yesterday's carpet removal adventure."

"All right. It's a date."

"Let us go then, you and I," I say, grabbing my purse.

I lead the way to the glass door, unlock it, and out we step into the sunshine.

Riviera Avenue is the main street that runs fourteen blocks through Santa Caterina's downtown area—from the historic mission with its palatial façade and problematic history, straight to the glittering stretch of sand and sea known as Cielo Beach. Gertrude's is near the middle. In the upper blocks, toward the mission, there are historic buildings, offices in Spanish-style complexes, a few museums, the castle-like library, and a gothic-looking church. In the middle, where Gertrude's is located, the blocks buzz with shopping, coffeeshops, bars, and restaurants, with the neoclassical *Santa Caterina News* building overlooking Pensador Park. And on lower Riviera, it gets clubbier, noisier, upscale fish restaurants and souvenir shops all selling the same I LEFT MY ♥ IN SANTA CATERINA shirts.

My favorite block is ours, the sixth block, of course. As Zofie and I amble in the direction of lower Riviera, toward the beach, we pass the bead store, then a record store Iggy's with posters and albums in the windows, then a place with a fancy cursive sign that says *Chat Auberge*. It means "cat hotel" in French. It's a cat rescue with wide windows looking in on a white room filled with cat towers, cat toys, screens showing birds in trees that cats watch lazily from perches.

"Now that's the life," Zofie says before we continue on. I'm not sure if she's envying the cats or the establishment, but either way, I concur with an *mmmm*. Next we have an ice cream shop that was a T-shirt shop two months ago that was a dumpling restaurant last year. An upscale furniture store on the corner that I've, quite honestly, never seen a patron inside and wonder how they survive. Like residential, commercial rents are not cheap around here.

At the corner, Zofie and I wait for the light to change so we can cross. She gives me a look, eyes wide and exaggerated, a little sigh.

"What?" I ask her.

"I'll miss it here," she says. "It's been home, you know?"

I'm surprised to hear this admission. Zofie's tough, ever-confident, perpetually forward-looking. When she zeroed in on LA and acting full-time as her next step, I knew there was no stopping her. And I have no doubts she'll succeed. I just hope she'll remember me when.

"It has been," I agree.

The light chirps and we cross and hit Tchotchkes. A wide-open room lit with funky lamp after funky lamp, artfully arranged furniture, occasionally interrupted by racks of vintage clothing. Everything's for sale, and it's easy to forget it–to wind up in a perfect, retro corner with a Persian rug and chaise lounge and a Victrola playing old records and realize you haven't stepped into a magical living room from days of yore. You're in a store. It's all got a price tag.

"You need shelving, yes?" Zofie asks, pointing to a long shelf with glass doors.

"Seems unwise to put that much glass in a bar."

"Mmm, the drunkies."

"Always got to consider the drunkies, Zof. I'm a bar owner."

"You're a bar owner." She comes toward me, squeezes my hand, her eyes light up momentarily, and we move on.

"Can you believe it?" I ask as we pass a row of records, jazz musicians whose names I don't recognize. "Back when you and I first met at Study Hall, would we have ever guessed that I'd have my own bar someday?"

"I knew you'd be doing *something*," she says, pulling the straps on her flowery backpack to give it a lift. "I figured you'd be a famous poet."

I see myself in a mirror on a vanity. Glasses still on, tired eyes, pajama pants. I look away.

"There's still time for all that, though," Zofie says as we move ahead, as if she is unnerved by my silence. "I'm so proud of you. I wish I could be here to see it. Oh! Isadora Valenti!"

Zofie loves to proclaim my name in dramatic moments. When she does, there's a tinge of an Italian accent that only she can pull off because, well, Zofie.

She beckons me toward her and points to something gasp-worthy: a stunning wall of ceiling-to-floor walnut bookshelves with a ladder on wheels in front. The shelves are only half-full. There are random tea sets, doily sets, and even an abandoned CD box set on the shelves. But Zofie and I both see the potential. We exchange a look and cover our mouths with our hands.

I wonder, do I dare? And "Do I dare?"

"It must be for sale," Zofie whispers. "It's all for sale."

"I can see it in the front," I say. "You know, to the right if you're looking at the stage?"

"If you're looking at it from the inside," she continues.

"Right. The bar to the left, the shelf to the right."

"Basically, it would take up the whole wall opposite the bar," she says. And after a pause, "I love it."

I walk to the front, terrified of what the price will be. You never know in Santa Caterina vintage stores. You might get a steal, or you might get robbed. The girl at the front has a short, blush bob of Marilyn curls and silver cat-eye frames. She's so engrossed in an engorged paperback she doesn't notice us at first. Then, cheeks pinking, she slides her book under the countertop. I'll bet she's not supposed to be reading on the clock—that's how it's been for me at every job I've worked. But it's not how it will be at Gertrude's.

"Can I help you?" she asks.

"We were wondering about the wall shelving in the back, with the ladder," I say. "Is it for sale?"

"Oh! Yes. Let me look it up! But yes." Pink Marilyn turns around and opens a binder behind the counter, laminated pages crinkling as she flips through to find something. "Six hundred."

Zofie and I exchange a wide-eyed look. Six hundred for shelving that large? With a gliding ladder like an old-fashioned library?

"I'll take it," I say.

I charge it on my credit card and try not to think about the growing balance. We're in the anxiety-inducing time period when all I do is spend with no income to counterbalance. But in just thirteen days, we'll be open.

"Are you taking the shelving now?" Pink Marilyn asks me.

"We can come back for it Tuesday with your truck?" I ask Zofie. "The floors will be done tomorrow, the walls should be painted by then, and you'll be back from LA."

"Works for me."

"I work right up the street," I tell Pink Marilyn as she writes up a receipt with a purple pen. "At a bar that's about to open."

"Brady's?" Pink Marilyn asks. "The football bar?"

"No," I say, fighting irritation. "Next door to it. It's called Gertrude's. A bar for book lovers."

"Oooh!" Pink Marilyn looks at me. "That's what the shelving's for?"

"Yeah."

"How fun! What's the date you officially open?"

"Two weeks. Thirteen days, actually."

"I'll definitely be stopping by for a drink, that sounds right up my alley," she says, handing me the receipt. "I'm Eva, by the way."

"Isadora," I say. "And this is my friend Zofie."

Eva flashes us a lipsticked smile. "So nice to meet you both."

"See ya," Zofie says, jingling her keys.

The combination of the serendipitous furniture find and meeting someone genuinely excited about visiting Gertrude's has brightened my mood. The stress from earlier lifts for a moment and I see through the clouds—the clear blue sky of my future, the excited wind of knowing that I've escaped the sad fate of a dream deferred; I'm daring to risk everything to open a business I'm passionate about, in my favorite city in the world. So I'm next door to a sports bar run by an obnoxious jock, so the wall needs replacing. Life's imperfect. But I'm so lucky. I must remember that.

I hold onto that thought throughout the day, until the finished floors are done, the workmen have gone home, and all I smell is glue. I hold onto that thought as I ride my bike under the dark night sky and its bold silver shrapnel of stars, back to my apartment a few blocks behind the mission. I hold onto that thought in the apartment, where Zofie's bedroom door is open, littered with clothes and half-packed boxes. She's spending a couple nights in LA moving some stuff to her new apartment, then she's meeting with an agency Monday morning. I'm lucky. I'm so lucky she's my friend, even if she's moving away, even if I'm so scared of being left alone again. Of always being alone.

I'm so lucky, I think the next morning when I arrive at Gertrude's and lock my bike out front. I stop a moment to look at Brady's and notice a handwritten sign promising GRAND OPENING SEPTEMBER 20! Of course. The same opening date as my bar. I peek through the glass doors but it's hard to see anything besides dropcloths, paint cans, and a chaos of tables and chairs. I need to stop comparing.

I'm lucky, I think, unlocking the front door and admiring the gorgeous, finished oak floor for a split second before my smile disappears and I see the wall between

Brady's and my bar has a person-sized hole in it. And guess who's standing there on the other side, grinning like he's been waiting for this moment to relish the look of horror on my face?

"What the hell, Chuck?" I ask him. "Couldn't even give me a heads up?"

"I texted you," he said.

I pull out my phone. "You texted literally seventeen minutes ago. And all you said was 'its happening.' Missing the apostrophe, by the way. No context provided."

"I'm busting up the wall," he says, showing me a sledgehammer proudly. "Electrician's coming this afternoon."

I lose the train of conversation as he yawns and stretches. I regret to acknowledge that he's apparently built —his brawny biceps are the kind I'd like to circle my fingers around to test their strength. I am overcome with unwanted thoughts as he continues stretching and his T-shirt lifts to offer a peek of a freckled stomach. I wonder what else is under there; I detest myself for wondering. Finally, thank God, he finishes his stretch.

"Electrician," I say, to remind myself of what we're talking about. "Okay."

"You look tired," he says.

I glare at him.

"You look mean, too," he continues.

"You really know how to boost a girl's confidence."

"What? I wasn't insulting you. I could stare at your gorgeous, hateful face all day long."

Is he flirting with me as a method of torture? Who

knows with this exasperating man. "I'm sorry, don't you have a wall to bust up?"

"You're welcome."

"Excuse me?"

"You're welcome for taking care of the wall."

"You are maddening."

It's like he's knows exactly which buttons to push to completely annoy the shit out of me. His overconfidence bordering on arrogance, his too-pleasant demeanor, his perpetual grin. I stare at his head and think maybe he does have a big toe face. It makes me feel better to think that about him.

"I have work to do," I say. "So I'll go to the back and let you finish the wall here."

"Will you?" he asks. "Will you let me do that? How generous of you."

I just stare at him, about a million things flashing through my mind to respond to him with, beginning with the old classic *fuck you*. Instead, I take the high road and say nothing at all, walk back to my office, and shut the door. I open my laptop and work on reformatting the drink menus for what feels like the hundredth time. It's hard to concentrate, however. I can hear the sledgehammer hitting the wall repeatedly and my skull throbs with the sound of it like a headache.

Opening a tab, I search "Brady's Santa Caterina" and immediately come upon not only the Santa Caterina Wire article, but a few blurbs in sports news outlets and even a national paper. Besides being owned by a hotshot ex-football player, there doesn't seem to be anything special about

Brady's. But of course, they've gotten significant coverage anyway. They have the advantage of celebrity I can't even begin to compete with. I search Cory McCaffrey and learn he's married to Aislin Gray, a former runway model. Hard to imagine that obnoxious twerp out there came from such perfection. Then again, it explains a lot: he's beyond privileged, not only born and raised in Santa Caterina, but born to class-C celebrities. Maybe I'd have a shit-eating grin on my face twenty-four hours a day if life had always been that easy.

The painters text that they're on their way so I get up to unlock the front, but when I turn the doorknob to my office door, it breaks off in my hand.

"Come on," I say to it. "Really?"

I figure I just need to wedge it in somehow to pop open the door, but after several attempts, and some door-pushing and kicking, I realize I am locked inside this windowless room. The painters will be here in a minute. And I need to pee. Sitting at my desk for a moment, first I do some breathing exercises.

Then I do the last thing I want to do.

I text Chuck and ask for his help.

chuck

"WELL, LOOK AT THIS," I say, reading the text back again.

And then, an afterthought:

How polite of her. A true class act.

Lucky for her, all thanks to me and my trusty sledge-hammer, there's half a wall missing. It only takes me a couple seconds to step through it. Place looks decent. Still needs a paint job and furniture. Doesn't even have a bar set up yet. Narrower than my space. Nice new wood floors. Her ceilings are somehow much higher than ours next door, which opens the place up, and her front window is much brighter because it's not tinted like ours. I make my way down the back hall toward the shut door and try to open it.

"Oh thank God," she says, hearing me.

"No, it's just me, Chuck," I say. "You know, I really didn't have you pegged for an all-caps texter."

"It was for emphatic purposes. I was yelling. And I definitely had you pegged as a person who can't tell the difference between 'you're' with an apostrophe and 'your' without."

"Lot of good your big smart brain's doing you in there, huh, all locked in a room with no doorknob."

Isadora makes a sound between a moan and a scream.

"Hang on, okay?" I say. "I need to get a screwdriver."

She sighs audibly. "I have to pee."

"Well, you should have thought of that before locking yourself in your office."

"The *knob* broke off in my *hand*."

"Why are you locking yourself in your office anyway? You're the only person here right now."

"To get away from you."

I shake my head, laughing silently. I go get a screwdriver from my bar and come back and pop the pins on the hinge. The door opens toward me with a groan and reveals Isadora's closet-sized office decorated with ripped magazine pictures and crammed with boxes that say BOOKS on them. There's something less than sane about this whole setup, especially the wild look in Isadora's blue-gold eyes when the door opens.

"Thank you so much," she says, sprinting past me. "I have to go to the bathroom."

I stay standing here a moment, taking in the cramped room she was in. Thinking about how different it is from the office on the other side, twice this size, with a custom-made mahogany desk my dad ordered and THE BOSS placard he also had custom-made that sits on the edge of it. On the walls, Dad's already framed the articles that have come out about Brady's in a couple papers. The whole room stinks peaty, because my Dad's a scotch man and he keeps the good stuff in the file cabinet in there. But Isadora's office smells sweet and clean, like coconuts.

"What?" Isadora asks behind me, wiping her hands on her jeans.

"Just looking at your office. What are all those magazine pictures?"

"Nothing."

She reaches to shut the door. I stop her from shutting it by putting my hand over hers. "You might want to fix the knob before shutting it again."

After an oddly electrifying second, she pulls her hand away. "Fine. You can go now."

"Oh, you're dismissing me?"

"I mean, thanks." She says it so flatly it could pass as an insult.

"I'm getting the feeling you're not a morning person."

"Goodbye, Chuck."

"I could have left you locked in there," I say, backing

away from her toward the hole in the wall and pointing at her. "Remember that."

"And why didn't you?" she asks, softer, almost curious, tucking a loosened curl back into her messy bun.

"Believe it or not," I tell her with a look of complete seriousness on my face, "there's a heart underneath these amazing pecs."

She gives me a witheringly blank look before heading back into her office. It's truly amazing how she can, without moving a facial muscle or making a sound, tell me I'm the world's biggest idiot. And it doesn't even bother me. In fact, I kind of enjoy her prickliness.

Back through the hole I go, to the other side. The Brady's side. The slick, marble-countered, marble-floored room with twenty-one TVs mounted on the walls. Before I pick up the sledgehammer, I take a look at my hand.

I can still feel the exact spots on my skin that touched her.

I've broken up with four women in my life.

Allie Lawson, seventh grade. Sweet soul, pink glossy lips, first kiss, loved video games as much as I did. But after a couple months, I got bored. I wrote her a note telling her I'd like to be friends. We were friendly after that, but she's still never given me back my handwritten fanfiction epic about Mario going to the moon and fighting aliens.

Cassie Bluth, eleventh grade. Oh, Cassie. Tall, freckles,

swim team, hair to her thighs, funny as hell. Together a year, which is practically a generation when you're in high school. We were each other's firsts. When her family moved to Jersey, we tried the long-distance thing. Didn't work out. I broke up with her via email and she said she'd never forgive me, but she forgave me. We're still social media friends and message sometimes.

Tatum Woods, senior year. Blue colored contacts, bleached hair, spray tan, rhinoplasty at sixteen. Smart as hell but never had much of a chance to lean into it because everyone around her was so focused on her looks. My relationship with Tatum was basically the teenage equivalent of an arranged marriage: my mom's buds with Tatum's dad Dr. Liam Woods, and the fact Mom's that chummy with her plastic surgeon should tell you everything about her. Mom harangued me into dating Tatum by constantly harping on how cute it would be if Tatum (budding model) and me (budding football player) got together. Just like Mom and Dad! A carbon copy of a love story! I went out with Tatum for a few months but that spark wasn't there. I broke up with her by sending a single text and she responded it was all good because she had never found me attractive. Touché! All water under the bridge now. Tatum's married to a photographer and living in Italy. I see her sometimes around holidays when she visits her family.

Then there was Samantha Lewis, who I dated for the first few years of my twenties. This one hurt. Razor-sharp wit, made me laugh until my belly hurt daily, dark pinup girl hair, cat eyes. I met her in a city college English comp class before I became a city college dropout. We lived together in an apartment in the hills. She got a scholarship to Oxford and as much as I wanted to chase her there, I knew it wouldn't be what's best for her—some uneducated goof waiting for her at home every day like an attention-starved dog. Dad sat me down and said, "Charles, you can't follow a woman halfway 'round the world to a country where they don't even play proper football. Stick around here and we'll make something big happen for you." He had nothing to do with me calling it off with her in what must have been the saddest coffee date of all time. Still, Dad's convinced he had everything to do with it. Like he saved me from some sad-sack fate. I guess, a year and some change later, Brady's is the consolation prize he landed on for me. Sam and I still talk every couple of weeks. She still makes me laugh til my guts are in pain. In her social media pictures, she looks happy. Like she's where she belongs. She's pretty in scarves and sweaters, smiling against a backdrop of Gothic buildings.

Those are my four breakups. Every time I knew they were coming, nausea struck like food poisoning. And that's exactly how I feel right now, hearing the knock on the door of Brady's. It's Tyrus. I invited him out here for a drink and to tell him I have to quit coaching the Sea Lions.

"What's up, my man," Tyrus says, coming in and giving me a fist bump. He looks around at the countless TVs, the pool table, electric dartboard machine. The shiny row of two dozen draft beers, the pint glasses lined up with our custom logo. "Damn, this place is *slick*."

I go behind the bar, which pulses with blue light. Can't lie, I still feel like I'm a kid pretending to bartend when I step back here. Which I guess I am. I've never bartended. Dad's hired bartenders who will do the work mixing drinks. Shit, I hope Tyrus doesn't want a cocktail.

"What can I getcha?" I ask.

"I'll have one of those 805s," he says.

"You got it."

Relief. Don't need to look like a complete dummy having to search for a cocktail recipe on my phone. I fill two pint glasses up and hand one to him, hoping he doesn't notice how much foam's on top. I really need to get better at pouring beer.

We cheers.

"Congratulations, man," he says, and takes a sip. "This spot's where it's at. Remember the dive that used to be here? Lou's? Man, they had three-dollar drink night. Back in my college days I used to get sauced up in here."

"You know, I passed by it, but I don't think I ever came inside."

"Shit was legendary." He strokes his goatee. "But what you've got going here's professional. Real sleek. I think I could bring Monique out here and call it a date night."

"You should, man. You know it's always on the house."

"You must be real busy, being a business owner," he says.

Business owner. Technically, he's right. The business license, the lease, the bank account are all in my name. But it was my dad who filled out my forms. My dad who co-signed. My dad who deposited the chunk of change and paid every bill.

"Yeah," is all I say.

Tyrus leans in. "Which I'm guessing is why you've been distracted at Sea Lions practice lately. Why you're thinking of quitting."

He knows. Christ on a moped, I need to learn how to hold my cards closer to my chest. I step out from behind the bar, slide onto a stool, join him at the bar. He's right, this place is slick, but right now it's dead as a library. No music pumping, no games flashing on the TVs, no people except us.

"Has it been that obvious?" I ask him.

"Nah. I'm just good at reading people." He sips his beer. "Don't feel bad. I get it. You're loyal and you don't want to let anyone down. But this is important, man. This is about your passion, chasing your dreams."

I nod at him, surprised the conversation's taken this turn. That he reads how my heart's in coaching, how this whole bar thing was never my idea, how worried I am about letting my dad down after everything he's done to get me here. Then it hits me: I had it backwards. Tyrus thinks opening this bar is chasing my dreams. That I don't want to let *him* down, not my dad.

"I already found someone to assist in coaching the team," he says. "So no worries. We'll be all right."

"You found someone?" I ask, surprised that this conversation stings the way it does.

"Yeah. That kid Owen? His older brother played college football and he's been looking for an in with coaching."

"That's great," I say.

I stare at my beer, at the bubbles that keep rising. I

don't even want to drink it but I do anyway because I don't know what to say. The food poisoning feeling has settled into something different. Tyrus came tonight to cut me loose. He doesn't care that I was going to quit coaching the team. I'm replaceable. I'm nothing.

"Maybe you can swing by next practice and give the boys a proper goodbye," Tyrus says.

"Sounds good," I say. "I'll be there."

"Now tell me how many TVs you've got up in here," Tyrus says, standing up. "I've never seen this many TVs in one room in my whole life."

"Twenty-one," I say, standing up to behold the ridiculous array of TVs with him. "Something, right?"

"And what are these?" Tyrus points to the biggest ones on the far wall facing the bar. "Eighty-inch screens?"

"Eighty-six. Or eighty-three. I don't know, they're fucking big."

"How much that cost you?"

"Not sure exactly. We got some kind of a deal."

"Where'd you get them from?"

"Online."

You know those old movie clips with chimpanzees dressed up like people? That's what I feel like right now. I don't actually know where we got the TVs or how much they cost or even how big they are. Rather than continue bumbling through this conversation, I get up and use the master remote to turn the TVs on all at once. We don't have cable yet so it's just the channel three news. Tyrus is hypnotized by the set up. I show him the subwoofer speakers and how I can control the stereo with my phone.

"This is *dope,* man," he says.

I hand him my phone so he can play with it. He's got a look in his eyes that I used to have when I played with remote control cars as a kid. Such power in the palm of your hand. He puts on a rap song about—here's a surprise—how great the emcee thinks he is. Cranks the bass so loud the pint glasses clink on their shelves, turns it back down. Turns the entire volume up a notch.

"Shit. My feet are buzzing," he yells in my ear.

I grin watching Tyrus as he nods his head to the music and laughs at the phone in his hand, switching to a classic rock song about hard women with a guitar riff that makes us both headbang for a minute. But I soon realize this version is weird. It has a track in it I never noticed before. Maybe it's because it's so ear-splittingly loud? There's a screeching sound. Tyrus and I both seem to notice it at the same time and look at each other. That's when I notice the movement in the background—the flapping. Flapping of arms.

Over there, behind the bar.

It's a woman screaming and gesticulating so wildly she's resembles a human trying to fly. Why the hell is there a woman behind my bar, trying to fly??

Oh. Shit.

It's Isadora.

I grab the phone from Tyrus's hand and turn the music off. There's a split second of Isadora screaming, then she stops. Her hands fall to her sides.

"Do you have no sense of conscientiousness?" she yells.

"Of, like, other people existing? I was on a very important phone call."

Tyrus's mouth is wide open. "Who are *you*?" he finally asks.

"I am the woman from the other side of the wall," he says, pointing to the hole, which Tyrus doesn't seem to have fully noticed until now. To be fair, there's a lot going on what with the ten thousand TVs, blinking lights, electric sports posters. It's easy to miss.

"The woman," he repeats, "from the other side of the wall."

"My neighbor," I tell him. "The new love of my life. Her name's Isadora."

Oh, that comment *really* pissed her off. She's turning pink. "Chuck, if you ever play your music that loud again, I swear."

"What?" I ask. "You'll what?"

"You don't want to know."

"*You* don't even know, do you?"

"Do *not*," she says again, slowly, "mess with me."

I can't help myself. I press a button on my phone that's under my thumb to unpause the song and she jumps about a foot in the air. I press it again to pause it, doubled over laughing. Tyrus is busting up, too. Not Isadora, though. She looks like she's about to cry.

"I'm sorry," I say.

Not sure anyone's ever given me such a spiteful look in my life. "You are *such* an unbelievable asshole." She spins on her heel. I shouldn't enjoy the sight of her stomping away from me this much, but she makes it impossible in those tight pants. She disappears through the hole.

Tyrus is still laughing. Wiping away tears, actually.

"She seems fun," he finally says.

"Yeah. I feel bad. I should apologize to her."

"You just did."

"I mean, really apologize."

"I'd wait a day, man. When Monique gets that look in her eyes, I call it her 'steer clear' look. And I thank baby Jesus we have fifteen hundred square feet to occupy in our house."

"Your wife gives you looks like that?"

He laughs. "Man, nobody *but* my wife gives me looks like that."

We finish our beers. Tell a few jokes. Talk some shit about the Sea Lions boys, about poor Aiden and his obsessive dad.

"You don't even know," Tyrus says. "I made the mistake of giving that man my cell number and now I get him texting me ideas for plays all day long."

"You should ban parents from practice," I say.

"Wish I could. Parents are the hardest part of that job." He finishes his beer, checks his phone, stretches, gets up. You know, the goodbye routine. "Be proud of this place, Chuck. This is the life. But we'll miss you over there. You've got a gift with kids, you know—even temperament. Smart head on your shoulders. Wicked sense of humor. And a big heart. I appreciate you, man."

"Appreciate you too, Tyrus," I say.

We high five and he heads out to go meet Monique for

dinner somewhere up the street. I wipe up the counter, clean the pint glasses. Go into the office for a couple minutes and just sit at the desk. My dad's been out of town for enough days now I almost can't smell him in here anymore. I can imagine this is my place. That I did this. That I can do this.

Remembering the scene with Isadora earlier, I get up and poke my head through the hole in the wall. Shit, place is dark.

"Isadora?"

I step in, flip a switch behind the bar that lights up the hallway. Nothing. No one. Just the stink of new paint. Walls look done now. A deep blue. Bunch of wood lined up near the front, maybe for the bar. She still has a lot of work to do. Down the hallway, I can see the door to her office there, still missing its knob. The knob's there next to it on the floor.

Back in Brady's, I grab my toolbox. Head back over to the hole and cross through to the other side. Weird how the energy's so different—two worlds separated by a single wall. Like people, I guess. I used to feel that way when I held Sam. We were whole worlds separated by nothing but a few thin layers of skin.

I kneel, pick up the knob, and study it. Study the place it fell from. Ah, yes. There's the problem. Quick tutorial on YouTube, then take my screwdriver and get to work putting it back together again. And when I'm done, I shut off the lights and duck back through the hole, to my side.

isadora

WHEN I CONSIDER how my day is spent before half of it is done, I am impressed with myself. Well, not *myself*, I suppose. With Zofie, because Zofie did most of the work helping get this massive walnut shelving into Gertrude's. And the electrician came in to install the copper sconces and the black chandeliers above the bar. And the carpenter Jacques finished building the long bar this morning and is now spending the afternoon staining it. I could give some credit to Chuck for finally building his side of the wall and closing the gate to hell as well, but that man deserves no credit. He is privilege in flesh form.

Jacques, on the other hand, is possibly the most attractive man I've ever seen in my life. I have a weakness for long-haired men, strong arms, and French accents, so Jacques truly is the trifecta of male perfection. It's been hard to not stare at him as he hovers over the bar he lovingly crafted and applies stain to it in long, gentle strokes. I imagine that's probably how he might run his fingers along my skin as we read Baudelaire by candlelight.

"Isadora," Zofie whispers in my ear. "You are *gawking*."

She's right. How mortifying. I'm standing here frozen with a stack of books in my arms, objectifying a carpenter. Let's not even acknowledge the fact I was staring at *Chuck,* at Satan himself, with lust in my heart for a fleeting moment the other day. I clear my throat and turn around and shelve the books, magnificent hardbacks of classics I got at an estate sale. This complete collection of Shakespeare's works cost me a flabbergasting five dollars.

"Is this the reason you're wearing your contacts and lipstick today?" Zofie asks, giving me the side-eye as she unpacks a box of her own.

"Shut up," I whisper. "He's right behind us."

"He's at least fifteen feet behind us and he speaks not a word of English," Zofie says—horrifically, at a normal volume.

She's right though. His English is terrible, which should be a dealbreaker for me, considering I majored in it. But somehow the trifecta of male perfection previously mentioned makes up for it. Plus, I'm almost positive he fixed the doorknob to my office, so he's also an angel. When I tried to thank him for it, though, he said something to me in French that was sexy but indecipherable. God, why did I take Spanish in high school?

"You need to get laid," Zofie says—again, horrifically at normal volume.

I don't disagree with her. Times are getting desperate. It's been, what, since my last semester at SCU? Damien, the philosophy major. A paramour of opportunity, nothing more. He lived in my building and there was really only one way to get him to shut up about Derrida.

There's something about filling the shelf with books that makes my heart skip a beat. Stepping back with Zofie, admiring the gleam of antique hardback spines and the glorious, musty scent of ink and paper, my dream has finally manifested. It's *real*. So real that my eyes burn with emotion; either that or wood stain. Or maybe the fact that I'm wearing contact lenses for the first time in months.

"You're doing it, babe," Zofie says, her arm around me as she gives me a half-hug. "You're *so* close."

"I feel like once the bar is done, we unpack that mountain of furniture in the corner, and the liquor gets delivered tomorrow, it's going to be official," I tell her. "We'll pop some Dom Perignon this weekend."

Zofie's arm drops from behind my back. "I'm out this weekend, remember? I have to finish moving the last of my stuff."

"Oh, right. Well, next week."

Zofie chews her cheek. It's a habit she's been trying to break after her new housemate in LA warned her it would give her wrinkles. Now that Zofie's serious about breaking into acting, she's started worrying about things I've never seen her care about before, all superficial. Wrinkles. Contouring. Heels that can give her a few inches. When she came back from LA this week, she'd had a blowout and was wearing full makeup. I'd never seen her like that.

"Gotta play the game," she'd said when she came back

to the apartment, put her hair back up into a baseball cap, and changed into sweats.

I want to keep pretending she's going to stay this person always. That playing the Hollywood game won't change her. That landing that agent isn't some life-altering step leading her in a direction away from me. That if I leave that room open in my apartment, she might come back. But isn't that distasteful of me? To secretly, selfishly hope somewhere dark and deep within me, that she might fail?

"I need to tell you something," Zofie says to me as we stand in front of the stunning array of books. "I'm so sorry."

Oh no. I get a pitch-forward falling feeling in the pit of my stomach.

"I got offered an audition a week from Friday. For a commercial. It's a really, really good opportunity for me. But … it's your opening night. And I know I told you I'd drive up weekends and help bartend Friday and Saturday nights until you hired someone."

"Can't you go to the audition and drive back here?"

"It's at four in the afternoon and I have no idea how long it might take. Plus, a Friday, rush hour? Traffic's going to be terrible. I don't want you to count on me and then end up disappointing you."

You're disappointing me right now, Zof, I want to say. But I don't. I don't know what to say, and I so dislike that about myself—that I'm a poet, a lover of words, and when the important moments sneak up on me, I never know what to say.

"You're mad," Zofie says.

"How can I not be?" I ask quietly. "You were supposed to be there for me on the most important night of my life."

"I'll still be there, I'll just be getting there later. And I want to make sure you have someone else to help you out since it's opening night and all."

"It's fine," I say. "Don't worry about it. I'll figure it out."

"No, but I have a solution!" Zofie says.

"What," I say flatly.

"That hot-ass girl at the antique store where we got the shelf from—Eva? When I picked up the shelving, we were talking and she asked if we had any job openings. She used to bartend *and* is a book nerd *and* is kind of obsessed with the idea of a literary bar."

"Great, I'll just hire her with all that extra cash I have lying around."

"You can afford to pay someone for Friday and Saturday nights, come on. She's perfect."

"I'll run it by myself. I'll be fine."

I've been having this conversation with the bookshelf, basically, while Zofie stands next to me, because I don't want her to see how upset I am. But Zofie comes to stand in front of me and forces me into eye contact.

"Babe, you have that *Santa Caterina News* article coming out next week. You're going to get a lot of buzz when that comes out. If you try to run this place alone opening weekend, you're running the risk of disappointing a shitload of customers who won't come back again. First impressions and all. You need someone here."

I sigh. She's right. And it all hits me right now: Zofie is leaving. She's really leaving. Somehow in the back of my mind I imagined that she was still my partner in crime. That this is *our* bar. That I could convince her to come back weekends, at least, and it would be like the good old days at Study Hall, late nights filled with raucous laughter, music, and the joyful noise of cocktail shakers. But that's not happening. It was never going to happen.

"I'll go talk to Eva, I guess," I say.

Zofie reaches out and hugs me. We hug for a long time, tightly, her head on my shoulder. We hug so long that Jacques finally clears his throat behind us and tells us he's done staining, by saying the word *fin* and pointing to the bar.

"Back with seal," he says. "Tomorrow, maybe."

Takes me a moment to register that he's not talking about the sea animal, but the protectant coating.

"Great," I say, probably too enthusiastically.

"Text in morning if still wet, okay?" he says.

"Okay," I say. "Thanks."

I unlock the front door for him, relock it, and turn around. Zofie's waiting there with a mischievous twinkle in her eye.

"Text him tomorrow if you're still wet," she says. "Hubba hubba."

"You are the absolute worst," I tell her.

She cackles like the exquisite little witch she is.

~

I might have spoken too soon when I said Chuck built the wall back up. Because now that I'm back here over the weekend by myself doing last-minute work like painting the wall behind the bar and next to the liquor shelves, I notice the tiny window of space he left open, about four by four inches two feet above the floor near the electrical outlets. Honestly, wouldn't surprise me in the least if he did it on purpose. I can imagine Chuck's name in the intersection of "asshole" and "pervert" in a detestable Venn diagram.

It's interesting though to get a window into his world over there. Not that I can see much—a gleaming sink behind the bar, some rubber mats on the floor. But I can hear the booming voice of someone else who seems to be on the phone talking about money and/or sports occasionally. A voice that isn't Chuck's. I can hear him talking to a bank about a business loan, arguing about rates with the cable company, and then shooting the shit about sports. I'm assuming it's Chuck's dad, Ginger Asshole Senior, and it makes me think Chuck's just a puppet in this whole operation and it's his dad running the show. Which makes Chuck even more of an entitled brat. I should sue their family for almost busting my eardrums the other night when he was playing with his abominable stereo.

I'm sitting on the floor high on paint fumes, finishing the trim, when I hear the sound of someone moving around the other side after hours of silence. I see some Converse high tops and muscular calves and then hear an unmistakable muttering of "Christ with a hockey stick" and know exactly who it is.

"Hey," I call through the tiny window-hole.

The legs go still.

"Down here," I yell. "The peeper window."

Takes the legs a moment to turn, facing me, and for Chuck to squat down so he can peek through. His hair is falling in his face and there's something about this angle that makes me realize what long eyelashes he has. Of course he does. He even has privileged eyelashes.

"You scared the shit out of me," he says.

"Somehow I think you'll still manage to be full of shit," I say.

"Ahh, I see. So you made me crouch all the way down here just to insult me."

"I want to know why you left this creepy peeper hole in the wall. It's repugnant."

"Don't flatter yourself. Your nasty cowboy boots aren't worth peeping."

"How do you know I'm wearing cowboy boots, then?"

"Because it's literally the only thing you've worn every time I've seen you. Pajama bottoms and cowboy boots."

Okay, he has a point.

"I left the window because the cable line's in there and we still don't have our cable set up. I'll cover it up when that's done," he says.

"You could have at least closed it up on my side."

"I was being a gentleman, in case you too needed access to the cable line."

"We're a book lover's bar; we don't have television."

"Wow. Thanks for reminding me, once again, that you're so much better than me."

I stand up and consider whether or not my cowboy boot would fit through the hole and be able to land on his face.

"Why are you wearing lipstick?" he calls through the hole. "And where are your glasses? And … wait, why aren't you wearing pajama pants?"

Jacques came by earlier to collect payment. I wish that was a euphemism, but the sad truth is, he didn't even seem to notice the fact I had a physical existence at all. He looked at the bar, then looked at his phone while accepting my payment, then left without so much as a *merci*.

"It's none of your business what I wear and why I wear it," I say, reaching behind the bar for duct tape, and then kneeling on the floor.

"Doesn't seem fair that a girl as smart as you also gets to be that beautiful," he says with a grin that barely fits in the four-by-four inches. I ignore the reflex of my flattery. Somehow, even his compliments land like insults. There's no line between sarcasm and sincerity with this man.

"Bye, Chuck," I say.

And then I seal the Window to Hell with duct tape.

Another reason I dressed up today and spent my entire weekend painting, unpacking booze bottles, arranging furniture, and spit-shining Gertrude's is because I knew Saturn Martinez was coming this afternoon to interview me for the *Santa Caterina News*. Yes, her name is Saturn. And even more excitingly, she writes feature articles that almost always end up on B1, the front page of the local section. It's my first real press opportunity and I'm elated to finally get to drum some media interest the way Brady's has.

I expected Saturn to be whimsical, a young woman with rainbow hair and tattoos, maybe, but instead the woman who shows up is a no-nonsense brunette with bronze skin, impeccable eyebrows, and a pantsuit that commands to be taken seriously, despite the fact she could pass comfortably for sixteen. Saturn is accompanied by a bald man old enough to be her grandfather, with a flash-bulb camera that is likely even older than he is.

"Reggie's going to be taking pictures," she says as we sit down at a wooden table together. "Don't mind him. Look casual. Pretend Reggie doesn't exist."

I look at Reggie, who assures me, with a cheerful smile, "I don't exist."

"I'm not photogenic," I protest.

"Oh, you're gorge. No worries." Saturn takes out her phone and sets it on the table. "I'm recording this, FYI."

I am so grateful that my vanity and lust for the French carpenter compelled me to doll myself up today, because Reggie is pointing his camera only about two feet from my face as I smile and say, "Sure, okay."

I am a poet, okay? An introvert. I am the person, at a bar, who brings a book with her, which led me to right where I am right now. Being the center of visual attention is not my forte. I can wax poetic all day long. There wasn't a worry in my mind about this interview. But now that there's a camera in my face, I'm almost disassociating.

Saturn asks me how to spell my last name and it takes me about thirty seconds to remember. Finally, Reggie backs off and starts wandering around the rest of the bar, snapping away like a paparazzi, and I can breathe again.

"Your name is fascinating," I say. "Were your parents …" I want to say *hippies,* but that seems disparaging. "… artists?" I finish.

"My father's an astronomer. My mother's an astrologer."

"Oh," I say, interest piqued.

"Enough about me, though," Saturn says, waving a hand in the air. "I can't tell you how thrilled I am to talk to you right now. Downtown Santa Caterina needs some culture, you know, hubs outside your dime-a-dozen sports bars." She points to the left, toward Brady's, and gives an eyeroll.

"Right?" I lean in. "Brady's is opening *the same night* as Gertrude's."

"The contrast is uncanny," Saturn says. "Knowing the ownership, it was probably calculated."

My jaw hangs open a split second. "You think it was?"

"Oh, I'm kidding," she says without a smile. Actually, I haven't seen a smile from Saturn yet; for all I know, the woman has no teeth.

"Wouldn't surprise me if it was calculated," I say. "Knowing how much the owner and I have already butted heads."

"Have you?" she asks, eyes widening.

"Chuck McCaffrey has basically been the bane of my existence for the past two weeks," I say.

"You mean Charles McCaffrey—Cory McCaffrey's son?"

Charles. He doesn't deserve a dignified name like Charles. I suppose he's less a Dickens, more a Bukowski.

"Yeah, he's the owner," I say. "On paper. But Cory's pulling all the strings. He's basically written a check for everything, furnished the place, and handed his entitled son Brady's wrapped up in a bow."

"Interesting." Saturn doesn't sound very interested. "Well, let's get started with the interview. Tell me about your inspiration for Gertrude's."

With Reggie out of eyesight, I'm able to concentrate, delving into the oral equivalent of my autobiography. I start with my mother, of course, and her love of literature; describe my upbringing in Ohio, our two-bedroom run-down Tudor, the elementary school where my father taught across the street; my dreams of living near the ocean, city college, then transferring to SCU; my English major, my poetry workshops, the job at Study Hall and the almost seven years I spent scrimping and saving in and out of college while I dreamed of opening the first literary bar in Santa Caterina county. By the end, I've picked up so much steam I'm out of breath and for the first time, I spy a smile on Saturn's lips.

"Wow, what an inspiring story," she says. "To be starting a business like this at your age."

"Life's too short to put off your dreams," I tell her, thinking of my mother.

"Beautiful, just beautiful." Saturn presses a button on

her phone. "I think that about does it for me. Reggie, you get everything you need?"

During the impassioned reverie of my life story, I had, in fact, forgotten that Reggie existed until now. He stands in a corner like a hat rack, holding his camera.

"If I could get one more of the young lady against the backdrop of the bar," he says.

"Of course!" I'm so high on the experience of riveting a reporter that the thought of having my picture taken doesn't inspire the urge to vomit anymore. I get up, beaming, and stand against the bar, smiling with my hands on my hips.

And that's the picture that makes it to B1 two days later.

The headline?

COLLEGE GRAD'S NEW LIT BAR GIVES 'ENTITLED' SON OF EX-FOOTBALL STAR A RUN FOR HIS (INHERITED) MONEY

chuck

OUR GRAND OPENING'S three days away.

I should be pumped. Or nervous. I should feel *something*. But my heart's drawing blanks. My buddies text me and ask how the bar's going and I say I'm busy. Yeah, busy killing time. Busy figuring out ways to look busy as I walk around the bar polishing things that are already polished. Coming to the bar just to sit and watch the cable guy do his thing. Watching YouTube tutorials on how to make basic cocktails, getting buzzed all afternoon.

More bored than hungry, today I head out for a meatball sub at Gio's and spot Isadora outside the bar, locking up her bike. Oh, so it's hers. The beach cruiser with the fake flowers wrapped around the handlebars I've seen here every day. Her hair's down today. I've never seen it down. It's long, curly, wild, nearly black, and it's weird how much I want to run my fingers through it. In the sun right now, I can see the outline of her legs through her long skirt. She's beyond beautiful. She's the kind of beautiful

66

who doesn't think much about being beautiful, doesn't let it rule her or occupy her. My favorite kind.

Too bad she hates my guts.

Just wait and see that dreamy smile melt right off her face when she notices me lurking here in the doorway of Brady's.

"Hey," I say to her.

She turns around and subtly flinches at the sight of me, blocking out the sun with a hand above her eyes. But to my shock, she doesn't respond with some quip. She gives me a smile. An almost nervous smile, like I caught her off guard.

"Hey," she says sweetly.

Sweetly?! Now I'm *really* waiting for a dig.

"How are you?" she asks.

"I'm … fine," I say. "And you?"

"Doing well. Excited for Friday."

"Same."

For the first time since I met Isadora, I'm at a loss for words. She crosses to her front door and fiddles with her keys.

"How's the interior looking?" I ask.

She turns around. "Good! Pretty much ready."

"Nice. Well, I'm going to Gio's—you want anything?"

"I'm okay. Thanks so much." She turns around and gives me a little wave. "Have a good one!"

"You too!" I say.

She closes the door and I'm left here gaping on the sidewalk. I step aside for a woman in a dress walking a poodle wearing a matching dress and then turn the opposite direction of Gertrude's, past Brady's, and head to Gio's. I pass a spice shop called Beyond Bay Leaf where the same bored man stands behind the counter staring into space. Punch the button at the crosswalk, waiting for the light to change.

It's the usual blue-skied seventy-two degrees in Paradise City, but I'm in the Twilight Zone. What the hell just happened? What changed since I last saw Isadora to make her act so pleasant? Maybe she's one of those people with wild mood swings. But no. As I cross the street and head toward Gio's, I realize what happened.

It's the doorknob.

I fixed her doorknob.

That's all it took for her to warm up to me.

I shake my head, laughing to myself. Some women are so easily won over. I eat a meatball sub in Gio's with a dumb smile on my face, thinking about how gorgeous she looked with the wind blowing in her hair. Would she ever go out with a guy like me? Nothing's impossible if a screwdriver, a YouTube tutorial, and five minutes of my time melted the ice queen. Damn, Chuck. You still got it.

I give myself an invisible pat on the back.

Which soon turns into an invisible slap in the face.

Because then I get back to Brady's. My parents are at the bar—both of them. My mom's first time inside the place as far as I know. She looks like she came straight from the gym, leopard print leotard over spandex leggings, high blond ponytail. They have a newspaper spread out in front of them.

"Oh, Chucky, what a travesty," she says. "How embarrassing for you."

"What?" I ask, frozen in the doorway.

"Charles," is all Dad says, shaking his shaved-bald head.

"What?" I say, louder.

He points to the newspaper. I walk closer. My mom watches me closely, her hand on her mouth, as I look down at what his finger's pointing at. First I see the picture: Isadora, looking radiant against the backdrop of a bar, the smile lighting up her face like Christmas. My eyes linger on her a moment before falling to the headline below it.

COLLEGE GRAD'S NEW LIT BAR GIVES 'ENTITLED' SON OF EX-FOOTBALL STAR A RUN FOR HIS (INHERITED) MONEY

"Oh, fuck me sideways," I say, grabbing the paper.

"We should sue them," Mom says to Dad. "Libel."

"Not libel, defamation," Dad says.

"Saturn Martinez," I mutter as I see the byline. "She went to my high school."

"So it's personal!" Mom says. "She has a vendetta!"

"No, Mom. I hardly knew her."

"She didn't interview you, huh?" Dad asks. "What kind of a journalist is that, only getting one side of the story?"

"Yellow journalism, that's what it is." Mom takes out her cell phone and starts swiping. "I'm going to give the publisher Jennifer Carson a call right now and rip her a new one. No one talks about my son this way."

"Please don't," I say.

"What? Someone's got to stand up for you because you won't stand up for yourself." Mom's acrylic fingernails are giving her trouble so she hands it to my dad. "Hon, search for Jennifer's number right now for me."

"I like the idea of suing them," Dad says to her, taking her phone. "Could actually be great publicity for Brady's."

"Oh, I hadn't even thought of that!" Mom says. "Good point."

It's like I've disappeared.

"Stop!" I yell at them. "Can you give me a minute to process this?"

"Chucky, you don't need to shout," Mom says. "Take a breath and count to four. Let it out and count to four."

"Don't yoga me right now," I tell her. "I need a minute."

I go into the office and close the door. My office. It's supposed to be my office. But my dad's coffee cup, windbreaker, sunglasses are on the desk. For some reason, a foam hand has made its way in here along with some golf clubs. I sit at the desk and kick back in the chair. Take a deep breath but don't count to four. Let it out but don't count to four.

And I read.

Literature has been central to 27-year-old Isadora Valenti's life since she can remember. Growing up in a small Ohio town, Valenti credits her mother's love of Emily

Dickinson and her father's lifelong teaching career for instilling her passion for poetry and prose. Now Valenti is poised to finally achieve her dream: a literary bar called Gertrude's opening in downtown Santa Caterina this Friday, September 20. The catch? She just so happens to be competing with Brady's, a sports bar next door, opening on the same night.

Brady's, owned by former Grizzlies quarterback Cory McCaffrey's son Charles McCaffrey, offers a stark contrast not only in style, but in story. Valenti worked for years through college to afford her bar, while McCaffrey comes from a family of millionaires.

According to Valenti, "Cory's pulling all the strings. He's basically written a check for everything, furnished the place, and handed his entitled son Brady's wrapped up in a bow."

And the two neighbors have apparently been butting heads since day one.

"Chuck McCaffrey has basically been the bane of my existence," Valenti said.

Even so, Valenti has forged forward, building her dream from the ground up all on her own. While initially Valenti dreamed of opening a bookstore after graduation, a side job she got at a local bar led her to instead blend her love of literature and devotion to drinks into something fresh: a bar for book lovers.

Valenti's literary bar Gertrude's is set to open this Friday, September 20, and will be hosting Saturday Poetry Open Mic Nights and Lit-Up Trivia Tuesdays. Gertrude's has a library-like interior filled with classic books customers are encouraged to borrow, elegantly antiquated décor, and drinks named after famous writers.

Then, at the bottom, in italics and what looks like size eight font:

Charles McCaffrey did not respond to a message seeking comment.

"The hell I didn't," I say to the size eight italicized font. "Who reached out to me?"

I'm about to go out there and join the "sue em all" bandwagon when I open my email for kicks. There, about half a page down under all the useless garbage in my inbox, is an email from Saturn Martinez from the day before yesterday requesting an interview.

"Damn it," I mutter before putting my head on the desk.

"Charles," Dad says, opening the door. "You all right in there?"

"Fine. Please tell me Mom didn't call the newspaper."

"I convinced her to wait."

"Well, they apparently emailed me for an interview and I didn't see the email until now. So it's not their fault. So you can tell her to lay off."

"You're *kidding* me."

"Wish I was."

"You know, part of being a responsible adult is checking your email. Look at me when I'm talking to you."

Reluctantly, I sit up and stare my red-faced father in the face.

"How the hell are you going to run this place on your own?" he says, hands on hips. "I leave for a week and the cable's not even hooked up when I get back. *I* have to set up the appointment. You blew a media opportunity because you're not checking your email. I'm surprised you got yourself dressed this morning—though honestly, I can't even tell if you're dressed right now in that outfit."

I don't say anything. It's happening; I'm becoming Charles, the Incredible Shrinking Man-Boy. It's an effect the man has on me.

"You're letting some stupid smartass woman rip you to shreds," he says.

Stupid smartass is an oxymoron, Dad, is what I would say if I hadn't shrunk to half my size.

"You're just going to sit there, saying nothing. You drive me crazy when you do this shit," he says. "I don't have a clue what's going on in your head sometimes."

"Chucky," Mom says, now joining Dad in the doorway and holding my dad's bicep. Tag team, right here. Good cop, bad cop. "Don't worry. I'm at least going to talk to the paper, get another feature on this place."

"Don't," I say. "Just let me handle it."

"You know, the best revenge is going to be your own success," Mom says, coming in and sitting on the edge of the desk.

Dad snorts. "He did it to himself, Aislin. Kid didn't check his email box and see the interview request from the *Santa Caterina News* for that story."

"Oh no! Poor Chucky!"

"It's his own damn fault!"

"Can you just stop?" she says, turning around. "Go get some nachos or something."

My dad huffs and leaves the doorway to the office. I hear the front door open and close. The man will do anything my mom says, and vice versa. They drive me up the wall but I've never known two people more in sync. Maybe that's why I've always had a hard time connecting with them: I was born a third wheel.

"Listen, the first time you get bad press, it hurts." Mom reaches out and puts her hand on mine. Everyone always says my mom's a fifty-foot-fakeout because of her age. She looks flawless and like the model she once was from a distance; but I think she's best up close. Right here you can see my mom's freckles, her clumpy eyelashes, her crow's feet creeping through the Botox. You can see her humanity. "Believe me, I know. When I was modeling, that tabloid *Rumor* put my picture on it after I'd had some tacos and circled my tummy and splashed me on the front page with the word PREGGO on it in all caps. That hurt."

"Tragic," I say.

She slaps my arm. "It was!"

"Worse than the Holocaust."

"You are such an asshole, you know that?" she says with a smile.

"I've heard. Girl next door said the same thing. Guess that's why she tore me a new one in that interview."

She sighs. "Well, she's only half right. You're an asshole with a heart of gold."

I snicker.

"You going to be okay?" she asks. "You want me to go over there and kick her ass?"

"You can't kick anyone's ass."

"Hey, I took cardio kickboxing!"

"I'm okay, Mom. Really. I'll be okay."

She stands up over me with that worried look in her aqua eyes. Sometimes I miss the days when she towered over me instead of me towering over her. "Don't worry about that woman. Her bar's a joke. Who on this earth goes to a bar to read *books*? You'll be putting her out of business in no time."

"Don't you have things to do?" I ask. "I got this. I really don't need a pep talk. I don't need you to beat anyone up. I'm a grown-ass man."

"Well, don't be a doormat. You should do *something*. I'll leave it at that." She glances at her smart watch. "Oh, I need to go meet Anna. See you at the opening Friday?"

"Sure."

"I'm so excited for you, hon!"

"Thanks, Mom. Tell Anna I said hi."

Anna's her masseuse. Also one of Mom's friends, I guess? The woman's come over for multiple Thanksgivings. It's weird that a lot of my mom's friends—Liam Woods, Anna, her housekeeper Maria—are people she pays. She doesn't seem to find it weird though. Money's toilet paper to my parents. They go through business ventures like hobbies. They were both born middle-class, but they don't even remember that life anymore.

And me?

The worst part about that article, the thing that clenches my stomach up, is that every word of it was true.

Taking out the newspaper again, I gaze long and hard at that picture of Isadora. That everywhere hair. That come-closer stare.

So proud. So gorgeous. So *smug*.

Even if she were right, did she really need to work those digs into her interview? Why couldn't she be proud of what she's building without tearing me down? I don't deserve that. I didn't do anything to her. I fixed her doorknob, for shit's sake!

"You want it to be like that?" I ask the picture, a slow smile spreading. "You want to be rivals? To be enemies? Well then. Game. Fucking. On."

She thought I was an asshole before?

She hasn't seen anything yet.

isadora

HAD we but world enough and time, I would have booked something more exciting our opening night than a string quartet. Perhaps obtained a food license, considered catering. A moveable feast! Shakespearean breakfast sandwiches, The Red Queen's stolen tarts, fried green tomatoes. Now it's two days before we open and I've bitten my nails to the quick fretting over this stunning first impression I so desperately want to make. That *News* article has stirred a bit of a buzz, with neighbors stopping by to say hello and even a local bookstore calling me to see if I might be interested in collaborating for future events. *This is all good*, I tell myself as I fight a panic attack.

"It's going to be amazing!" Eva assures me from behind the counter. She does a twirl. She must be wearing a petticoat under her polka dot dress, it's so puffy. "I'll bet you'll sell the place dry!"

Eva is bubbly, coquettish, and with her cotton-candy pink bob, she reminds me of a glass of sparkling rosé.

She's adorable. She's also, I gathered from our first hour working together, a bit of an airhead. I'm trying very hard not to be hypercritical, but she pronounced "pinot" like "peanut" and, while admiring my bookshelves, actually said, "George Eliot? I've heard people love him."

I miss Zofie.

"You're fine," Zofie says when I hole myself up in my office, calling to whisper-complain to her. "Stop being such a judgmental bitch already."

"When I asked her about her favorite book, she said it was *Verity*."

"And?"

"Zofie," I whine. "You know how I feel about Colleen Hoover."

"You know, listening to Eva's tastes might not be the worst thing for business. I mean, love the crap out of what you've built, babe, but ... maybe featuring some actual books from the twenty-first century that weren't written by crusty dead white dudes would bring in a new clientele."

"Great," I say, throwing up my hands even though she can't see me. "Yeah, I should just ditch everything I've built and go with Reese's Book Club picks from now on. Take all the typewriters out and put tablets in."

"I mean ..."

"It's supposed to be retro, Zof!" I say. "It's supposed to evoke another place and time!"

"Look, you hired her to make drinks. Can she make drinks?"

"I don't know. She hasn't made any yet. She mispronounced 'pinot' so my hopes aren't exactly sky high. She just got here an hour ago."

"Oh my God, get off the phone and go train the poor girl and stop calling me to talk shit. I'm about to go get my brows waxed anyway."

"You wax your brows now? I love your brows."

"Yeah, my agent says they make me look too ethnic."

"First, that's racist. Second, what? You're Slovakian."

"She's also trying to convince me to change my stage name to Sophie Kidman."

"I hate your agent. This is like the tragedy of Norma Jeane Baker all over again."

"I wish. Anyway, stop being ... Isadoraesque. I'll call you."

"Fine."

"Later."

I hang up, glaring at the dark phone in my hand, as if it's to blame for Zofie being as far away as she is, doing unnecessary and unprecedented treatments to her impeccable face, considering butchering her name. To Kidman! As in Nicole. I don't care what the Oscars say about *The Hours*, she's no Virginia Woolf.

"Everything okay?" Eva asks, leaning on the counter when I come in, the menu in her hand.

"Yeah, checking in on my friend." I sit on a stool on the other side of the bar. "So tell me about what drinks you can make. You said you previously worked at a bar at hotel, right?"

"*Near* a *mo*tel. It was a place called Glug, a real dive.

But, um, I feel kinda dumb saying this," she says, holding up one of the menus. "I don't know any of these drinks."

"Let me explain." I pluck a pen from the bartop—we have an assortment of pens in jam jars, of course, along with notepads and a Remington typewriter. I pick up a stray menu and begin writing the translations of the drinks. "All the drinks are named after classic writers or books. So *Catcher in the Rye* is just a scotch and soda."

"Oh! I'd have thought it would have rye in it."

"You'd think so, but scotch and soda is a drink featured in *Catcher in the Rye*. And the Ernest Hemingway? That's simply a mojito. It was his favorite drink."

"That I can make!" Eva says.

"Related, there's a tequila sunrise called *The Sun Also Rises*."

She looks at me blankly.

"Related because Hemingway wrote *The Sun Also Rises*."

"Oh! Okay."

I scrawl the translation on the menu. "William Faulkner —mint julep. The Anne Sexton's a martini."

"I can make all of these!" Eva says, with an excited hop.

"The Jack Keroauc's a margarita, the Maya Angelou's a glass of sherry, and the Dorothy Parker is a whiskey sour."

"This is so cool!"

"Dorothy Parker's also who said those words up there," I say, pointing to the stencil that's over the back wall, the one next to the hallway that leads to my office and the restroom. The stenciled lettering reads:

I'm not a writer with a drinking problem, I'm a drinker with a writing problem.

"Wow!"

I've never known a woman whose dialogue was so punctuated by exclamation points. In literature, they're considered garish. But I must admit with Eva, it only seems to render her enthusiasm more infectious. My phone rings in my pocket and I pull it out. Blocked number. I consider rejecting it but who knows, it could be one of our vendors.

"How about you mix one of those drinks for me and I'll be right back?" I ask.

"Sure!"

I head toward the hallway and pick up. "Isadora Valenti speaking."

"Ms. Valenti? Delighted to reach you. This is Grayson Soiree. I'm a writer for the *New Yorker*? I was hoping to speak with you about your bar, Gertrude's, for an upcoming feature."

The floor drops out below me and I swallow to contain my gasp. Making my way to my office, I close the door behind me and collapse upon my chair, in the event I indeed faint.

"Hi Mr. Soiree. Wow. How … did you hear about Gertrude's?"

"I'm an acquaintance of Saturn Martinez," he says. He has a velvety voice with an ever-so-slight continental accent. Proper, sedate, educated, just what I would imagine a writer for the *New Yorker* to sound like. "I saw her writeup on you and thought it would make a unique story to highlight some of the various literary bars that are cropping up in smaller cities around the nation."

If only my father could see me now. My father, who bought me a subscription to the *New Yorker* last Christmas. I have a stack of *New Yorkers* in my apartment. And now I'm being interviewed by them? When only last week I was lamenting my lack of media coverage? This must be a dream!

"Wonderful," I murmur.

"I'm actually in town right now—I'm technically on holiday, road tripping on the west coast. Stayed in Los Angeles last night, now I'm on my way up to San Francisco."

So classy, the way he pronounces things. Vaguely European, but not in a pretentious way. Just a touch. Los Angel-*ees*. San Fran-*ceesco*.

"… I thought since I was out here, I might as well stop by for an interview in person. Seems utterly serendipitous, that I happened to see the article this morning right before I hopped into my car for the next leg of my journey."

He chortles. I don't normally chortle, but my joy overwhelms me, and I join him.

"Are you at Gertrude's at the moment, by chance?" he asks me.

"I am, just training our new bartender."

"Well, I believe I'm outside right now, but if there's a better time later today …"

"Right now?" I ask, scrambling to my feet and desperately fishing around my purse for lipstick. "Oh, I … yes. Wow. Yes, let me just … let you in. Give me a moment."

"Looking forward to it," he says.

In the hectic minute of locating my mirror, applying lipstick, and hyperventilating, I also somehow manage to have an extensive fantasy that Grayson—a dashing essayist in a dapper dress shirt with the top button unbuttoned and slicked-back dark hair with a peppering of gray —will hit it off with me. That perhaps his day in town might turn into an overnight trip. That he might happen to be wildly attracted to women with unruly hair and big noses.

Zofie's right; I do need to get laid. First I'm drooling over a carpenter who doesn't speak any English and now I'm indulging in romantic fantasies about a writer I've never even seen in person.

"Eva," I whisper as I go out to the front. "A writer from the *New Yorker* is here to interview me."

"Wow! I love New York. I saw *Hamilton* there last year—"

"New York*er*," I emphasize. "As in, the literary publication."

Her eyes widen. "With the cartoons?"

"Yes, Eva. With the cartoons." I flash her a huge smile. "How do I look?"

"Stunning! But you have lipstick on your teeth."

What a doll. She's a keeper, this one. I reach across the counter and squeeze her arm. "Thank you."

I rub my teeth and flash another smile.

She gives me the thumbs up. "Break a leg!"

Not sure that's the proper sendoff for this occasion, but I take it. I take a deep breath and stride outside, into the sunshine, using my hand as a visor as I peer up and down the street, on the lookout for that dashing man with the carelessly unbuttoned dress shirt. But all I see is a rather old, balding man in a Hawaiian shirt sitting on a bench next to where my bicycle is locked up. I admit I'm disappointed. But really, what was I expecting? Isadora, this is the *New Yorker*! Who cares what Grayson looks like?

"Hi Grayson, I'm Isadora," I say, coming over and putting my hand out for a handshake.

Grayson looks at my hand, then at me—as if he's just as surprised at my appearance—and shakes it.

"I can't believe the perfect timing of your trip out here," I say. "I'm elated to get to speak with someone from the *New Yorker*. I've been a subscriber for years."

Nine months, technically. Gift subscription. But who's counting?

"Is that so?" he asks.

I gesture toward the front door of Gertrude's, which I've left open. I can see Eva peeking out from behind the bar with a hungry stare. "Would you like to come inside to conduct the interview, or ..."

Grayson's mouth is half-open and he shakes his head. "I'm—I'm sorry, young lady, but I have no idea what you're talking about."

I step back, confused. His voice sounds different than it did on the phone. Perhaps I've identified the wrong person?

"You're not Grayson?" I ask.

"My name's Bill," he says. "My wife's in the bead store and I'm just sitting here catching some rays while she does her shopping."

"I'm so sorry," I say, stepping back from the bench, mortification blooming from my face to my toes and back to my face again. "I thought you were someone else."

"That's all right. You have a good day now."

"You do the same."

I step back toward Gertrude's and look up and down the street. A party of teenagers taking a selfie. A bicycle courier. A throng of businessmen and women with to-go boxes waiting at the crosswalk, clearly on a late lunch break. My heart plummets—he had a blocked number, so how am I to reach him if Grayson is outside the wrong establishment? What if I miss my opportunity?

"Looking for someone?" a voice says.

I whip around, but it's just the disappointing sight of Chuck standing in his doorway, dashing and bright-eyed. Ugh. I am still experiencing guilt about the article. Not that there was anything but the truth in it, but I hadn't expected him to be part of the headline and lede, or part of my story at all, really.

I smile at him. "Oh hi, Chuck. Have you seen anyone … waiting around here?"

"Mmmm. There was a guy who came in and asked for you a minute ago. But I told him that you were up another block and sent him on his way."

My smile drops. "Why the hell would you do that?"

He shrugs. "For fun, I guess."

"For *fun*?" I step over to him. "Chuck, that guy was a writer for the *New Yorker*. He's coming to interview me."

"Fancy."

"You've probably never heard of the *New Yorker*. Let me describe it in terms you might understand: it's like *Sports Illustrated*, but for people who love literature."

"Wow, that sure does sound special."

"It is. And you know what? As much as I don't like you, I would never send a *Sports Illustrated* reporter in the wrong direction if they came to interview you and popped into Gertrude's by mistake."

"Gosh, that's nice of you," he says. "You're so kind."

I sigh exasperatedly and check my phone. Nothing! So I head in the direction Chuck said he sent Grayson, but Chuck says, "You *would* throw me under the bus for a local newspaper interview though. But that's different, right?"

I stop in my tracks. "That *is* different. And that wasn't my intention, okay?"

"Of course not," he says incredulously. "You would never."

I close my eyes and everything goes gold a moment, then open them back up again. "Chuck, can we please discuss this later? I need to find this guy."

"Sure. Okay."

"I need to find him and I have no idea even who I'm *looking* for."

"I can help you there," he says. "He's tall, maybe six-two."

I nod.

"Reddish-brown hair. Well built. Casually dressed. Charming, handsome."

I wait, liking what I'm hearing.

"Talks a little bit *like this*," Chuck says, softening his voice, adopting a vaguely European accent. "Like a quite educated fellow who simply cannot *wait* to interview you as he gallivants from Los Angel-*ees* to San Fran-*ceesco*."

Wait.

What is happening right now?

My heart forgets how to beat. My mouth goes dry. My skin tingles and first all I feel is confusion, then despair, then white-hot rage.

"Ms. Valenti, delighted to meet you," he says in Grayson's voice.

"That," I say, barely able to make out the word. "Is the meanest trick anyone has ever played on me."

"Really? Meaner than you *defaming* me in the local paper the week before my *grand opening*?"

Now that I hear the voice coming from him, I can't believe I fell for it. I hate myself for being a fool. But I hate him even more for making a fool of me.

"I never want to speak to you again," I say. "I hope you fall in a hole and die."

I spin on my heel and go back toward Gertrude's.

"Have a nice day, *dahling*," he says, one more taunt in Grayson's voice. "And you're welcome for fixing your doorknob."

There is no word in the English lexicon to properly describe the cocktail of wrath, shame, and disappointment evoked within me—with a splash of surprise that the boor who evoked the aforementioned cocktail of emotions was the angel who fixed my doorknob.

"Isadora!" Eva says from behind the counter. "How was your interview?"

"Didn't work out." I sit at the counter across from her. "I'd rather not discuss. In fact, I need a drink."

"Oh! I made you an Anne Sexton here," she says, pointing to a martini with a crescent of pink lipstick on the rim. "I had a sip or two. Just to make sure it tasted right."

I wave my hand. "That's okay. I need something strong. Make me a Hunter S. Thompson."

She blinks at me.

"Wild Turkey, neat."

"Got it!"

After Eva pours me a drink, I drink the fire thirstily and then send her on an errand to buy some potpourri for the bathroom. This afternoon and the unsavory turn of events demand an additional Hunter S. Thompson, so I help myself and sit at the bar alone for some time, brooding. I parse the interaction with Chuck in a horrid loop in my brain and imagine all the better replies I could have delivered. To know he's right there, behind the shelves of bottles, maybe even just a dozen feet away, is aggravating.

But as the anesthetizing effects of the whiskey manifest and my muscles unclench, I also recognize my shock that the Grayson voice—that proper, educated, well-spoken man I imagined—came from him. That he's even capable of faking class and eloquence. That he, apparently, fixed my doorknob. Snuck through the gate to hell just to do something thoughtful for no reason. I have to admit my intrigue. The man contains multitudes.

You know who else contained multitudes? Walt Whitman. Powerful poet. Repulsively racist.

Chuck might be more complex than I initially thought. But that doesn't mean I'm not still going to take any opportunity I can to get him back for that horrendous trick he pulled today.

Do I contradict myself?

Very well then, I contradict myself.

chuck

IT'S THE AFTERNOON. Grand opening is three hours away.

You'd think I'd be running around like a headless chicken. Instead, my ass is parked in my office chair, feet kicked up. I'm eyeing my phone's clock. Right now, the Sea Lion boys at Oceano Valley Junior High are practicing; wish I was there for it. Still doesn't make sense to me why Dad was so insistent I quit. Can't I do more than one thing? Have a hobby? Like that poem by that old, bearded dude: I contain multitudes.

"Knock knock, brah," Brayden says, coming into my doorway.

Brayden is the bartender my dad hired. Dad hired him and another dude without consulting me. He hired them less for their bartending experience or work ethic and more for the fact they are both obsessive Cory McCaffrey fans who kissed up to him in the interview. Oh, and he's friends with their dads. Nepotism wins every time. I should know.

Brayden is, to put it mildly, a bro—a boat-shoes-with-board-shorts-wearing, tribal-tattoo-on-the-arm bro. He talks like a surfer but does not surf. His mode of transportation is a longboard. He is the reason "no shirts no shoes no service" signs exist. I have worked with him for two short days and he's already driving me nuts.

"Please stop calling me 'brah,'" I say, putting my phone down. "I don't like to be referred to as lingerie."

He laughs a machine gun laugh, *he-he-he*. "Copacetic. Br—I mean, Charles—"

"Chuck. Call me Chuck."

"Chuck, I was going over inventory, yeah? And it's lookin pretty kosher, but we've got no Jameson. Which, you know, we *need* Jameson for opening night."

"It was supposed to get delivered yesterday."

"They weren't in that delivery. I loaded what came in myself and unpacked it."

"We'll order some next week. We have, what? A dozen other whiskey brands?"

"What about Irish car bombs, man?"

I have never had an Irish car bomb. I guess I look like a guy who should know what an Irish car bomb is, but honestly, I've never even been much of a drinker. I'll have a beer if I meet up with someone. I tinkered with cocktails the past week or two, just to educate myself. Samantha took me wine tasting a couple times when we were together. But I didn't go to a four-year university, never lived in a dorm, and frat parties suck.

"You don't know what an Irish car bomb is?" Brayden says, in horror.

"I do," I lie. "And yeah, you're right. I should get some Jameson. I'll see if I can pick some up to tide us over before next week."

"Tight. Hey, your dad's gonna be there tonight, yeah?"

"I mean, it's opening night. Of course."

"Sick. I invited a shitload of my buds. Told them Cory McCaffrey'd be there and maybe they could snag an autograph."

"Great," I say, trying not to clench my teeth. "Hope they buy drinks."

"Irish car bombs," Brayden says, pointing at me.

"Sure."

He lingers for an awkward beat, and then another awkward beat. "Hey, you think the Dodgers are going to make the playoffs?"

This guy is a walking headache. It's excruciating having him around with nothing to do. Now he's asking me about baseball, as if I give a shit? Baseball is the worst sport. I suffer through summer every year just waiting to get to football and then basketball season again.

"Hey, actually, would you mind taking some petty cash and making a grocery store run to see if you can snag some bottles of Jameson?" I ask.

"On my board?"

"I mean …" I raise my eyebrows, "unless it's too heavy for you."

"Nah." He flexes a bicep. "I can do it, actually. It's casual."

He leaves my office. The sound of the front door opening and shutting.

Silence. A sigh of relief.

In the quiet, I can hear laughter faintly through the wall. Women's voices. Isadora, I'm sure. I get a sick rise of guilt in my stomach, thinking of how excited she looked yesterday when she came outside looking for the man I made up. How hungry she was to find him. Then how her face fell when the joke was exposed—like a kid realizing Santa's not real. I wanted to get her back, and it was funny … but I also wondered immediately if I'd gone too far. If fucking with her emotions like that actually hurt her in some way. I didn't want to hurt her; I just wanted to play around with her a little, give her a zing to make things even.

She's got this magnetic force that makes me want to toy with her.

Picking up my phone, I first search "Irish car bomb" recipe and gag. Next I search "Isadora Valenti" and open her Insta. She's a lot more active on there than I am. I scroll backward through image after image … Isadora with that rude-ass friend of hers at a concert at the Santa Caterina Bowl, bikinied Isadora lying on the beach with a book (I hang on that one a second too long), Isadora giving *what the fuck you lookin at* face in sunglasses, dim shots of Isadora bartending and laughing, Isadora on campus with a backpack in front of a schmancy building. She's got a joyful smile, a smile that almost can't be contained and spreads all over her face.

"You are intoxicating," I admit.

I scroll back up to the more recent pictures, all of the interior of Gertrude's. The latest one, posted today, has an interior shot of her with arms open in the doorway, with the caption *it's opening day// the long-shot dream's come true// have a drink. have two!*

"Haiku," I say, recognizing the pattern from the poetry class I took senior year in high school. "Cute."

Then I look closer and see a stack of boxes next to the doorway. I zoom in and peer closely at my phone. *Jameson* the boxes say. I zoom a little more and see 1171 written on the side. Brady's address.

"Did you steal my whiskey?" I ask loudly. "Seriously?"

I turn off my phone and shake my head at the air.

Of course she stole it. She probably thought it would be a fun way to get back at me after the shit I pulled Wednesday. Come on, though. Sure, what I did was low. But stealing?! Now she's moving into criminal territory.

So I get up and head next door to reclaim what's mine.

The cardboard covering the windows must have come down from Gertrude's this morning, because I can see inside for the first time. String lights in the window under a cursive sign that says *Get Lit*. Honestly, I would have passed the place thinking it's an antique bookstore. She could use some signage telling people it's a bar. She could use some signage, period. Brady's has a neon sign with a foaming beer and a football on it. But I'm not about to give her pointers.

I try to push the glass door open but it's locked. Isadora's behind the bar, on her phone. When she looks up and notices me she ducks behind the counter. Christ in a parachute, are we playing such immature games?

"Come *on*," I say, knocking harder.

Slowly, she rises. Walks toward the front door as if she's walking through molasses. She's wearing a va-va-voom leopard print dress like something a classic movie star would wear, but I'm not about to get distracted by her fantastic figure. Or how irresistible her legs look when they're in high heels.

No, I'm staying focused.

"What," she says, opening the door just a crack.

"I'm missing a shipment of Jameson."

She delivers a deadpan stare.

"And I'm pretty sure it got delivered here," I continue.

"What makes you think that?"

"Just a hunch I have."

She raises an eyebrow and scans me from head to toe and back to head again. "That's what you're wearing for your opening night?"

I look down. Shorts. Long socks, Converse. My Sea Lions sweatshirt. "What, you think I should wear a tux? It's a fucking sports bar."

She abandons the door, as if she's lost interest in the conversation. Heads back to the bar and damn her for the way her ass looks in that dress. Sits on a stool and turns her back to me. I follow her inside, annoyed, but can't help myself from studying the raven tattoo on her back shoulder peeking out from her leopard-print sleeve.

No, not about to be distracted by a tattoo, or the thought of what other secrets might exist underneath that dress. Focus.

I give a gentle kick to the cardboard boxes of Jameson next to the entrance, just like they were in the picture. The bottles clink. She turns to me, her elbows leaning on the bar, her chin resting in her hands. Her nails are painted red. Imagine how good they'd look running up and down my—

Come on, man. Getting turned on by a manicure? Focus.

"You stole my whiskey," I say.

"It was delivered here by mistake yesterday."

"And when exactly were you planning to tell me?"

"At some point in the future."

"So you were just going to keep them stacked here."

"Maybe."

"Leaving me without Jameson. On opening night." She shrugs.

"Look," I say, "I know what I did the other day was … rude."

"Humiliating. Malicious. Heartless. Possibly psychopathic."

"Okay, Lady Thesaurus. Yes. All of those things."

"You came here today to apologize?"

"No, I came here because *you stole from me.*"

"I didn't steal, someone delivered it here."

"And you knowingly didn't tell me."

"I didn't realize a delayed shipment of Jameson was enough to get you red in the face," she says.

Is my face red? Fuck, I hate when my face gets red. A little anger gives me the complexion of a sunburned Oompa Loompa.

"There's a popular drink we serve that uses Jameson," I tell her.

"Is it called a 'shot'?"

"No, it's called an Irish car bomb. I'm sure your bar is too good to serve those."

"We have them. It's called a James Joyce."

I pick up the three boxes. "Portrait of the Bartender as a Pretentious Snob," I say.

Isadora raises her eyebrows and opens her mouth but doesn't say a word.

I push the door open with my sneaker and head to Brady's.

Our doors open at four PM, Dad arriving with a bunch of hooting, guffawing friends who order pitchers and take up all the tables. Food trucks park out front at five PM. It would have been too much a pain in the ass to build our own kitchen in Brady's, so Dad arranged local food trucks to rotate through each night. Opening night, it's a burger truck and already there's a line forming on the sidewalk. I watch it all wondering what I should be feeling. Nerves? Pride? But I come up empty.

In back of the food truck, a van's parked; a string quartet unloads their instruments and heads into Gertrude's. A string quartet. We have DJ BLASTER setting up inside at the moment, so this should be interesting. The dress code is a higher bar over there. Dresses, coats, some ridiculous guy wearing a top hat. Their female to male ratio is much more even than Brady's. Conversations happening out on the sidewalk in front of Gertrude's contain phrases like "contemporary novel," "CoHo is over-rated," and "film adaptation." Conversations happening outside Brady's contain words like "killer quads," "fuck Lincecum," and "sick waves."

Brady's has a decent crowd forming inside, baseball games and boxing matches flashing on the many TVs. Brayden and Sean are both working tonight. I much prefer Sean: bearded, rag over his shoulder, monosyllabic responses, scowling, efficient. I wander, slapping hi-fives with Dad's friends, stopping to chat with a couple old buddies from high school who showed up. Take a few minutes in the office with the door closed, sitting at my desk. That blank feeling. That non-of-this-is-real feeling. That Charles feeling.

Not to have a one-man pity party over here, but I'm real-izing in real time that even if I could feel joy right now, I'd have no one to share it with. After high school, I floated around from entry-level job to entry-level job, the profes-sional equivalent of throwing shit at the wall. Tried a carpentry apprenticeship, city college, took a graphic design course, finally thought I was getting somewhere when I started coaching. Met nice folks everywhere I landed, but never landed long enough to make a lasting friendship. Then Sam and I got together and it all happened so fast. She moved into my apartment and absorbed me into her circle of friends. But when she left, I didn't stay in close contact with anyone. And now here I am, handed a bar, living a just-add-water life. And, well, there's no other way to describe it: I'm still thirsty.

Back out in the bar, I plaster a smile on my face and walk around with a pint. Hey! Hi! Yeah, great place, right? So dope! Thanks for comin' out, man! The music's started, loops of *mmm-chh, mmm-chh,* the sun's gone down. People are anywhere from lightly buzzed to already snockered. Brayden comes by with a mop and bucket and yells in my ear that "someone snarfed in the pissroom sink, brah," and I'm just so fucking glad I have my own private bathroom and don't have to deal with the public bathroom whatsoever.

My dad grabs me to introduce me to a tall guy with an intense spray tan, shouting, "My son Charles! He owns this place!"

"Nice spot!" the man yells over the music. "We should talk about doing events together sometime!"

"Nate owns Nate's Sporting Goods store, down on Palmera," Dad explains.

"Definitely!" I say, pocketing the guy's card.

Over near the door, I spot Tyrus and a woman I assume is his wife Monique: tall, thin, with a short afro and blue lipstick that matches her dress. She is not smiling. They stand near a high top with glasses of water.

"Good turnout, man," Tyrus says, clapping my back. "Have you met my wife, Monique?"

She waves at me, offers a tight-lipped smile.

I shake her hand. "Haven't met you, but Tyrus talks about you nonstop."

Monique's smile spreads, revealing perfect white teeth. She beams at Tyrus. "Awww. Does he?"

Tyrus slings an arm around her back. "What? You're surprised?"

"Psssh, I don't know what you say to your boys when I'm not around."

"All good stuff, I swear," I tell her.

"We wanted to swing by and say congrats," Tyrus says. "I think we're going to head out though … not sure this is really Monique's scene."

"It's just a little loud for me," she says. "I'm more about a mellower vibe."

I'll be honest, mellower vibe sounds amazing right about now. A vibe so mellow I'm back in my apartment in my slippers and robe, watching TV. "Might want to try the place next door," I say. "They've got a string quartet. Good wine selection. Nice cocktails."

I step outside and point them to Gertrude's. While I'm out here, I take a couple pics on my phone of the food truck, Brady's with the sign lit up and the crowd in the window, post them to Brady's social media pages. I look up and there's Isadora outside, hugging a man with gray hair. Her eyes are closed. There's a flower in her hair that wasn't there earlier. She hugs him so tightly. Is that her boyfriend? I look away, trying not to stare, eavesdropping as much as I can over the chatter of people waiting in line for the food truck.

"You came!" she's saying. "How?? Seriously, this makes tonight absolutely magical!"

He responds quietly. I can't make out what he says.

"Didn't see it coming at all," she says, linking her arm in his. "Well played, Daddy."

Right at that moment, my mom comes running up to me in stilettos, jeans, and a tank top, tiny purse swinging on her arm. "Chucky!" she squeals. "You did it!"

"I did it," I say to her.

Hands up in the air, she gives me a double hi-five.

"You're a business owner. I'm so proud of you. Come here, hon."

Mom opens her arms and gives me a hug, her head on my chest. I'm a little embarrassed by this display of affection, but what are you going to do? When I look up, Isadora's holding hands with her dad and heading back into her bar. She stops mid-step and catches my eye for a moment, something new in her gaze. Soft. Curious. Shining. I lift an arm up from my mom's embrace and wave at Isadora, and she smiles at me before heading inside.

You know, all in all, it's been a pretty damn good night.

isadora

IF YOU CAN KEEP your head when all about you are inebriated, when the chaise lounge has been stained with cabernet, when the bathroom toilet has flooded and you have run out of limes—you'll be a bartender, my lady.

After Eva, Zofie, and I finally send the last patron on her merry way (a woman snoring at a writing desk with a copy of *The Bluest Eye* covering her face), we get to work. Those two cherubs clean up while I count the drawer and lock the money up in the safe in my office. Then the three of us sit at the bar and pop a bottle of brut and go over every outrageous moment we had no time to process or gossip about at the time.

"Look at this," Zofie says, shuffling the pages of a manuscript. In a silver dress and wedges, she's a disco-era wonder tonight. "The man-bun in the zebra-print jacket? He gave me his self-published autobiography."

I sip the bubbly. "Bold."

"You know only a man would do that," Zofie muses. "No woman would be that presumptuous."

"Mmmm!" Eva says, finger in the air. She leans behind the bar, extracts a stack of papers, and waves it in the air. "He gave me one too!"

"I wonder if it's any good," I say.

"It's called *And On The Eighth Day, God Created Me*," Zofie says. "It's written in what appears to be Comic Sans. And it begins with a twenty-page chapter called 'MY BIRTH.'"

"Next," I say.

Zofie clicks her heels over to the recycling bin, raises the manuscript over her head, and drops it in with a *thunk*.

Eva downs her champagne in one gulp and picks up her purse. "Mind if I take off?"

"Not at all," I say. "Thanks so much for everything today."

She flashes me a faded pink smile. "You got it, Boss."

After the door slams shut, Zofie raises her eyebrows at me. "*Boss*. A hot young bartender just addressed you as *Boss*."

I turn on my stool to face her. "I can't believe this is my life, Zof."

She comes to hug me from behind. "I'm so fucking proud of you."

"And I'm so glad you're here. Super appreciate you jumping behind the counter and helping us once you got here."

"Of course! Felt like old times."

"How was your audition?" I ask. "I didn't even get a chance to ask you."

She drops her arms from me and groans. "It was crap. No way I'm getting a callback. I had to cluck like a chicken while running on a treadmill and it was a disaster, I have the hugest bruise on my ass now."

I'm opening my mouth to demand more details, but she keeps going.

"Babe!" she says, jumping to sit up at the bar. "Your dad! Your *dad* came."

A gigantic sigh escapes me as I recollect that moment. I was flabbergasted that he showed up. He's terrified of flying. He hasn't been out here to visit me since he came to send me off to college. Since then, it's been me flying back to Ohio a couple times a year to see him, and our "Saturday morning coffee" that we have together on a video call each week.

I wipe a tear away. "That meant so much to me. Probably the highlight of my night, to be honest."

"Where's he staying?"

"The Ramada. For a week! I'm going to get to show him around Santa Caterina."

She pours more champagne into our glasses. "He seems sweet."

"He is absolutely the dearest man in the world."

"Well, except for my dad," Zofie says.

"Fight me."

"Eh, too lazy."

We drain the bottle and lock the place up. Outside, I unlock my bike. Brady's light is still on and I can see someone wiping a table. Peering in, I see it's not Chuck. It's the guy with the tribal tattoo who said "hey you sexy lil leopard" when I encountered him out back as we both threw away garbage earlier. Chuck's hired some real winners, apparently.

"Looking for your special friend?" Zofie asks.

"He's not there," I say. "And he's neither special, nor my friend."

She shakes her head at me. "So cute. Falling for the boy next door."

I pucker my face.

"Come on, babe," she chides. "You totally have a thing for him."

"I do not."

"You always do this."

"What?"

"Go for the most obnoxious people."

"Says a lot about you."

"I was the exception."

Zofie gets on the back of my bike. We used to ride this way home from Study Hall after long nights, her arms around my waist, the wind in our hair, a sea of stars illuminating the black sky, our voices carrying along the empty streets.

There is such comfort sometimes in a little déjà vu.

Not that I would ever describe myself this way out loud, but I am very much a daddy's girl. If you met him, you would understand. He worked as an elementary school teacher for forty years and finally retired last year. He watches competitive baking shows the way some men watch sports, and now he's elevated himself by learning to bake his own extravagant cakes. He's the sweetest, most supportive man alive and he gives the best hugs. If Santa Caterina weren't one of the Most Expensive American Cities in the Country (according to *Forbes* magazine), I could probably convince him to move out here. Then again, he loves Brockman. He loves our old Victorian house with my mom's portrait greeting him in the foyer above the coatrack, and the sunroom he built with his own two hands where he has coffee every morning and watches the birds in the cherry trees.

Today, though, he's traded cherry trees for palms, and the crisp-aired, red-leaved Midwestern autumn for a breezy, blue-skied California day where you'd never guess summer is over. We're eating brunch together at the Tides Café, an upscale diner right on Cielo Beach, with a view of curling blue waves, surfers, and occasional dolphins. Tides Café has everything from crab cake benedict to goat cheese frittata, but my dad, as usual, just opts for buttered wheat toast and black coffee. He even bought a paper to accompany his breakfast, same routine he has at home. Only it's a paper copy of the *Santa Caterina News* instead of reading the *New York Times* on this tablet.

"Guess it's time for me to accept this really is home for you," he says. "I think for a long time, I kept hoping you'd come back."

"And do what? Work at the rubber company?"

Brockman's entire economy and culture is centered around the enormous rubber factory at the edge of town. In fact, the town's motto is *Where the boing gets going*. On certain days, a faint rotten-egg stench of sulfur dioxide blows through our neighborhood. My dad has lived in Brockman his entire life and claims he can't smell it.

"Open a bookstore or a bar of your own there, maybe?" he says, as if even he realizes the absurdity of this suggestion.

"Dad, I love you," I say, "but I do not love Ohio."

"I know you don't. This place fits you." He sips his coffee. "Your mom's up there looking down on you, and she's so proud of you, you know."

I offer a tiny smile, push my tofu scramble around the plate. Dad has the best intentions. But it makes me so sad every time he brings her up in that cheerful tone, as if she's right out of eyesight. How he claims the cardinals that visit his porch in the mornings are her spirit.

"I'm sure she would be proud if she were here," I rephrase carefully. "And it's bittersweet that part of the reason I had the money to open the bar at all was the money from the settlement."

"That and saving every extra penny you made for, what, four years?"

"Almost six."

He gazes at me with such adoration teeming in his brown eyes.

"You know how incredible you are?" he asks. "I hope someday you find a man—or *woman*," he corrects himself, because he's ever careful to honor my sexual orientation, "who loves you even half as much as I do. Because half of—"

"Infinity is still infinity," I finish. "Yes, yes, I know."

"You have me memorized."

"Well, your catchphrases, anyway."

"Fair enough." He waves a waiter down for a coffee refill and then clears his throat. "*Are* you … seeing anyone?"

"No. I don't have time for that right now."

He rubs his hand on his beard. Every time I see him, more white has crept into his beard and hair. If only life came with a pause button because I ache watching him grow older. "I hope at some point you make time for yourself," he says. "You know, your mother was your age when we met."

"Really? I thought you met when you got the job at Brockman Elementary and Mom was teaching special ed."

"No, that was when I asked her out. We'd actually first met when I was in grad school. Thank you very much, sir," he says to the waiter who refills his coffee. "These are some fine beans." When the waiter's left again, he sips his steaming coffee and studies the air and his lips perk up. "She didn't like me much that first time we met. She worked in the university library. I was eating at one of the long study tables. In fact, the first thing she said to me was, 'Interesting that you are able to digest Proust, but cannot read a five-word sign.' And then she pointed to a placard that said NO EATING IN THE LIBRARY."

"The woman had a point, Dad."

"She did, she certainly did. Then I didn't see her for

five years and the first thing she said to me when we met at Brockman Elementary was, 'Oh, it's the man who left crumbs all over my library table.'"

I laugh. "Wow, Mom sure could hold a grudge."

"Well, I wore her down with my charm pretty quickly after that."

"The rest is history."

"Or romance," he says, looking out at the ocean. "The rest is a romance story."

Romances shouldn't have sad endings, I think. But I guess it all depends on where you end the novel.

We sit for a bit finishing breakfast, me emptying my email inbox, Dad reading the paper. After the check comes, he points to a story on the bottom corner of B1. LOCAL SPORTS FANS HAVING A BALL AT NEW DOWNTOWN BAR. A pic of Chuck next to his dad, both of them smiling. His dad is towering, bald, tan, brawny. He resembles a man you'd hire to work security with confidence. Next to him, Chuck appears different to me. A far cry from a tough guy despite his build, his ruddy hair curling up around his ears, eyes piercingly blue. Even so, I brace myself, assuming he's sought revenge for my B1 story by getting a story of his own.

"Let me see that," I say.

I read through the article, scanning for my name or the word "Gertrude's," but see nothing until I get to the end.

"There's nothing entitled about my son opening Brady's," Cory McCaffrey says. "If you want entitlement and snobbery, go to Gertrude's, the bar next door where you need a bachelor's degree to even understand the drink menu."

"That is not true," I say as I shut the paper.

"What's not true?" Dad asks.

"Never mind. Not worth an explanation."

As we get up and head to the mission (my first of many touristy activities I plan to take my father on while he's here), I admit I'm a little peeved. Though I was expecting worse. And honestly, if anything, I expected it to come from Chuck himself. Or "Charles" as the article calls him. But now his quasi-famous millionaire dad is taking potshots at me … though I guess that's appropriate for a man whose father does everything else for him in life.

The part that irks me most is that I've never thought about how Gertrude's menu, the bar, the inside jokes actually *are* inaccessible to people who aren't well-read in classic literature. But that just makes it niche. Not snobby.

Right?

While I may have prejudged her, Eva, it turns out, is a goddess in cat-eye glasses and swing dresses. The woman makes a mean Manhattan (though we call it a "Miss Lonelyhearts" at Gertrude's), she's efficient and organized, sweet as a sugar cube, yet she's got a shocking fierceness to her she can summon when needed. In the two weeks since the bar opened, I've seen her take a drunkard's keys so he wouldn't drive home, slap a lecher's face who touched her ass, confiscate a fake ID, and chase two intoxicated fist-fighters out the door while she brandished a bottle of brandy.

And she covered for me extensively last week so I could traipse about the county, showing my dad the unforgettable sunset vistas, the quaint zoo, the historic carousel, the beach vendors and landscape painters on the pier, wine tasting, and every other memory I could make during our too-short visit. I fought tears when we parted at the airport —though my dad promised me he'd come back again, I wonder if it will take another momentous occasion to get him here. A house purchase, which, in this expensive town, feels about as farfetched at this point as a wedding.

But while I was out basking in every Dad moment I could get, Gertrude's was in capable hands. And business has so far been good. Nothing like opening night, of course, but our two Saturday poetry open mic nights have now had some repeats who I hope will become regulars and our Tuesday trivia nights have attracted a good number of college students. And today, Eva suggests we offer discounts to book clubs that want to hold discussions here.

"Think about it!" Eva says, while washing pint glasses in the sink. She's wearing an apron with cherries all over it and looks like a *Good Housekeeping* photo a la 1950. "Weeknights only, right? Slow times. We tell people they can bring their book discussions here. And not only do they get to hang out in a pretty literary space, but who knows? Maybe they get new members to join. Livestream it on BookTok! So, it's, like, social."

I nod, contemplating this idea. The bar opened an

hour ago and right now there are only a few students sitting at a table, studying over pints of beer. I'm intrigued by Eva's suggestion. My nagging thought, though, is that we're going to attract … a different clientele. Folks who read mass market paperbacks and best-sellers. Middle-aged women who love romance novels. I don't say this out loud though, because, well, I've seen the covers of some of the books Eva reads: the shirtless men, the lusty, locked embraces. I would offend her if I insinuated romance was inferior to literary fiction. And though I'm quite sure it *is*, I might come off as snooty for saying it.

Even worse, I might, in fact, be snooty.

Oh my God, am I?

I hate to think that. I don't want to foster elitism. I want to be inclusive.

"Let's try it out," I say. "One night a week to start. Monday nights, maybe, because they're the slowest. We can call it Book Club Night and give book clubs half off if they bring their book for group discussion."

Eva squeals. "It's going to be so fun! I'll make some fliers for the bar here so we can let people know about it." Her expression falters a moment though. "Though Monday is one-dollar shot night at Brady's. Last Monday it got kind of wild."

"Was that the night the cops came because someone started hitting someone else with a pool cue?"

"I think so." She eyes herself in a cocktail shaker, takes a finger to perfect the outline of her lipstick. "Maybe I'll go next door and talk to the owner." She puts the shaker down. "You know him, right? The guy who looks like a younger, hotter Prince Harry?"

"*Chuck?*"

"Yes," she says with a coy smile. "Chuck."

Did she seriously compare him to Prince Harry? Because Chuck's not hideous, but let's be realistic here.

"We generally try to steer clear of each other," I tell her, coming behind the counter and straightening bottles on the shelf. "We didn't exactly hit it off."

"What happened?"

I open my mouth to try to tell her but realize it's beyond words. "We're just very different people."

"Do you know if he's single?"

I turn around. Eva is smoothing her hair.

"I have no idea," I say. "Are you thinking of asking him out?"

She shrugs. "Why not?"

There's something I want to say. It's on the tip of my tongue, or more like on the tip of my brain. I want to dissuade her, badly, suddenly, but why? Why would I care if she wants to date him?

I beam an assuring smile her way. "You should, then."

She unties her apron strings and hangs it up on a hook. "Since it's slow, you mind if I go over there and try to catch him? I'll talk to him about Mondays."

"Sure, go ahead."

"I won't be too long."

"Take your time."

She walks around the counter, catches her reflection in the mirror behind the bar, and pulls her dress down a smidge to highlight her cleavage. Eva's undeniably hot and Chuck's one lucky dog. He's lucky to have such a gorgeous gem interested in him.

Takes about three minutes of staring out the front door to realize I'm standing here behind the counter, grinding my teeth, forgetting to exhale.

chuck

BRADY'S HAS BEEN UP and running three weeks.

In that time, we've gotten so busy we've had to hire another bartender. Our social media accounts have exploded with followers. We've sold out of that tower of Jameson I had to reclaim from next door. We're raking it in.

And I don't give a shit.

Brady's instantaneous success is boringly predictable. No shock in the fact that men flock here every night in baseball caps yelling at TVs. Big fat yawn for every middle-aged guy who comes strutting in here in their number six Grizzlies jersey, asking if Cory McCaffrey's in for an autograph. Brayden's got an ever-flowing parade of friends coming in to visit him, the floors are grody, and our pool table somehow lost its eight ball.

Still don't give a shit.

I have learned that I, Chuck McCaffrey, am gifted with the power of invisibility. Each day I come in, greet Sean, Brayden, or our latest addition Chadley with a head nod, then duck into my office. Behind the closed door, I spend hours scrolling the internet or playing Farmtopia on my phone. Sometimes I kick my feet up and enjoy a nap. When I come out, the bartenders stop snickering or guiltily usher a friend out the door and I realize that I am now The Boss and I invoke fear just by entering a room. What a joke!

Every few days, usually after he's hit the gym in the early afternoon before the place opens, my dad comes in and I come out of the office. He proceeds to walk me around Brady's giving me a tour of criticisms: "Do these tables look clean to you?" "Someone didn't refill this napkin dispenser." "This nail right here's a lawsuit waiting to happen." I nod and thank him and when he leaves, I go back into my office.

Or I don't.

I have also spent a lot of time away from Brady's. Running "errands" that involve me going home and sitting on my couch watching TV. Or visiting the gym for dawdling hours in the middle of the day. Long meandering lunch breaks and dinner breaks. Walks on the beach.

So Eva has been a welcome distraction.

Knock, knock.

"Ready?" she asks, poking her head in my office.

Pink bobbed hair shining, pale glossy lips perked up, looking serpentine in her green dress with its snaked curves. It's silly that she looks at me this way. Me sitting here in a Slayer shirt and checkered Vans with no socks and hair I cut myself over a kitchen sink.

"Ready," I say, getting up.

I hear a thump in the wall. Wait a moment to hear more, imagining Isadora there. It's so odd how some wood and drywall's enough to pretend another person isn't with us.

"Ready?" Eva asks again.

I'm no sophisticated literate like you'd expect from next door, but I am smart enough to realize our dialogue needs work.

"Ready," I confirm, grabbing my sweatshirt.

We go outside. It's early evening and fog's still clinging to the palm trees. It gives Riviera Avenue a mysterious air to it, like something out of a film noir movie. Eva looks like she could have stepped right out of one as a classic femme fatale. But I'm a far cry from Humphrey Bogart so I'm not sure what I'm doing in this movie. We pass the spice store, the tattoo shop, cross the street, and continue walking up Riviera.

"So how was your first book club night at Gertie's?" I ask Eva.

"Just one club showed up," Eva says.

"Better than zero."

"True! Though I'd hoped it would be more."

"How'd you advertise it?"

"I made these cute little fliers and added it our calendar on our website."

"Maybe try the library's bulletin board," I say. "And if you have a few bucks to throw at it, some targeted social media ads can help."

"I don't know anything about advertising," Eva says.

"You'll have to teach me."

"I mean, that about covers it," I say.

Long awkward silence.

Is it obvious I suck at this dating thing? Because I do. I suck. Small talk's excruciating and I don't know how to flirt. The best relationships I've had are with people who I became friends with first, girls who I genuinely had things in common with and didn't have to wrack my brain to jumpstart a conversation. I've had a single one-night-stand in my life and I didn't even enjoy it. I was uncomfortable and overthinking it the entire time. I joined a dating app for a half day earlier this year and deleted it. Back when we were together, Sam told me that she thought I was "demisexual" which means someone who needs emotional connection to enjoy sex with someone. Sounds accurate, but I'm not about to go around telling people I'm a "demisexual." Dating is just one more area of my life where I feel like a fraud pretending to know what I'm doing.

We get to the sushi restaurant. Nice place I've passed but never eaten at. Paper lanterns, bonsai trees, candles on the tables. I picked this place after searching the internet for "best first date spots Santa Caterina" and now that we're here my pulse picks up a little because the ambience is romantic and I'm feeling the pressure. Also I probably should have worn something fancier, based on what I'm seeing in here.

It's fine. Deep breath and count to four, let it out and count to four.

"You doing okay?" Eva asks after we sit down.

I look up from the menu. "Yeah, great. You?"

"I'm good." She smiles. "What do you think of my dress? It's my first time wearing it."

"It's nice. I like that green color." I go back to the menu. "How about we order some rolls and share?"

"Sure!"

"You like unagi?"

Eva leans in, blinking, smile frozen.

"Unagi," I explain. "You know, eel?"

She makes a face and laughs.

"Okay, so ... no unagi."

"I'm sorry," she says. "I'm not really a fish person."

She's not really a fish person. The girl who, when I suggested sushi earlier, replied, "Sounds amazing!!"

"What do you usually order when you go to sushi restaurants?" I ask.

"Um ... chicken teriyaki?"

I haven't been on many dates, but I do believe a person's eating habits tell you a lot about them. And the fact that Eva goes to a sushi restaurant and orders chicken teriyaki is not a great sign. The fact that she asks the waiter for no teriyaki sauce and whether or not they have French fries instead of rice is an even worse sign. I order an unagi roll and try not to think about how much fun it used to be when Sam and I went out on dates. We shared plates. We liked to order something on the menu neither of us had tried before. And I never had to sit there in silence, wondering what to say next.

"I've always wanted to go to Japan," says Eva.

"Yeah? Me too," I say, grateful for some common ground. "What about Japan interests you?"

She shrugs. "I don't know. The food?"

The ... ? But you just ordered chicken teriyaki with no teriyaki??

"Interesting."

The waiter comes, takes our order, and brings us two miso soups.

"So you enjoying working at the bar?" I ask.

"I am!" she says. "Isadora's a great boss."

"Is she?" I lean in, genuinely intrigued. "What makes her a great boss?"

"She's, like, passionate, you know? She cares about every little detail in the bar, getting them just right. She's inspiring to me, I don't know, being a young woman like her and knowing exactly what she wants and making it happen."

"It's pretty impressive," I say, sipping my soup.

"I mean, same with you!" Eva says. "Brady's seems to be really taking off."

It's not the same. Not at all. But I don't tell her this.

"Has Isadora hired anyone else?" I ask.

"Not yet. I don't think she can afford to."

"So she must be in there all the time."

"Yeah, that's another thing I love about her: she's out sweeping the stoop every morning. She cleans the bathrooms every day. I've worked other places where the bosses are above all that grunt work. Like, you can tell they think they're better than you. But Isadora's not like that. She takes pride in every bit of work she has to do."

Unlike me, who farts around in the office all day long playing video games on my phone.

"Guessing she doesn't have much of a life outside the bar then," I say.

"Yeah, doesn't seem like it. I mean, her dad visited her recently and she spent a lot of time with him. She doesn't date though."

"At all?" I ask, surprised. "Why not?"

Eva sips her soup with a horrible slurping sound. Slurping, chewing with your mouth open, anything involving weird squishy sounds while eating is a major pet peeve of mine. I smile, clenching my teeth.

"I don't know," Eva says. "I haven't asked her. I just know I've seen a couple guys ask her out and she's told them she doesn't date."

"What kind of guys?" I ask, curiously.

"Customers. You know." She smiles. "When you're a bartender, you get asked out a lot. I'm sure it happens to you too."

I'm rarely behind the bar. And look at me. Look at our clientele. "Not really."

"I mean, *I* asked you out," she says with a flirty smile. "So it does happen to you."

I smile. "Oh. Right."

As we finish our soups and I pretend to ignore the sounds of Eva's slurping, I try to imagine what kinds of guys are Isadora's types if not nerdy book-loving customers at her bar. And just writing off dating? Saying you don't date … at all? How does that work? She's young and gorgeous and sharp as hell. She has so much going for her. Anyone who ends up with her would hit the jackpot.

"Chuck?" Eva says, waving her hand. "Where'd

you go?"

"Sorry," I say, snapping back to reality.

Eva smiles at me. Her mouth is a little pink around the edges, like her lipstick smeared. "I was asking if this soup has tofu in it?"

"Yeah, miso soup always has tofu."

"Oh." She rubs around her mouth and sticks her tongue out almost like she's gagging. "Oh no."

"Not a tofu fan?" I ask.

That's when I notice the hives forming all around her mouth.

"I'm allergic," she says.

So we leave before the main course and go to CVS for Benadryl. I take her home in my car as she itches her poor face.

"At least my throat's not swelling up, so that's a plus!" she says brightly as we pull up to her place. "Want to come in?"

The place we pulled in front of is a Spanish-style mansion surrounded by a lush, elaborate garden. I raise my eyebrows. "*This* is your place?"

"I live in the guest house in the back. Want to see it?"

Eva's giving me a flirty look covered in hives, which is just making me sad.

"I should probably get going," I say.

"Oh. Okay."

Her face falls so hard so fast that my gut buckles in guilt.

"I mean, maybe for a minute?" I say. "I'm still kind of worried about your allergic reaction."

"This?" she says, pointing to her face. "This is nothing, believe me. It's when I start wheezing and turning blue that you have to worry." She laughs and gets out of the car. "Come on!"

I'm left alone in the car a moment, wondering if I should do a quick YouTube tutorial on administering CPR if this date is going to continue.

She knocks on her window. "You're coming, right?"

"Sure," I say.

I reluctantly follow her up a long set of stone steps on the side of the mansion. Automatic flood lights come on and a window lights up on the side. An old man's wrinkled, squinting face appears in the window and he opens it yelling, "I'm calling 9-1-1!"

"It's okay, Mr. Harrow!" Eva yells. "It's just me! Eva!"

"Who?"

"Eva!" she yells. "The girl who lives in the back?"

"Who's this man you're with?"

"This is a gentleman I work with. Well, he works at the bar next door. He owns Brady's. Have you heard of it?"

"No," the man shouts back. "Can't say I have."

"He's Cory McCaffrey's son. You know who Cory McCaffrey is?"

"Politician?"

"No, a football player. For the Grizzlies."

"Didn't they play the Superbowl last year?"

May I silently ask what the fuck is going on? We are standing below a row of blinding security lights having a shouty conversation with a bewildered, grumpy old man who lives in the main house.

"No," I speak up finally. "They made the Superbowl three years ago. And lost."

"Well, don't worry son. You'll get there." The old man salutes us, for some reason. "Have a good night, Evelyn."

"You too, Mr. Harrow."

Eva leads the way up the steps and the old man continues squinting after us. When we get to the top, there's a Spanish-style guesthouse with a squat palm in front of it. Eva opens the front door without unlocking it and steps inside, kicking off her shoes. In the dim light, I can make out an aquarium bubbling on the countertop, a dress rack, and at least five creepy mannequins.

"Those are my roommates," she jokes, flipping the light on.

"Um, hi," I say to them.

The place is adorable, but tiny. She has no living room. She has a bed, a sewing table, clothing racks that face the kitchenette. I'm not sure where to sit. It would be weird to sit on her bed, right? I barely know her.

"Something to drink?" Eva asks, heading over to behind the counter.

"That's okay," I say. I'm still starving because we never ate dinner.

She takes some wine out of the fridge and pours herself a glass. "You sure? You won't join me for just one drink?"

"I mean, I ..."

She's already pouring a second glass. She hands it to me and we cheers.

"To a wonderful first date," she says, in a velvety voice, with no irony whatsoever.

She's very beautiful. But right now it's hard to not look at her hive-covered face without feeling extremely alarmed. She's giving me bedroom eyes but I clear my throat and walk over to the mannequins.

"So tell me about your roommates," I say.

Excitedly, Eva shows off her sewing table and dress patterns. She tells me she made the dress she's wearing, which is legitimately impressive. I had no idea. When she slips off into the bathroom for a moment, I quickly search "how long allergic reaction last" on my phone. It says it can peak up to two hours later. So what if it gets worse? I'm about to search for some quick CPR tips when she comes back out and puts on some Taylor Swift and sits on her bed.

"You sure you're feeling okay?" I ask.

"Me? I'm wonderful! Sit!" she says, patting the bed next to her.

I don't know what the alternative is except to stand here awkwardly. So I sit.

"You're such a sweet guy to worry about me," she says. "Thanks for taking me home."

"Yeah, I'm just sorry about the tofu."

"Psssh," she says, putting her hand on my leg. "Not your fault."

She's definitely looking to kiss me right now, and I can't. I cannot put my lips on that hive-covered face as I worry about whether or not I might have to suddenly perform CPR.I get up and pretend to be interested in her fish.

"Wow, these are amazing," I say. "Tell me about them."

She has tetras all named after characters from *Stranger Things*, and she describes each in detail. That's nice. That fills some time up. I still have a half glass of wine left to drink though. Not sure how I can continue to avoid the bed since it's the only piece of furniture you can sit on in this entire room-sized house, so I ask if I can check out the plants outside on her porch I spotted on the way in. You know, because I'm so interested in plants.

So I go out here and slam the rest of my wine and breathe a few minutes. Look up at the mess of silver stars and make up my own constellations. A mountain, a shopping cart, a sad face. Is there something wrong with me? There's a smoking hot girl who clearly wants to sleep with me inside and I'm getting hung up on a few itchy blotches she has on her face. What does it matter?

You know what, it doesn't.

It doesn't matter.

This is exactly what is wrong with me. This is textbook brainfucking Chuck. I get so hung up and in my head I can't enjoy anything. I'm over it.

I'm going to walk inside right now and sit on that bed and put my lips on hers and close my eyes and turn my brain off. And see where this goes.

Deep breath. I push the door back open and step inside.

But Eva's collapsed onto her bed. Oh fuck. Is she ... dead? No, she's snoring louder than a freight train. Benadryl and white wine. Phew. I take the empty glass from her hand and go put it in the sink next to mine. I pull a blanket from the end of the bed, drape it over her, and sneak out.

Chump, I know, but relief floods me as I tiptoe down the stairs and back to my car. As I pick up a burger at the drive thru and go back to my apartment to eat it while watching cartoons in my robe and slippers, I think of Isadora. I think of her saying she doesn't date. I feel like, you know what? I get it. I do.

Hell, maybe I should start saying the same thing.

I text with Eva on and off over the next week and some change but make excuses about being so busy with World Series this week and all. I'm not sure how this thing that never was really a thing is going to end with her, but I would hedge my bet on disappointment. So when Chadley comes into my office to tell me I have a visitor on a Thursday right after we open, my stomach pitfalls. I should give her, us, another chance. But it fills me with such dread I might as well be telling myself I need to go to the dentist.

As for Chadley, he's standing in the doorway with a Jack-O-Lantern grin because he's some kind of sketchy amateur boxer. He thinks *Fight Club* is a moral philosophy. He tried to argue we need a gun at the bar for "protection." People talk about checkered pasts? This is a man with a checkered future. My dad hired him as a favor to the guy's uncle. Brady's runs on a steady fuel of nepotism and trust fund money.

"Is it a woman?" I ask Chadley. "Pink hair? Retro fashion?"

"Shit, I wish," Chadley says. "Just some old dude in a visor."

I stretch in relief. "Okay, be out in a minute."

When I stroll out to the bar, it's already semi-packed for happy hour. A table of office-goers with ties loosened and top buttons unbuttoned. Some girls who look like they came straight from the gym. A table full of pipsqueaks who make me feel old. My God, are they really twenty-one? I cross over to the bar to make sure Chadley checked their IDs, but am intercepted by a short guy in a visor with a surly look on his face.

"Chuck," he says.

It's only when I notice the yellow pad in his hand that I realize it's Aiden's dad. The most annoying dad in pee-wee football history, right here.

What the fuck is he doing at my bar?

"Ray Feinstein," he says, reaching out to shake my hand. "I'm Aiden's dad. Sea Lions?"

"Sure, sure, I remember you. How are you?"

"You know, hanging in there. Season's kicking off, so we're busy. Sea Lions beat the Penguins by three points last week."

"Nice."

"Hey, you have a few minutes?" he asks.

"Sure." I point to a high-top in the corner. "Have a seat. You want anything? A beer?"

"That's all right, I'll be quick. I know you're busy."

Hilarious how everyone thinks that. We sit across from each other. I've never sat down and had a chat with this man before. Has he yelled at me from the sidelines?

Shouted suggestions I've ignored? Indeed. But I've avoided conversations with him because he was pretty much the worst thing about coaching the Sea Lions.

"So I wanted to ask if you had any plans to maybe return to coaching?" Ray asks. "I mean, again, I know you've got a lot on your hands here, and I've asked Tyrus, and he says he doesn't think you have the time. But it's ten hours a week, tops, including games. And Aiden's performance was a lot stronger with you around—I think he looked up to you. Since you left, his interest has been flagging. He's not doing drills at home. This replacement they got for you? Owen? He's inexperienced. And I wanted to show you some of the plays he's had the kids do, they're just—"

He's pushing the legal pad toward me, but I gently push it away and cut him off. "Listen, man. Ever think that Aiden's interest might be waning because you're going at him a little too hard with this football stuff?"

Ray stares at me as if I just spoke to him in Pig Latin.

"Just let him have fun," I say. "Stop worrying so much about it."

"If he wants to play pro, he's got to start early," Ray says. "Your dad was already a star player by the time he was a freshman in high school."

Great, so Ray's memorized the entire Wikipedia entry for Cory McCaffrey and is using it as a blueprint for his kid's life.

"Does Aiden even *want* to play pro?" I ask.

"Yes!"

"No offense, Ray, but he's, what, eleven? Your kid

doesn't know what he wants yet. And you following him around with your legal pad and being so pushy all the goddamn time is probably ruining any legit passion he had for the sport."

"Hey," Ray says. Clearly the "no offense" prefix didn't do its job because he's turning red in the face. "I'm trying to support my son."

"There's a difference between supporting and suffocating."

Ray gets up, collecting his legal pad and adjusting his visor. "You know, never mind. I came here because my kid looks up to you. I thought I might be able to pitch the idea of you coming back to the team, or even just having some one-on-one coaching sessions with my son. But instead, you're insulting me."

"Listen, I'm sorry if it came off that way," I say. "I'm just giving it to you straight, you know? As Cory McCaffrey's son. As someone who was highly pressured to play football myself. All it ended up doing was confusing me about what I really wanted. And I overtrained to overcompensate for the fact that I didn't have the build the other players did at the time. What did that do in the end for me, man? I injured myself so badly I can never play again."

Ray blinks, tight-lipped. "Thank you for your time."

He leaves the bar. Clearly my sob story didn't move him. Oddly, it stirred something in me, though. Because I don't know if I've ever articulated that before.

The table of pipsqueaks has gotten louder and there are a few people waiting at the bar, but Chadley's nowhere to be seen. Annoyed, I go behind the bar and pour a few beers for people. Chadley comes out of the bathroom with some guy he's chumming it up with who walks out the back door. Jesus. Where do I start with this one?

"Hey boss," Chadley says, coming behind the counter. "Thanks for holding up the fort for me while I whizzed."

"Who was that leaving out the back door?" I ask, ringing someone up on the register and handing them change.

"Oh, buddy of mine."

"You know we don't let customers use the back door."

"Yeah, but, I know him."

"Yeah, but, I don't give a shit," I say.

That wipes Chadley's jack-o-lantern grin off his face. "All right, man. It's chill."

"And did you ID everyone at that table over there?" I ask, pointing to the pipsqueaks.

"I mean, the one buying had a beard, man," he explains.

"That's peach fuzz. That's chin pubes. That's not a beard. And a beard is not an ID."

"It's chill," he repeats.

I point a finger at him. "Do it again and you're fired."

Back in my office, door closed, I plop in my chair and stare at that stupid placard my dad made that says "THE BOSS." I take it and break it in half with a satisfying snap and chuck it in the garbage.

THE ART of closing isn't hard to master. Garbage cans to empty, counters to shine, bathroom to be sanitized, floors to be swept, et cetera, et cetera. Though I can manage it myself, if Eva's working a shift with me, she always lingers behind. I'm beginning to think it's less about the closing duties and more about a free, impromptu therapy session for Eva. Which is a perfectly acceptable transaction in my mind: she's willing to mop, I'm willing to listen to her lament about her love life—Chuck in particular, which is an added bonus because that obnoxious man so piques my curiosity. And it seems everything I learn about him surprises me.

"So when I woke up, he'd put a blanket on me and tucked me in and snuck out the door," she's saying. "He's such a perfect gentleman. We didn't even *kiss*."

Never would I have used either the word "perfect" nor "gentleman" to describe Chuck. But I raise an eyebrow as I polish glasses. "Maybe it was less about him being a gentleman and more about the fact you had hives all over your face."

"He was just so *sweet*. And you know what he told me when we were talking one day? That he likes to move slow. Which … I don't think a guy's ever said to me in his life."

"Really." I hang a wine glass up.

"Or maybe it's just his way of saying he's not into me."

"I'd be surprised. You're quite the catch."

"Thank you!" She stops mopping to put a hand to her heart. "Oh my gosh, that means so much!" She goes back to mopping, her face contemplative. "I worry he's too smart for me."

I laugh and pick up the rag bag, cinch it, and walk it to the back, where we leave dirty laundry for the service each Thursday. "Eva, there are many things to worry about in the world. Chuck being too smart for you is not one of them."

"The last woman he dated seriously is going to Oxford University. You know, the place that wrote the dictionary?"

I stare at Eva from the hallway, frozen, as I both debate whether or not to correct her statement about the Oxford dictionary and simultaneously experience consternation over the fact that Chuck dated a woman who now attends the best university in the world.

"Huh," is all I can manage.

As Eva continues worrying out loud, I try to imagine this woman—this intellectual, this sophisticated, literate, ambitious woman—falling in love with Chuck. It's astonishing. Perhaps, I begrudgingly acknowledge, there's more to him than I previously imagined.

"Do you think I should?" Eva's asking when I snap back to the present moment.

"Should what?"

"Ask him out again? Or should I wait for him this time?"

"You should wait for him this time," I say. "Just give it a little. He'll come around."

I take the drawer to the back to count it, because it's the only way Eva will give me a moment of peace. As I reconcile the drawer, I lose count as I stare off into space and something in me whispers—did I tell her to wait because I think it's best? Or because I'm bothered somewhere deep within me that Eva and Chuck could possibly become romantically involved?

No, that's ludicrous.

Yet after I reconcile the drawer, I pull my phone out and search his name to find his Instagram account, scrolling through a scant total of eleven pictures over several years. One from two years ago has him kissing the head of a brunette in a beanie, who's laughing and closing her eyes. The caption just says, "She gets me." There's something so tender and sweet about the picture, I find myself gazing at it for far too long. They look genuinely smitten and happy. She's striking. Is this the woman that went to Oxford? Who is Chuck, really, if he's able to land a girl like that and make her smile like that?

"Boss?" Eva says behind me.

I gasp and guiltily shut my phone off before turning around. "Eva, you scared me. And please just call me Isadora."

"Sure. I can do that. You ready?"

"Yeah."

We walk around, shutting off the lights. Outside, it's chilly. Well, chilly for Santa Caterina, which means it's probably about sixty degrees. As I unlock my bike, Eva goes over to the window to peek in Brady's.

"Stop obsessing," I tell her.

"Just seeing if he's in there."

"Didn't you already go in there today?"

"Once right when they opened, once on my break," she admits guiltily. She comes over, hands in her peacoat pocket. "He wasn't in. And they were so busy inside. It was bananas."

"Yeah, I'm sure they're busy," I say, not without bitterness.

If it's a contest, I hate to admit it, but Brady's is blowing us out of the water. Our book clubs and open mics can't compete with one-dollar beer nights and the World Series. It's depressing.

"Oh my gosh, I forgot to tell you something," Eva says, coming over and whispering to me. Why she's whispering on a dead, dark Riviera Avenue is beyond me. "I used their bathroom today when I went in on my break."

"I'm sure it was disgusting."

"It was. It was so gross. I would bet my life they don't

clean it daily like we do." She leans in. "I wasn't sure if I should tell you this or not. And I'm sure it's, you know, all in good fun. I'm sure he didn't mean anything by it."

"Mean anything by what?" I ask, mounting my bike seat.

"Your picture is in there."

The silence stretches so long a distant siren comes and goes.

"My picture," I repeat, "is in Brady's bathroom?"

She grimace-smiles. "You know that picture from the *Santa Caterina News* article? Yeah, it's in there. In the urinal. With the headline under it and everything."

"My picture," I say again, out loud, just to be sure I am hearing correctly, "is in the urinal at Brady's."

She nods, still with that grimace-smile.

"So customers are regularly pissing on my face," I say.

"I would guess so."

"Chuck put my face in a toilet," I say. "And you think he's a perfect gentleman?"

"Who knows if it was him—"

"Of *course* it was him," I say, and a rage that had been sleeping for weeks rouses like a hungry bear from hibernation. "God, what a complete and utter asshole."

"I knew I shouldn't have told you," Eva moans.

"Did you try to remove it?" I ask.

"I'm ... sorry. I didn't want to stick my hand in there. It's, like, glued on or something. Waterproof."

I emit a petite scream. "I hate him. I seriously—I hate Chuck. And I know you think he's so great, but come on!

What does that say about him? *Gigantic* fucking red flag right there."

"I'm sorry," she says in a small voice. "I'll talk to him about it."

"No, please don't. I want to talk to him myself."

"But don't—"

"I won't tell him you told me. Don't worry." I take a deep, cold breath, let it out. "Are you okay getting home?"

"Fine. You know I live a block away."

"I know, but if you want me to walk you …"

"That's okay. I have a knife in my purse," she says with a sweet smile.

So off she goes, flouncing down the sidewalk under the streetlights with a secret knife in her purse. And I pedal home, uphill, imagining how satisfying it would be to stab Chuck with it.

The next day, the moment Brady's opens its doors, I'm there, elbowing my way through a crowd of Neanderthals clad in baseball jerseys to make my way inside. I've never been in here since it opened; it's appalling. Black marble countertops and floors with about ten thousand TVs set up, country music inexplicably blasting over it all. The environment is overstimulating, charmless, and stinks like someone spilled Budweiser all over a wrestling room. Just stepping foot in here fuels a new fire within me: oh, how desperately I want to take this place down and see it fail. This establishment is simply a commercial manifestation of toxic masculinity. The sign on the wall says maximum occupancy is a hundred people, and there's already a hundred people here. There's no way that stoned-looking bartender with the rattail who opened the front doors is checking IDs. As I make my way past the bar, I calculate the myriad ways I might bring this place down. Call the fire marshal? The sheriff's office? OSHA? The possibilities are endless.

I'm not about to ask permission to find Chuck because I'm pretty sure I know where he is. I've heard him clearing his throat through the wall on the other side of our supply closet, so it's got to be the door I'm striding toward right now that says EMPLOYEES ONLY. I open the door and sure enough, there he is, the worst man in the entire world: feet kicked up, eating a meatball sub with one hand and scrolling on his phone with the other.

The décor in his office is predictably minimal and male. Some framed news clippings of his quasi-famous dad. Golf clubs in a corner, and, for some odd reason, a foam hand. If someone's office is any indication of who they are as a person, this confirms that there is nothing to Chuck McCaffrey other than the soulless detritus of his father. Chuck appears utterly shocked to see me right now, taking his legs down from the desk. I close the door behind me. He takes a moment to chew and swallow.

"Um, hello?" he says finally. "Just walk right into my office?"

"As if you'd hear me knocking with the horrid commotion out there."

"'Horrid commotion?' Try 'joyous festivity,'" he says,

looking amused as goes in for another bite of his sandwich. "It's possibly the final game in the World Series tonight."

My blood pressure is rising. "I don't give a fuck, *Chuck*."

"Christ on a unicycle, calm down." He raises his eyebrows. "You also could have texted me rather than barging into my private office. What the hell is going on?"

"What's going on?" I ask, hands on hips, eyes turning to slits. "How about, I don't like getting my face pissed on? How about that?"

He carefully puts down his meatball sub, wipes his face with a napkin, sits back, takes a breath, and finally says, "What?"

"I don't even have words for what you are. I was up half the night, rehearsing all the insults I'd like to sling at you. Just practicing ripping you to shreds."

"Okay," he says slowly. "I guess I didn't realize you still had a vendetta. Can we back up a minute and go back to the pissing on your face thing?"

"My question is, what does it feel like to be such a casual misogynist?" I go on. This is the part I practiced at home. "I've always wanted to know what it's like to be inside the brain of a chauvinist pig. How can you have a mother you love, yet disrespect women so much?"

"I don't disrespect women," he says. "I disrespect *you*."

"Clearly!" I yell.

He gets up. "Who do you think you are, walking in here and launching into a tirade about me hating women? What did I even do? You make absolutely no sense. Last time I saw you, I thought things were okay between us."

"You're such a chronic asshole, you probably forgot," I tell him. "Let me show you, Chuck."

I leave the office, pulling Chuck by the sleeve behind me as we weave our way through a throng of people in the narrow hall who are yelling about a foul ball. Finally, we reach the bathroom in the back, Chuck's hands in his hoodie pocket, his mouth a straight line. I'm not used to seeing Chuck's mouth a straight line. He looks like a different person. Someone leaves the bathroom and I pull Chuck in with me.

First, it smells like a porta potty. I would be shocked if anyone had ever, at any time, scrubbed the toilet. The walls have graffiti on them, and the graffiti is rife with misspellings and tasteless epithets, as one would expect. And there, where my shaking finger is pointing, is my face in the urinal, as expected. It's distorted, probably from all the urinary projections. And I know it's just a picture. But immediately, when I see it, my eyes well up.

"You're telling me you didn't do this?" I say, struggling to keep my voice angry when all I feel is embarrassment and sadness. "You're going to look me in the eye and tell me you had no idea that people have been pissing on my face? That *you* have been pissing on my face?"

"I haven't been pissing on your face. I would never do that," he says. "I'm so sorry. I had no idea this was in here."

"Right, no idea," I say, wiping my eyes. "It's just your bar. It's just the *one bathroom* in your bar."

"I don't use this bathroom. Ever. I have my own bathroom."

"Mmmm, of course you do. Wouldn't want to urinate with the plebians. You have a golden toilet too?"

"Isadora," he says softly, putting a hand on my arm. "Please. I know we haven't gotten along. I know I've been kind of an asshole—"

"Kind of? You are my *nemesis*. You are the nightmare that has cursed my life dream."

"Okay, sure, those things too. But I wouldn't do this. I wouldn't do something like this. And I'm going to find out who the fuck did this. You understand me?"

His hand is warm on my arm, with a grip that sends a wave all through me, makes me inhale twice, but I shrug it off.

I shake my head. "The most disappointing thing about you is that you are exactly what I thought you were. There's nothing more to you. You are every jock who cajoled me in high school. You are every guy who I went to college with who made me, my body, the butt of some mortifying joke. I'm so sick of being unsurprised by men like you."

"Isadora," he says imploringly.

I leave him there in the abhorrent bathroom. By the time I get through the sweaty, hooting crowd, I'm positive I need a shower. My arm is still tingling from where he clasped me. I hate how it felt so warm and inviting for him to touch me that way—that men's comfort can be so enticing even when they're humiliating you.

Back in Gertrude's, it's dead as a library. Eva is playing

Blossom Dearie on the speakers and four students are nursing a pitcher while discussing art history. The jubilation next door is thumping the walls. I'm still livid, but more so, I'm miserable. Instead of vindicating me, that whole interaction absolutely drained me. Revenge sounds delicious. But what would I even do? Put his picture in my toilet bowl? I'm better than that. My revenge must have some class.

"You okay?" Eva asks.

I nod, flinching at the rise and fall of cheering next door. The students look up, hearing it too. The raucous sounds of our neighbors make this place somber and pathetic by its juxtaposition. I turn around and thump the wall, but it's no use. They can't hear me.

That's when my eyes fall to that miniature box-shaped hole in the wall. The sight of it lifts my heart and perks a smile to my lips.

"What a shame it would be," I tell Eva, as I lean over. "If Brady's cable were to suddenly fail?"

"Oh—I don't think you should—"

I rip the cord out, leaving it hanging there with the outlet askew. Beholding my work, adrenaline courses through me. I did enough damage there that they'll certainly need a cable technician. They'll lose all their business tonight. Eva puts her hand over her lips and we stare down at the mess of wires. A chorus of boos rises from the other side of the wall.

"You can't do that," Eva says, her hand still over her mouth. "Can you?"

"I just did," I tell Eva. "It's called payback."

"But how do you even know it was Chuck?" she asks. "Did he say it was him? I'm sure it wasn't him."

"Eva," I say, annoyed. "Whose side are you on?"

She takes a deep breath and turns around, straightening the menus. And she doesn't say whose side she's on. She doesn't say.

chuck

MAYHEM. When the cable goes out at a sports bar on the night of the final game of the World Series, that's what you get: mayhem. Pint glasses hurled. TVs frantically slapped. The pained screams of grown men. Someone punches a crater in the wall. The crowd trickles outside, leaving a trail of *motherfucker!*s behind.

I tell Chadley to call the cable company while I pull Brayden into my office. Because honestly, I care less about how we just lost all our business on one of the most hectic nights of the year and more that I'm still stinging with enraged embarrassment at the fact someone decoupaged Isadora's face in a urinal.

"Do you know how fucked that is?" I ask Brayden, door closed. "To put our next-door neighbor's face in a urinal?"

"It's been there since we opened, brah."

"Who put it there? You?"

"Nah, I think it was Sean." He grins. "You don't think

it's kinda funny? Your dad thought it was funny."

Oh, fantastic. So my dad saw it and gave this horrible idea his blessing. I inhale and forget to exhale for a minute.

"Brah, it's mad out there. I'd better go back out and help Chadley."

I finally exhale. "Fine," I mutter. "Go."

Alone in my office, I pace back and forth, trying to think of what I should do. Good thing my dad's not here tonight—he hates baseball more than I do—because I might lose my shit. When I go out into the bar, Brayden's cleaning up broken glass with his bare hands like the imbecile he is, and Chadley is hanging out the back door talking to someone.

"Hey," I bark at him. "Get in here and help clean this shit up."

"Sorry, boss," he says, and closes the door to come back.

"What have I told you about that back door? Who're you talking to?"

"Just a customer."

"Don't. Let. Customers. Use. The. Back. Door. It's employees only."

Chadley grins and goes to help Brayden clean up glass, also with his bare hands.

"Hey," I say to them. "You call the cable company?"

"Left a message. Office is closed."

"Did you look at the box?" I ask.

"Yeah," Chadley says. "I don't know, man. I'm not some cable guy, you know?"

I grind my teeth and go into the bathroom with a putty

knife. There, I spend a few minutes scraping that picture of Isadora off the urinal. It is, hands down (in other people's piss), the most disgusting, foul thing I have ever had to do in my life. For the grand finale, I barf in the urinal when I'm done. Then I wash my hands for about half an hour.

Brayden and Chadley have done the most half-assed cleanup job you could imagine, but at least the broken glass is gone. There are only—count them—six customers left now, all folks who got too sloppy drunk to last through the seventh inning stretch. Two of them are asleep at the bar. One is crying on the phone asking whether the game's been called yet. Three are huddled around a cell phone trying to catch the last of the game. It's a pathetic scene.

"I'm taking off," I tell Brayden and Chadley. "I need a fucking shower."

Chadley salutes me and Brayden does a hang-ten sign.

Outside, I expect to see stragglers from the World Series event gone wrong. But no, just a typical Thursday night on Riviera Avenue: some well-dressed couples arm in arm, a parade of girls on bicycles. Next door, at Gertrude's, the windows are lit up with gold light. With the books on the high shelves and the velvet furniture, I could be staring into a scene from another century. I don't stare too long, though, because I see Eva's in there. I just don't have it in me tonight. So I turn to head down the street in the direction where my car is parked.

"So unfortunate," a voice says behind me.

I turn around. Isadora's there, purse on, keys in her hand as she stands near the bike rack, looking at me.

"What?" I ask.

"That your cable went out like that. On such a momentous occasion. Just so unfortunate."

She's smirking, with big, gorgeous, glossy lips.

"It is unfortunate," I say slowly.

"Did you figure out the cause?" she asks innocently.

"No. Why, you know something?"

She gives me that blank look that tells me what an idiot I am without doing a damn thing.

"*You* did it?" I ask.

"Did you not check where it's plugged in?" she asks. "Seriously?"

"I … Chadley was supposed to check into it."

"Chadley. Oh my God. Is that even a real name? You are all such stereotypes."

The rage that builds in me is a slow burn, beginning in my face, stretching down my shoulders and into my arms. First, I can't believe Chadley didn't check where the cable is plugged in. Actually, I can believe it. The people I have working for me are such buffoons Brady's should be recognized as a charity for employing them. Second, Isadora is fucking cutthroat. Yes, I know, the urinal. But this is so shady.

I want to ruin her in more ways than one.

"You want to do this, really?" I say. "You want to compete to see who can wreck whose business first?"

"I was getting you back for allowing your customers to piss all over me. Feels fair."

"Having your image in a urinal is not the same thing as losing an entire record-breaking night's worth of business."

"I don't know. Kind of hard to financially quantify the level of humiliation I feel."

I'm about to tell her I just spent ten minutes removing said image with my bare hands when she gasps and kneels next to the bike rack. Suddenly, the smirk is gone.

"Oh no," she says.

"What."

"My tires are slashed." She stands up and shoots me an indignant look. "What the hell?"

"You think *I* did that?"

"Wouldn't put it past you."

"Oh, come on."

"Or one of you minions did it," she says, jabbing a finger at me in the air. "You know, Chadley. Or one of your many rude customers who, by the way, came into Gertrude's shouting that they needed a TV like a bunch of junkies as soon as they abandoned your establishment."

I will be honest: I wouldn't put it past those drunken clowns who left my bar in a state of agitation to slash some tires. Have you ever seen footage of hometown city streets when a sports team loses? It's a goddamn war zone.

"Listen," I say. "I'll take you home."

"You? I don't want you knowing where I live."

"Fine, I'll take you to the general area and drop you off, then. What do you think I am? The Night Stalker?"

"Wouldn't put it past you."

"Just … shut up and let's take your bike to my car."

She unlocks it with a sigh bigger than an Arctic wind. I look up at the gold glow of Gertrude's windows and see Eva there, gazing out at us with a slack expression. By the time I raise my hand up for a wave, she's turned and left the window.

"I still hate you," Isadora says as we start walking down the brick sidewalk. "I don't accept this ride as any kind of peace offering. It's more like you owe me this and a lot more."

"Actually, I don't owe you anything," I say. "I'm doing this out of the niceness of my heart. If anything, you owe me thousands of dollars for unplugging my cable."

"I didn't just unplug it, I ripped it out of the wall. You're going to need to call a technician," she says, beaming.

God, she is obnoxious. I should have left her face in the urinal after all. I stop for a minute, looking into the window of the cat store with the pretentious French name. Look at all those fluffy little buddies, curled up in beds or sleeping on fancy towers.

"Maybe I should get a cat," I say.

"Psychopaths shouldn't own animals," Isadora says.

I keep walking. "If I were a psychopath, I wouldn't be able to feel such passionate dislike for you. Turn here."

We turn around a corner. There's moonlight catching Isadora's wild hair right now and dancing off her eyes. She's ravishingly pretty. If only she never opened her mouth. I take my keys out and beep my car open.

"*This* is your car?" she asks.

"What, this chariot not good enough for you, my liege?"

She's staring at my Toyota Prius like it's an alien spaceship. Sure, I know it's a dinged-up piece of shit, but what the hell was she expecting?

"I was expecting you to drive, like, a Tesla. Or an Audi," she says, like she can read my mind.

"I'm so sorry that my humble car didn't meet your lofty expectations." I open the trunk, pick up her bike, and shove it in.

"Aren't you a millionaire?"

"My *dad's* a millionaire," I say, slamming the trunk shut. "Big difference."

She scoffs and circles the car to climb in the front seat. I get in and buckle up. As she adjusts her seat, and our elbows bump, my pulse quickens. There's something unexpectedly intimate about inviting her into this tiny, contained space. That maddening, sweet coconut scent I sniffed in her office is back.

"God, what is that smell?" she asks, making a face at me as I back out of my (amazing) parallel parking job.

"Coconut?" I say. "You smell like a goddamn bakery."

"No, it smells like pee. Your car smells like pee."

I move the car to drive and pull onto the road, a side street that runs parallel to Riviera, with rows of Victorian houses converted into offices. "It's not my car. I smell like pee."

I can feel her eyes searing holes in the side of my face.

"Because," I say, rolling down my window and putting my arm out, pointing left. "I personally scraped your picture out of the urinal."

"Really? I don't believe you."

"The lasting scent of piss you just commented on

should be sufficient evidence."

She faces forward as we wait at the light. "Well, if you expect me to thank you, I'm not going to."

"Fair."

"You don't get a cookie for attempting to erase a misogynistic hate crime."

The light turns green and I turn left.

"Also," she mutters. "I should have known you're one of those people who doesn't use their turn signal." She turns to me. "May I ask what it feels like? To be a person who lives in a perpetual state of blissful selfishness, never considering how your actions impact other people? Why would you not perform the most minute of gestures—flip a switch—to help other people understand what direction you're going? To keep the world a bit safer? To make life just a little easier on other people you share the road with?"

"You really think you have me all figured out," I say. "Where are we going?"

"I live at Gardenia and De La Flora. Right below the Botanical Garden. And yes, I do have you all figured out."

"Do tell, then. Why am I a person who doesn't use my turn signal?"

"Because," she says. "You're a person who has been handed everything you ever got in life. You are fundamentally broken when it comes to thinking about other people."

I don't even know how to respond. Which is apparently fine, because she's nowhere near finished.

"You're the kind of man who is gifted a bar by his dad

and then sits in his office all day long scrolling on his phone while the peasants do the work. The kind who doesn't even know what the inside of the public bathroom in his own establishment looks like, and who probably doesn't even know how to make a cocktail, either."

Okay, this is painful. My hands are choking the steering wheel. This feeling is new, but comes with a dash of déjà vu, because she's calling out pretty much everything I fear about myself in the depths of my soul. I would imagine this is what getting socked in the stomach while being naked would be—humiliating. Painful. The last time I felt this bad I was being hazed in high school.

"Right here," she says, pointing. "That's my building."

I pull to a stop. I still don't know what to say. I'm a balloon that kissed a needle.

"Chuck," she says, almost concerned.

Her apartment building's a charmer, old-fashioned, vines creeping up the walls. I get out, take her bike from the trunk, put it on the sidewalk.

"Chuck," she repeats, getting out of the car. "Did I break you? Say something."

I run a hand over my hair, looking up at the sky, at the lopsided moon that hangs there like a dumb grin. "I thought you *wanted* to break me. Isn't that your goal?"

"Well … I've just never seen you so quiet." She holds her bike by its handlebars. "I'm worried you're having a stroke."

I look over at her.

"Number one, you're right about me," I say. "Okay? You win. You've got me figured out. I've been handed everything in life. I've been steered and pushed and propped up so much, I don't even know how to stand up like a normal person. It's great, Isadora. It's just the greatest thing in the world. What a *privilege* it's been. To be a puppet."

"I was a bit harsh," she says. "For that I apologize."

"Second," I say to her. "I didn't use my fucking turn signal because it's broken."

She and I exchange a long stare. Her expression is full of pity, which I dislike but am sure I deserve right now.

"As mean as you are, I envy you," I tell her. "You're passionate and driven. You know what you want."

"That's not fair," she says. "You can't envy me because I'm driven, as if it's something I was gifted with. You don't inherit ambition. I worked my ass off to be way I am."

"Exactly," I say.

"I went through hell," she says. "Years of working full-time while being enrolled in school. Twelve-hour days."

"Because you had a reason to," I say. "I never had a reason."

"I invented the reason!" she almost shouts. "Which you're perfectly capable of doing, too."

"What was it that made you like that?" I ask, curiously, leaning on my car. "Where does that come from?"

"Well, for one, knowing I didn't have a trust fund to buy me my dreams off the rack. I had to make them happen or they never would."

"Yeah, but why now?" I ask. "There are plenty of people without money. They don't open bars at twenty-seven or however old you are."

Isadora takes a deep breath and I think she's about to let me have it when she breathes it back out. She kicks the bike's kickstand, leaves it there, and then comes next to me, leaning on the car, too.

"When I was a teenager," she says. "My mom went on a diet."

In the long pause, you can hear crickets and the swish of cars on a nearby main road.

"She was incredibly smart," Isadora continues, "A teacher, an avid reader, a poet. But when it came to her body, she was so harsh on herself. It was this battle that she struggled with out loud all the time, you know? Counting calories, debating whether she could afford a piece of chocolate or another glass of wine. And one morning I stood there with her in the kitchen as she lamented about how much she missed cream in her coffee. She hated drinking it black. But she drank it black anyway. She said heaven must be a place where you can pour all the cream in your coffee and not worry about the conse-quences." Isadora looks up at me, her eyes filled to the brim. "And then she left the house, got T-boned by a drunk driver, and she died."

"Oh my God, Isadora," I say, reaching out and pulling her into a hug. It happens so fast I didn't think it through —but now we're here on the street, and I'm holding her, and she stays there, folded into me like a flower into itself. I feel her relent and I let her go, step back.

She laughs nervously and wipes her eyes. "So anyway, that's why. Because I want all the cream in my coffee. I want all the cream and I want it now. Because you never know how long you've got. Life is short and mean and fragile. There's no time for waiting."

"Wow. That's profound."

Isadora's sincerity is brighter than the moonlight we're standing in. She's a fresh pool of water I want to dive into. I wouldn't—I won't—but I can imagine how sweet her lips would taste, can imagine waking up next to her with her wild hair all over her pillow, and it takes me clenching my hands into fists to not reach out and try to hold her again.

"That wasn't on my bingo card," she says. "Nemesis hug."

"Mine neither," I say.

"You give surprisingly excellent hugs," she says, giving me a small smile. "Even if you smell like urine."

As she heads away toward her building with her bike, she turns back and waves. "Thanks for the ride. But if you think this means we're even—we're not."

Ugh. This again. My pleasant mood towards her is immediately washed away by that oh-so-familiar annoyance. "You lost me thousands of dollars in business tonight," I remind her. "And I'm pretty sure that cutting someone's cable is a crime. Like, oh, I don't know— stealing boxes of Jameson."

"But is it a hate crime?" she asks. "Because that's what having my picture in your urinal was."

"Can't we call a truce? Christ almighty."

"No," she says. "I'm not done with you."

Now we've got a stink-eye staring contest going.

"Well, then I'm not done with you either," I say. "And guess what? Since you were the one who cut the cable, and then I, hero of heroes, took you home out of the goodness of my heart—"

"Because my tires were slashed, likely by one of your customers, but please, continue."

"I believe it's my turn to get you back."

"Give me a break."

"I'm going to think of something *good*," I say, circling back to the driver's side of the car and beeping the door open. "And I won't need to break the law to do it, either."

"I'm just trembling in fear."

I lock eyes with her. "I can't wait to wreck you."

The moment hangs, swells with unintended meaning, and now I'm thinking of how good it would feel to walk over to her and take her head in my hands and quiet her with a kiss. To memorize her curves with the palm of my hand. Then I put the thoughts out like fires.

"I can't wait to see Brady's go out of business," she says, and turns to her building.

"I don't think you'd want that. Because when Gertrude's fails, you're going to need someplace to work. And I'm such a nice guy, I'll give you a job."

She walks away, offering a middle finger over her shoulder.

I drive home, a jumbled, contemplative mess of feelings. I want to kick her. I want to kiss her. I want to wrap her in my arms. I want to push her far away from me. I want to hear more about what's inside her. I want to shut her up. I want to get her back. I want to get her.

I've lost count of the ways she makes me want.

isadora

HOW DO I HATE THEE? Let me count the ways.

In the coming days, the initial mollifying effect of Chuck's vulnerability and comforting embrace wears off and I am left instead with a slow drip of remorse for telling him something dark and deep within me, for letting him even have the slightest glimpse of my mother and my pain, because now I'm terrified he's going to somehow use it against me. Additionally, I've begun an inventory of his wretchedness as I tally everything he's done so far to drive me bonkers: teased me like a uncreative schoolboy, humiliated me by faking someone's identity, and then the unforgivable face in the toilet incident. How I, for one moment, even buckled and leaned into him for a hug when he's shown me *exactly* who he is from the get-go is so far beyond me that I don't even know if I can trust myself around him at this point. Because who knows what might happen next time I'm alone with him—I might kill him, or worse, kiss him.

Because the night after our encounter outside my apartment, I had a dream I kissed him.

Perhaps I should call it a nightmare, but the eeriest part of it was that in the dream, I was utterly contented. I was standing in a forest, surrounded by butterflies that floated between the tree branches and landed like quivering, colorful leaves. He held my warm hand in his warm hand. I bent up toward him, he caressed my chin with a finger, our lips locked, my eyes shut, and I saw nothing but I felt everything. Everything, everything, everything.

Then my alarm sounded and I woke up with a gasp, jolting upright in bed, turning to my mirror to ask, "What the hell was *that*?"

I still don't know, but it's utterly chilling. More frightening than a Shirley Jackson book, more sensually disturbing than *Lolita*. I would rather turn into a cockroach than turn soft for that man. This is why I have gone to great lengths to avoid Chuck for a week and two days now and counting … and the threat, of course. The vague threat that I have something coming.

Perhaps I should have accepted a truce.

"I'm sure he was joking," Eva says as we open together on Saturday.

Eva suffers from a near terminal case of optimism, especially when it comes to Chuck. For example, he has returned ten percent of her texts since they started corresponding. We did the math. Yet she is sure he is interested in her. Another example? Last week the police visited Brady's on two separate occasions because customers out front were exhibiting drunk and disorderly conduct (shrieking, arguing, vomiting in a potted plant). Eva is convinced that the police presence is a positive sign that Brady's is a safe, protected place. And yet she hid behind the bar as if she were afraid a bomb was going to go off the whole time the drunk and disorderlies were arrested.

"Chuck's not joking," I assure her. "He's up to something."

"He didn't mention anything when I was with him last night," she says suggestively, raising her eyebrows.

Well, listen to that. And I thought her affections were unrequited. This romance between them is moving slower than *Wuthering Heights*.

"Oh really," I say, clearing my throat. "Do tell."

Her lips part, but we're interrupted by a loud, brash, "Greetings, bibliophiles."

Standing in the doorway, pulling an amplified speaker on wheels, is Callista Chang. Callista is a local poetry phenomenon whose self-published book of poetry *Self-Published Book of Poetry* adorns every bookstore front in the tri-county area. Her humor is martini dry, her physical aesthetic would best be described as Morticia Addams meets Lady Gaga, and her poetry is unreadable. Example:

standing/ in my misunderstanding/ missing/ ms. understanding

That's it.
That's the whole poem.
Still, she's not here for my literary critique. She's here

to run the open mic night on Saturday nights, and I'm grateful she does it.

"Hey Callista," I say. "Drink?"

"I'll have my typical," she says as she lifts the speaker up to the stage and starts setting up.

Her "typical" is a screwdriver, known as the Truman Capote here at Gertrude's. I nod to Eva, who goes behind the counter and starts pouring.

"What's with the line out there?" Callista asks, gesturing outside.

I hadn't noticed a line, but now that I peer behind her out the main window, I do see people queuing up. At first I imagine it's people waiting to sign up for open mic night, which starts in an hour. Wouldn't that kind of popularity be amazing? But even from here I can see the prevalence of males in backward baseball caps and flip flops. It's something happening at Brady's.

I look to Eva, who shrugs exaggeratedly.

"Not sure," I say. "I'll go check."

Annoyed, I note they are blocking our sidewalk and my sandwich board advertising open mic night has been carelessly pushed into the gutter. I prop it back up again. It's now been relegated to the street but I'm unsure where I'm supposed to place it if this crowd has swallowed my sidewalk. Brady's has been open for an hour already (they open at four, we open at five) so I'm not sure what would be going on to draw this kind of crowd. It's a Saturday evening, generally one of the busier times. But even on the night of the final game of the World Series there wasn't a line.

"Hey," I ask a guy waiting, scrolling his phone. "What's going on?"

"Meet-and-greet with Cory McCaffrey," he says. "And they're doing a raffle and stuff."

"Thanks," I say.

Fabulous. So now the rowdy, obnoxious football fans are going to be out here all night. "Excuse me," I yell. "Can everyone move back? This is my business and you're blocking our entrance."

A couple people snicker at me like I'm a librarian *shhh*ing them. But they don't move.

"I'm serious," I say. "I'll call the police. You can't congregate on a sidewalk."

"Okay, Karen," someone yells.

My blood is boiling. Although Chuck is the last person on this turquoise earth I'd like to have a conversation with at this moment, I also realize no one else is going to have the authority to right this situation but him. Though it's a long shot—perhaps this is his latest revenge?—I push my way through the crowd and go inside Brady's.

There's an enormous banner announcing *MEET-AND-GREET WITH GRIZZLIES STAR QUARTERBACK, brought to you by Nate's Sporting Goods.* People are walking around with swag, green T-shirts emblazoned with Nate's Sporting Goods logo and similarly branded foam hands. Along with the usual yahoos hooting at the TV screens and guzzling pitchers, there's a line that snakes to the far-right corner of the room where Cory McCaffrey is taking pictures with fans against a Grizzlies backdrop. I turn instead to the left, past the bar and near the hallway, and barge into the EMPLOYEES ONLY door. Chuck is doing his usual nothing, slouched in his office chair like an overgrown boy in his daddy's office. Which he is.

"So this is your newest plan to make my life miserable?" I ask. "Advertise a C-list celebrity meet-and-greet and have them hog the entire sidewalk outside on my busiest night of the week?"

"Gertrude's has a busy night?" he asks.

"You're so rude. Yes, we do. Saturday nights we draw a modest but dedicated crowd of local poets for our open mic night."

"Open mic night, wow. That's gotta be huge. You'd better hire a bouncer or two for that one."

"You need to tell your patrons to move their line or I'm calling the police, who apparently are frequent visitors to your bar these days. If you thought this was a good idea to get me back this way, well, you should have researched local sidewalk ordinances related to loitering."

Chuck puts his phone down with a clank on his desk and runs a hand through his hair. "Have you ever, for one second, considered that not every decision I make is about you? I'm trying to drive business here. I don't care about your open mic night. If I wanted, I could ruin your open mic night much easier than throwing some big splashy meet-and-greet event for my dad."

"Yes, I'm sure your genius mind is just teeming with brilliant ideas."

He puts his fingers up in a little tent and scoffs. "Don't test me."

"You're bluffing," I say. "You have nothing up your

sleeve but this stupid stunt."

"Oh, I could come up with something."

Chuck is full of shit. He looks so charming, so confident, and yet it's all bluster with him.

"Come up with it, then," I say.

"You are childish."

"No, Mr. Mastermind of Deviance. I want to see you come up with something."

He sits back for a moment and watches me, nostrils flaring. He looks behind him at a stack of boxes in the corner and a slow, reptilian smile creeps onto his face. Immediately I regret challenging him. I don't know why I did that—I wanted to see him fail in real time. I wanted to tear him down and prove how incompetent he is. But I've just upped his game again.

"What," I say.

"Oh, nothing. Just came up with an idea."

"What? What are you going to do?"

"I'm not going to *tell* you. That would ruin the surprise."

He doesn't have anything. He's toying with me.

"What time does your open mic thing start?" he asks.

"At seven. Just … tell your patrons to leave space on the sidewalk," I say, and turn for the door.

"Hey," he says.

I turn. He's studying me with eyes that are aggravatingly blue and enchanting.

"You want a hug? I've been told, by certain prickly women, that I give very good hugs."

"I never said that."

"You most certainly did. Your exact words were that I give 'excellent hugs.'"

"I was intoxicated."

"You were not."

"I'd had a glass of rosé before leaving the bar."

"Admit it," he says with a grin. "You liked hugging me."

"Never have I regretted anything more."

"Just wait until you see what I have in store for you later."

It almost sounds like an innuendo the way he says it. I think he realizes this too because he quickly adds, "I mean —revenge-wise."

I don't dignify this horrid conversation with a response and leave him without bothering to shut the door behind me.

Back at Gertrude's, the sandwich board has fallen down again and I pick it up. The line of McCaffrey syco-phants seems to have thinned, leaving a bit more space on the sidewalk. Inside, Gertrude's has filled with the usual Saturday night crowd—local poets, college students, a couple musicians, the man with the self-published autobi-ography, the woman who recites erotic couplets. I slip behind the bar and make a Raymond Chandler (AKA a gimlet) and an F. Scott Fitzgerald (a gin rickey) for a couple, then go to the back to fetch more Tanqueray. When I come back with the bottle, a guy in a suit jacket with shoulder-length hair is waving me down for a drink at the end of the bar, and as I near him, I recognize who it is.

It's Guy.

The most pretentious person in my senior year poetry workshop, who called my sonnets "antiquated and contrived" and who mansplained everything from Chaucer to Adrienne Rich to me. Ugh. And now he dares to smile at me as if we're friends.

"Guy," I say. "Hello."

"Isabella!"

"—dora."

"Sorry. Dora."

"*Isadora.*"

I beam my wish to the universe for this conversation to be over already.

"So you work here now?" he asks.

"No, I just enjoy wearing an apron and standing behind the bar."

He stares at me and then laughs. "Right. Yeah, ridiculous question."

"I *own* this bar," I say.

"You do?" he asks, clearly surprised and impressed.

Yeah, take that, you pretentious lover of experimental free verse. My antiquated, contrived ass owns this place.

"What can I get for you?" I ask.

"I don't drink. Clouds the mind."

Of course he doesn't. My inner eyeballs are rolling.

"May I ask then why you are sitting at a bar on a Saturday night?" I ask.

"Came for the open mic night, to read from my latest manuscript," he says, holding up his (of course) moleskin. "It's a series of deconstructed haikus about capitalism and consumer culture."

"Fascinating," I say.

"I'd love a club soda with crushed ice and a kiss of lime," he says, flirtatiously.

This is what Guy does. He flirts with everyone, while constantly peppering in sly critiques along with reminders of his superiority. While many women seemed to fall for his schtick, I am not one of them. I silently get him a club soda, with no ice and no "kiss of lime" and I charge him four dollars for it. He slinks away, unamused, his precious moleskin pressed against his chest.

At seven, the open mic night starts with an intro from Callista where she thanks everyone for coming and then dives into reading a poem about all our inevitable deaths from climate change.

"Is this the biggest turnout yet?" Eva whispers in my ear.

"Seems like it, right?" I whisper.

A deafening honk interrupts our conversation and causes everyone in the bar to collectively jump.

"What was that?" Callista asks.

Another honk. People are now covering their ears.

Honk, honk, honk.

Pandemonium ensues as the honking increases, our crowd shuffling to get out of their seats or leave the bar to peer outside at the source of the noise.

HONK.

I push past everyone to peer outside and see, who else, but Chuck McCaffrey out there with a grin on his face and an air horn in each hand.

"What are you doing?" someone yells at him.

"Just celebrating," he says. "We're having an event at my bar, I'm just outside drawing some attention to it." He points one of this Converse All-Stars at the cardboard box next to him, filled with air horns. "Hey everyone—free air horns, courtesy of Nate's Sporting Goods!"

People hanging out on the sidewalk outside Brady's clamor to the box, picking out air horns, and immediately honk them in an appalling cacophony. Everyone in my bar starts yelling from the doorway for the blowhards to shut up. I go and pull the door closed, but it does little to dampen the noise.

"Well, that sound is loathsome," Callista says into the mic.

HONK.

"Let's wait a bit and see if this passes, okay?" Callista asks.

HONK, HONK, HONK, followed by disappointed boos from the Gertrude's crowd.

I turn to Eva, seething. "So is he still wonderful? Chuck is still a real catch, huh?"

"He's just … celebrating," she says weakly.

"Ugh."

I can still see him out there, grinning ear to ear, blaring the air horns along with his horrible customers. I consider pushing him in the street to get hit by a car, but he's not worth going to prison. Instead, I stride up to the mic Callista has temporarily abandoned.

"Hey everyone, that atrocious man out there is Chuck McCaffrey," I tell them, speaking loudly to rise above the chorus of honking. "Owner of the sports bar next door, which has been hell-bent on putting me out of business. He's doing this to try to drive you away. Please—if you can—everyone get on your phones right now and rate his business, called Brady's, one star on Yelp. Write a review letting the public know what an obnoxious bully he is. Help me fight back against him."

The crowd applauds and customers take their phones out. Everyone except Eva, that is, who stays behind the counter biting her fingernails.

"If you love him so much, why don't you go out there and get a free air horn?" I ask her when I return to behind the counter.

"Don't be like this," she says. "I don't like being stuck in the middle."

"You're not stuck in the middle, Eva," I say. "You work *here*. Chuck isn't even your boyfriend."

"We kissed last night," she whispers. "And it was the most amazing kiss. I know you're not a fan, but he's an amazing guy."

Amazing, everything is *amazing* with him. I, too, continue to be amazed by him, but not in the way she means. I'm so bothered she kissed the enemy that I consider, for a split second, firing her.

I stare outside, where Chuck is now doing some kind of YMCA dance to accompany his honking, to the glee of a throng on the sidewalk.

"Amazing," I repeat.

The honking fiasco lasts a grand total of twenty minutes but feels like an ear-piercing lifetime. By the time it's over, a number of our customers have left. The open mic night continues, but flaggingly. And I can't help the lasting resentment that Eva's not taking my side. Zofie arrives late and comes behind the counter asking who the funeral's for. She's joking, but when I explain the way the night went, *she* at least takes my side.

"What an ass," she says about Chuck.

"Thank you," I say, giving a sidelong glance to Eva, who's watching a woman on stage weep through a poem about her cat.

"Your plan was brilliant, though," Zofie says. "Knock down their online reviews. I mean, air horns last ten minutes or whatever. But bad Yelp reviews? They can tank a business."

"Didn't make much of a dent though," I say, looking at their account on the app on my phone. "They still have a three-and-a-half-star average."

"Well, maybe you need a new special moving forward," Zofie says, putting her arm around me. "Give next door a one-star Yelp review, get a well drink free."

"That's brilliant, Zof."

"You came up with the idea. I just ran with it." She takes the Wild Turkey off the shelf. "Want a Hunter S. Thompson?"

"Do you even need to ask?"

We use the whiteboard to advertise our new special and hang it up behind the bar.

Chuck wanted to up the ante? Fine then. He destroyed poetry night, I'll give him that.

But I'm going to destroy his reputation.

chuck

THANKSGIVING'S never been about turkey and stuffing in my world. Since I was tiny, Thanksgiving was all about ordering to-go food and parking your ass on an easy chair to watch football. I say "my world" but I mean "Dad's world." Because let's face it, it's Dad's world and I'm just living in it.

This year, though, I have an excuse. We're keeping Brady's open (opening early, even) for the Cowboys and Lions games. We've got a turkey leg vendor outside— festive! You'd think people would have better things to do on a family holiday, but the place is packed by noon. By two p.m., a group of bros have already been kicked out for brawling. Turkey leg bones and spilled beer all over the floor. And even though Chadley and Brayden are short-staffed since I fired Sean for the urinal incident, I hide in my office because the ambiance of my own bar is, frankly, appalling. I can hardly argue with the one-point-five star average we now have on Yelp. Yep, our ratings have been tanking like the stock market in 1929.

Mom, blessed angel, sneaks into my office to deliver me a burrito. Dad's at home, of course. Wouldn't leave his easy chair if his house was on fire.

"What a scene out there!" Mom says as she closes the door behind her. She's in a pink jogging suit with her name custom-stitched on the front. "I got you carne asada, guac, no sour cream."

"You know me so well," I say, opening the plastic bag.

Mom sits on the edge of my desk, smiling at me. "Keeping open on Thanksgiving—was that your idea or your dad's?"

"Mine. Dad's been pretty hands off, lately." *Thank God*, I don't add. I peel back the foil on my burrito. "Thank you so much for this, I didn't realize how starving I was."

"And the turkey leg vendor, that's so cute. Was that your idea too?"

I bite into the burrito and close my eyes in a moment of bliss. "Mmm-hmm."

"I'm so proud of you, hon. And you know your dad is too." She watches me snarf a burrito like a slob and yet has such adoration brimming in her eyes. Moms.

I swallow and thank her.

"How's it going with that girl you've been seeing?" she asks.

What a mistake it was to mention Eva to her last week. I mainly did it to keep her off my back; Mom wanted to set me up on a blind date with some philanthropist's daughter. I said I was kind of dating someone, which is a stretch edging on a lie.

Eva and I have gone on two dates. There was the hives fiasco. Then, a couple weeks back, we went to see a movie and get a drink. Eva ordered one too many cosmos, stuck her tongue down my throat with no warning, and started talking about how beautiful our babies would look. Since then, I've made excuses to not go out again. I've had a backache, friend in town, other plans. She doesn't seem to read vibes well. I need to break it off with her. But really, do I? I never said she was my girlfriend or anything. It's not my fault she misread the situation.

"We're taking it slow," I tell Mom. "Honestly, not feeling any sparks."

"It's been, what, two years since Sam moved to England?"

"Almost."

"You haven't met anyone you felt that spark with in *two years?*"

She's eyeing me like I'm a freak, which maybe I am. But it's true. I'm ashamed to admit it, but the closest thing to sparks I've felt with anyone since Sam left have been fleeting moments with Isadora. My prospects aren't looking good when the only girl I've found myself dreaming about hates my guts.

"How about we don't talk about my love life?" I ask. "You want some of this burrito?"

"Looks delish, but I had a salad for brunch. Trying to keep that weight off."

"You don't need to diet. You're a twig."

"I'm a twig *because* I diet."

I shake my head, remembering that night outside Isadora's apartment, the story she told about her mom. How heartbreaking it was to think of someone depriving themselves when they should have just been living life to its fullest.

"Life's short," I tell her. "Eat a burrito."

She rolls her eyes and puts a hand on my head, inspecting my ears. "Did you cut your hair yourself?"

"Yeah."

"You need a stylist. Get some new clothes, too."

"Mom."

"You're an entrepreneur, a successful business owner. It's time you look like one."

Heat rises to my cheeks.

"Anything else you'd like to complain about?" I ask, putting the burrito on the table. "Any other way I'm not being the perfect son you wish I was?"

"Hon, no, I didn't mean it *that* way."

Christ on a jetski, I get so fed up with this shit sometimes. I play football, but disappoint them because I get injured. I coach, but disappoint them because coaching's not a real career. I fall in love, but disappoint them because Sam was geeky and silly and academic and they just couldn't wrap their heads around me being with a girl like her. I throw myself into Brady's but now I'm not dressing the part. Trying to be their son is so exhausting sometimes. It's a full-time job.

"I just meant—" she starts.

There's a knock on the door. Brayden pops his head in, the raucous noise of the bar spilling in.

"Brah, there's a brah here to see you."

"Who is it?"

"I don't know. But he's probably rich or something. He's wearing a suit."

Intrigued, I wipe my hands on my napkin. "Let him in."

A moment later, a wisp of a man-boy in a three-piece suit, who is probably too young to be in a bar judging by the four hairs on his chin and acne-ridden face, steps into my office.

"Charles McCaffrey?"

I stand up, not knowing what the hell to expect from this fancy man-boy visitor. I've never seen anyone this well-dressed in my bar. This is probably what Mom was hoping I'd wear to work each day if I hired a stylist like she wants.

"Son of Cory McCaffrey, right?" he asks.

"Yeah."

"Huge Grizzlies fan. First: he around? I was hoping to snag an autograph."

"No, he's not here."

"Ah, too bad. Well, then." The man-boy's smile disappears and he hands me a manila envelope. "Second: you've been served."

Mom gasps. "By who?"

"The city of Santa Caterina," he says. "Wait, are you Aislin Gray? Holy shit!"

"Get the fuck out of here," Mom yells, jabbing a fake fingernail in the air.

The man-boy's eyes widen and he slinks out of the room.

"We're getting sued by the city?" I say, ripping the envelope open. "For what reason?"

Turns out, for multiple reasons. Brady's has been deemed a "public nuisance" by the city for drunk and disorderly conduct outside the bar and for several drunk drivers being pulled over after leaving our bar. Which doesn't seem fair, really. Both things happened outside our doors. Why are we responsible? Part of me feels relieved. I mean, imagine this whole exhausting enterprise I never asked for might just end. I can move on with my life, spend my days somewhere that doesn't smell like BO and spilled Budweiser every day.

"Don't worry," Mom says, rubbing my shoulder. "We'll countersue. Even bad news is good publicity. It'll be the lead story on B1 every day for the next month, and it'll drive you more business than you could have ever dreamed of."

Thing is, I never dreamed of any of this.

And now I've got to fight a war I've got no heart in.

I've been so distracted planning Brady's Thanksgiving bash and worrying about the lawsuit, I completely forgot that Sam is in town for the holiday until she shows up on Saturday evening looking for me. The sight of her standing in my office doorway—bright-eyed, a new pixie-short hair-cut, grinning with that adorable gap between her two top teeth, her bronze skin glowing—turns me to goo.

"Holy shit." I get up and almost trip over my desk to give her a hug. "Come here, you."

"Chuck!" she says after we part, shaking her head at me. "This place is a *trip*."

"I know, right?"

She puts her hands in her leopard print coat's pockets. "It's got your dad's fingerprints all over it."

"Ya think?"

"I can smell the testosterone. I think I'm the only female in this building right now. Every patron at the bar turned around and ogled me like a bunch of hungry dogs."

"Yeah, this place sucks. Want to go get a drink some-where else?"

"What about that literary bar next door? I just popped my head in there. So cute!"

"Anywhere but there."

She gives me a funny look. "Why? Shitty drinks?"

"I've never tried one. No, it's because the owner and I don't get along that well."

"Oh, come on." She slaps my arm. "You've never had a drink and they're right next door? You should do it for market research alone."

I groan. This is Sam. This is what Sam does to me. She's always pushing me beyond my comfort zone. Every time I'm with her, I end up doing something I wouldn't have done on my own. Wine tasting. Watching foreign films.

Running a 5K. It's why I loved her so much. I loved who I was when I was with her.

"Fine," I sigh. "You know what discomfort awaits me? Just watch: if there's a girl with dark wild hair and glossy lips behind the counter, that's my enemy and she's prone to rip me a new one. If there's a girl with pink hair and glasses, she's trying to date me and it's awkward."

"Look at Casanova over here. This sounds fun, actually." She puts her arm in mine. "Come on, let's go."

Gertrude's is as dead as a weeknight at Brady's, even though it's happy hour on a Saturday. I fight pity for Isadora, thinking maybe driving her customers off earlier this month with the airhorns was a bit much. (But so funny. God, the staring-at-the-abyss look on her face when she saw me out there … every time I remember it, I crack the fuck up.) There's a woman setting up a PA on the tiny stage up front. Isadora's behind the counter scrolling her phone. When she puts it in her pocket and looks up at me, she rolls her eyes.

"What, come in to ruin another open mic night?" she asks.

"Eh, I'm all out of airhorns," I say as I sit on a stool. "Hey, this is my friend Sam. Sam, this is Isadora."

They both wave.

"I love your bar," Sam says, taking a menu. "If I still lived in the area, this would be my hangout spot."

Isadora is stiff, skeptical. "Where do you live?"

"Oxford, England."

"Ohhhh," Isadora says. "Okay. Sure. Oxford." She seems to perk up with that information, offering a small smile like the gorgeous snob she is. "What can I get for you?"

"I'll have a glass of pinot," Sam says.

"And you?" Isadora asks reluctantly, not meeting my gaze.

"Same. Though I'm a little scared you might spit in it."

"My saliva's too good for you," she says, and turns around to open a bottle.

Sam nudges me and points at the shelf.

"What?" I ask.

"The whiteboard," she whispers.

I squint to read what it says. GIVE THE BAR NEXT DOOR A 1-STAR YELP RATING, GET A WELL DRINK FREE.

"The fuck?" I say.

"Shhhh," Sam says.

"So *that's* why my ratings are tanking," I say as Isadora puts the glasses of wine in front of us.

"What?" Isadora looks confused, then glances behind her at the whiteboard. "Oh. Yeah, maybe. Or maybe your bar just sucks."

"She has a point," Sam says, smelling her wine. "It does suck pretty bad."

"That is seriously low, Isadora," I say, ignoring the fact Sam is a traitor.

"Is it low? Or is it only fair, considering the horror you put my customers through?" Isadora puts her hand on the counter in front of Sam and softens her voice. "Your glass is on the house."

"Awww, thank you!"

"And you," Isadora says to me, "Your glass is eighteen dollars."

"Eighteen—? I saw the bottle you poured that out of. That *bottle* didn't even cost eighteen dollars."

"Oh my God, Chuck, just pay her," Sam says. "You are being so obnoxious right now."

"He's not like this all the time?" Isadora asks, taking my twenty.

"No!" says Sam. "He's a sweetheart."

"Keep the change," I mutter to Isadora, and pull Sam's arm toward a table near the back. "I told you we shouldn't have come here."

"Are you kidding?" she asks, settling into her seat. "I love her."

I snort and take a sip of wine. "Of course you do."

"You clearly like her too," she says. "You're teasing her like a schoolboy with a crush. I've never seen you like that."

"A *what*? Are you kidding me? I am so pissed off right now. My Yelp rating is currently one and a half stars, and it's her doing."

"I'm getting the impression you're not exactly the ideal neighbor yourself."

"She unplugged my cable the night of the final game of the World Series."

Sam stares at me, unblinking.

"That's bad," I explain. "It was the busiest night we've had all year."

"Oh, okay. It's a sports thing."

"Yes, Oxford scholar. I own a sports bar."

"And so what have you done to her to make her that mad?" Sam asks, running a hand over her short hair.

"Well," I say, unable to contain my grin at the memory. "I kind of ruined her open mic night a few weeks ago by blasting an airhorn right outside her door and encouraging my customers to do the same."

"I can see why she hates you."

"But you don't understand. This vendetta goes way back."

"To when? You opened two months ago."

Behind the bar, Isadora's there, staring at me and Sam. When I meet her eyes, she takes out her phone again and pretends to be engrossed in it. But I can tell she's watching us.

"Testing," the woman on stage says into the mic. "Titillating tattletale. Transformative attachment."

Sam's eyes go big and she sips her wine again.

"Can we please pound this wine and go take a walk down the pier or something?" I ask. "I really don't feel like suffering through a bunch of amateur poets."

Sam sighs and takes a gulp. "Fine."

The fresh air outside has never smelled so sweet. It's not until we start walking that I realize how nervous I was in there, coiled up like a spring. I'm so pissed off about the Yelp thing. Isadora didn't even apologize! Didn't even blink an eye when it was pointed out. Like it's no big deal to shit all over my livelihood.

"You seem distracted," Sam says. "What's on your mind?"

"Oh, nothing. I'm just trying to think of how I can get back at Isadora for that stupid Yelp campaign."

We stop in front of Chat Auberge, gazing in at the lucky bastard cats. "For someone who's your enemy, you sure talk about her an awful lot."

I give Sam a sidelong glance and wonder if she's jealous. But it really doesn't seem that way. Since we broke up, she and I have slid pretty comfortably back into the friend zone I started in. That first visit hurt, I'll be honest. I wanted to hold her tight and call her "babe" and she wanted to give me a side hug and call me "buddy." But since then, I don't know. She seems a little different every time I see her, a little further from the girl I fell in love with.

"I've been thinking of getting a cat," I say.

"Aww, that's darling," she says. "What inspired this?"

"Something to be there when I get home, a warm body to cuddle at night."

"So … not dating anyone, I'm guessing."

"You know how I am, Sam." I look at her in the reflection of the window. "Sometimes I think there's something wrong with me."

"Has there been *anyone*? I mean, are you even trying?"

We walk to the corner, push the button and wait for the light to turn before continuing to walk toward the beach. There's a city worker stringing Christmas lights around a palm tree, a guy with a parrot on his shoulder sparing change, a street artist drawing caricatures. A couple holding hands. A family pushing a stroller.

"Well, there's that girl at Gertrude's next door."

"See? I *told* you you like her."

"Not her," I say, annoyed. "The pink-haired girl I mentioned. She's super into me. We've gone out twice. But I don't feel anything for her."

"You can just have fun, you know. It doesn't all have to be about finding The One."

"You're having fun out there in Oxford, huh?"

"Sometimes."

"Good for you," I say.

And I mean it. Once upon a time, it would have hurt. But now? I love this girl. Love her bigger than a lover can love someone. I love her enough to wish the best for her no matter what that best looks like.

Sam and I used to walk this same stretch of Riviera down to the beach all the time. She lived above the Domingo theater on upper Riviera in a tiny studio we practically lived in. I couldn't count the number of times we ate at the taco restaurant we're passing or split a bottle at the wine bar across the street. And the twenty-four-hour coffee joint coming up on the block before we hit the ocean? That was where Sam broke it to me that she had been accepted to Oxford. As we pass it, neither of us talk about it. It was one of the most painful conversations I think either of us ever had. But I know we're both thinking about it.

It's dark now and freezing, but we plop down, slip our shoes off, and stick our toes in the sand anyway. The waves are crashing, the shore is empty. The moon's full, its light dancing on the water.

"I'm proud of you and your bar," she says. "Even if it's not my cup of tea."

"Thanks. It's not my cup of tea either, but hey, it's a business and it's mine."

"Seems like you're doing well."

"Besides getting slapped with a bullshit lawsuit and sandbagged by bad Yelp reviews, yeah, we're doing okay."

"Lawsuit?"

"Not even worth going into."

"Are you happy?" she asks me.

I look at her, the ocean waves reflected in her eyes. Sam's always had this effect on me. She cuts through the jokes and the nonsense. She dives in deep.

"I don't know," I say. "I have no idea what I want. I'm like a broken compass."

"Sometimes I wonder if you'd be better off starting over somewhere else," she says. "It was so refreshing to leave Santa Caterina, Chuck. This place is so lovely, but hometown history's got such a grip, you know?"

"Oh, I know. I've wondered the same. But where would I go?"

Sam smiles. "You could come to Oxford."

"And do what?"

"I don't know. Be with me?"

We exchange a long heavy look. Heavy with what exactly, I don't know.

"Are you kidding me?" I ask.

"I mean, I'm just saying," she says. "I always wanted you there. You know that."

I almost take the bait and jump into an argument. The same old argument we had every night before she got on a plane and left: that I want a life of my own. I don't want to follow her to a city I have no interest in and play the supporting role of lapdog boyfriend. But then what the hell did I do? I stayed in Santa Caterina and played the role of lapdog son. Was that any better? Maybe I should have gone to Oxford. Who knows, maybe there was a life for me there, I just didn't have the imagination to believe in it.

"I'm sorry," she says. "I didn't mean to open up old wounds."

"No, no, it's okay. Just making me think is all."

"I should go," Sam says. "My parents are meeting me for dinner at seven. Walk me back?"

"Sure."

We walk back up Riviera, but Sam makes me stop in the whiskey bar we used to hang out in sometimes for a shot. Which turns to two shots. Which means she's late for dinner and then we have to power walk back up to the block Brady's is on and part ways. We're both laughing and red-faced from the alcohol and the walk when we hug goodbye. And as I watch her hurry up the street, I'm so exhilarated from everything—the whiskey, the conversation, the beach, the power walk, that I'm giddy.

I stand outside Brady's a moment, hearing the swell of people cheering. Thinking, I did that. That's my bar. Feeling nothing in return, nothing at all. It's like looking at a business I've never seen, don't recognize.

Next door in Gertrude's people clap. No hooting, no hollering like next door. It's dark out here now, and the light in there is radiant, glowing a warm campfire color. All those elegant shelves of books, that proper crowd standing to watch the open mic night. It does look busy in there now, which I guess is good for Isadora. I would feel happy for her if she wasn't trying to ruin me.

I'm still so pissed about the Yelp thing. Why does she play so dirty? I would never have sabotaged her to that degree. I mean, imagine if, right now, I strode in there, put my name on the open mic sign-up form, and …

I begin laughing under the streetlight.

I take a step toward Gertrude's.

Am I going to …?

Yes, I'm going to.

Irish courage, my friends.

I step inside the front door, weave my way through a bunch of cologne-heavy bodies and bulky backpacks. Onstage, a man is reciting a poem:

> *and the plastic bags will outlive humanity*
> *like gods immortal, microbeads like holy seeds*
> *while flesh is trash, is bone, is ash*
> *so let us worship at the feet of saint plasticine*

God, that poem sucks. Look, I know these people in this room think they're better than me. And in some ways, they probably are. But that objectively fucking sucks. I did take a poetry class that lasted all of senior year, so I can Carl Sandburg your ass if need be. I was also part of a football team, and we memorized some poems of our own.

I scribble my name on the clipboard. I don't dare order

a drink, afraid I might be spotted by either the lady who hates my guts or the lady who likes me too much. So I sit in a corner and wait my turn. And when they call my fake name, "Brady," I get up, mount the one step to the platform, and adjust the mic to my height. I grin and pause a moment to take in the eager, trusting faces in front of me, contrasted with the one face haloed in wild hair who is shaking her head and mouthing "NO" from behind the bar.

"There once was a man from Nantucket," I begin.

RAGE, rage against the wrecking of open mic night.

As soon as I see Chuck onstage, chest puffed with arrogance, my stomach corkscrews with the sense that something unsavory is coming. But when I hear the word "Nantucket," I spring into action, pushing through the crowd to try to get to him before he can continue. Unfortunately, after elbowing my own patrons and knocking down several drinks in the process, he has been able to belt out the second line, and let's just say it isn't "who kept all his cash in a bucket." I mount the stage in one step and tackle him like a …

Who's the tackle guy? A quarterback?

Anyway, I take him down. And now I'm on top of him. In front of a room of gasping people, sprinkled with nervous giggling. Chuck and I are one strange beast with two backs as we lay here, our wide eyes locking wildly, his tension oddly blending into my tension, our breaths so close I can nearly taste him.

"Is this performance art?" I hear someone ask lowly.

After a moment much too long, I stand up and grab the mic. "I'm so sorry. Please carry on, folks."

I lean down, offering my hand to Chuck to get up, internally planning his murder. As I help him up, I dig my fingernails into his hand and pull him off stage. Castilla announces the next act, who will be rapping about pronouns.

I pull him. He follows me, snickering, past the bar and Eva's stunned face. Past the hall and the line for the restroom. To my office, where I open the door and shut it behind us. Then, as the silence thickens between us, surrounded by my magazine cutouts like windows into a dream world, I ask myself, could I strangle him? Am I strong enough? Should I bludgeon him instead, perhaps with my stapler? Would a letter opener to the spleen do him in faster?

And there he is, laughing until there are tears in his eyes.

"Your face," he wheezes. "When I said 'Nantucket—'"

"You've gone too far, Chuck," I tell him, gnarling my fingers with anger.

"Oh, please." He folds his arms and perches on my desk. Perches! As if he's relaxed, as if he's not aware I'm about to either strange, bludgeon, or stab him. "You've been running a Yelp campaign to ruin me. When I do shit, it's a prank. It's funny. When you do it, it's *mean*."

I roll my eyes. "Come on."

"Why are you so mean to me, Isadora?" he asks, with a lazy grin, his gaze infuriatingly blue. For a moment, I forget myself, mesmerized by the flame of those eyes. He is charming. I get that. I get why Sam called him sweet earlier. Is that his charm? That beneath his insufferable tendencies, he is honey and warmth?

Stop getting soft, Isadora. This is your future at risk. This man could put you out of business. He's the son of a millionaire who runs through enterprises like they're disposable. He could wipe away everything you've built, vacuum up your potential.

"Because you deserve it," I say simply.

I turn to open the office door, my hand on the knob, thinking, you don't know how lucky you are, you grinning asshole. I had a stapler and a letter opener in here. And yet I let you live.

But then, a terrible twist of fate.

The knob breaks off into my hand.

The doorknob. Just like last time.

I'd be lying if I told you the first thing I think isn't that this would make a beautiful murder weapon.

My second thought, I utter out loud.

"Oh fuck," I say, turning around and showing Chuck the knob in my hand.

The smug grin evaporates from his face, his mouth now a mere crease. "Did you seriously break it *again*?"

"Why are you blaming me?" I ask, plunking it on the desktop. "You reinstalled it."

"Which you never even thanked me for."

"Well, I'm certainly not thanking you now."

Chuck steps over to the door and pummels it with his fists. "Hey!" he barks.

"No one's going to hear you," I say. "The only people who come down the hall this far are me and Eva when we're coming to the office or taking garbage out the back door."

He squats and peers out the knob hole. "I don't see anything."

"That's because you're facing a dark hallway."

He cocks his ear to it. "I can hear people clapping."

"This isn't helpful, Sherlock," I say. "You're going to need to call someone on your phone."

"My phone's dead," Chuck says, standing. "You call someone."

"My phone's behind the bar in my jacket," I say.

He and I remain at a standstill so intense it's statuesque. In this dim room, with nothing but a green desk lamp, I notice things about him I haven't before. Like how sculpted his face is, how square his chin. The smile lines around his eyes. And I am realizing that we are actually trapped in here and it very well could be until Eva closes up shop in four or five hours that she comes back to see I'm gone.

"Oh my God," I say, sitting on the edge of the desk. I put my face in my hands, emotion welling.

"We'll figure this out," he says. "You don't need to cry."

But I'm not crying. I'm shattering into laughter. Rolling, undulating, exhilarating peals of laughter in my hands. It's so absurd! Locked in here with this man after he paraded up on stage and recited a bawdry limerick to ruin me and then I tackled him in a mortifying dramatic gesture. And I can't escape him. Since I met him, I've tried at every turn and I can't escape him.

"Are you okay?" he asks. "I can't tell what's going on right now. Is this a medical situation or are you losing your shit?"

I pull my hands away from my face, the laughter fully in control of me now as I rock back and forth, tears falling from my eyes. He takes my hands in his and looks closely at my face with genuine worry, and then pulls back in shock.

"You're … laughing?" he says, his grin remembering its place on his face.

I finally gasp in some air and nod, laughing so hard it has no sound anymore.

"Oh my God, Isadora," he says, weaving his fingers in mine. "You're losing your fucking mind."

And it's uncanny how he does that—how he eases his fingers between mine like they belong there, like this is déjà vu and we've already done this before. Even more, how I let him. How, as my laughter dies down and I can take in air again, long relieving breaths, and the tears cool on my face, I don't pull away. I keep my fingers there because I like the exact temperature of him.

"Do you ever feel like we have an Elizabeth and Mr. Darcy thing going on?" he asks.

Did he … just make a *Pride and Prejudice* reference?

"You know about them?" I ask, pulling my fingers away from him, a bit embarrassed to realize how long we've stood that way.

It's highly inappropriate. I'm not sure what I was thinking, dissolving into girlish giggles and then holding his hands.

"I took an English lit class at city college when I went there for a couple semesters," he says. "I liked it, actually." He raises his eyebrows. "Don't look so surprised. The thing about me is, I'm not flashy smart. I'm not flaunting my intelligence all the time. You? You're like the Bentley of brains. I'm a trusty Prius."

I snort.

"So, Bentley, you got a toolbox anywhere in here?" he asks. "Because if we don't find a screwdriver, we're in deep shit."

"I have a letter opener," I say.

"Let me see it."

I walk behind the desk, open the drawer, and rummage to locate it. "I was planning to kill you with it when we first came in here."

"Good thing you didn't."

"That's still up for debate." I shut my drawer. "It's not in here. Maybe it's behind the bar." I slump into my chair, open the drawer back up to poke my finger around the desolate wasteland of paper clips and rubber bands. "What about a pen?"

"I mean, I'll try, but I need something sharper."

"Paper clip?"

"Sure, I'll give it a shot."

A paper clip, a rubber band, a pen, a staple, and an earring later, the lock still won't budge. I give it a shot and somehow get the paper clip stuck and we can't get it out. When he's started taking out his shoelace in one last desperate attempt to do something, anything, the light on my desk lamp burns out and leaves us in pitch darkness. We both burst into laughter. Then the laughter stops and dwindles into sighs and curse words.

"Eva has to come back here at some point," I say.

"I'm kind of in a meditative space right now, honestly," he says. "It's like I've returned to the womb."

"Mmmm. I'm actually supposed to be working. So I'm having a hard time returning to that nascent space."

"Who cares? So you miss one open mic night," he says.

I can hear him adjusting himself. His arm brushes against mine. We're sitting side by side now, facing the doorknob hole, a familiar voice out there rising and falling.

"I know this one," I say. "This is the rapping philosophy major. He has a song called 'Aristotle Didn't Scrawl No Twaddle' he does every week."

"Let me guess: he's white."

"Need you ask?"

"Ah, philosophy majors: the first line of sacrifice when the zombie apocalypse comes."

"Mmmm," I agree.

"Watch out: the poets are next."

"Damn. I was hoping they'd eat the rich and start with you."

"Always get the last word in, don't you?" he asks.

We're quiet a while. It is odd to be in here, in the dark, with only a tiny dim hole and the faintest sounds of unintelligible poetry and clapping now and then. It's how I imagine a sensory depravation tank might feel, if you were sharing the tank with your enemy.

Though in the dark, my mind keeps drifting and almost forgetting Chuck's here.

"Are your eyes closed?" he asks me after a while.

"I don't know," I admit. "Yes, I think so."

"Mine are closed," he says. "Hey, that was awkward earlier, when I came in for a drink."

"The Nantucket poem was more awkward."

"Yeah, but Nantucket really started when I came in for a drink. Prologue, if you will."

"Yeah," I say, turning my head toward him, trying to find him with my eyes. I see only the faintest silhouette of his hair, his nose. "So who was that? Your ex-girlfriend?"

He's quiet a moment. "How'd you know Sam was my ex?"

Oh, talking about you with Eva. Stalking your social media, I do not admit.

"Lucky guess," I say.

"We're friends now," he says.

"Is that hard, being friends with an ex?"

"I'm friends with all my exes. Aren't you?"

"Some," I say, thinking of Zofie, though we weren't official or anything. It was more like a temporary drifting out of the friendship lane. But others I haven't kept up with. I wonder what that says about my character.

"I'm curious what your exes are like," he says. "I have a hard time imagining you with anyone."

"And why's that?" I say, barbed and ready.

"Oh, I don't know. You're just …"

"A bitch?" I finish.

He laughs. "What? No. I was going to say special. Extremely special."

When I look for him in the dark, I can see the faintest shape of his eyes, lit by the weak light coming in through the doorknob.

This place we're in is lovely, dark, and deep. Like we've found ourselves lost in the woods and bundled up for warmth. Without the light and the noise, I'm not sure who we are right now in the dark. We could be anyone. Remember that junior high game, seven minutes in heaven? As the silence thickens between us, I see the outline of Chuck's arm beside me, only inches away, and wonder what ripple would sound the universe if I dared put my hand on it.

Tentatively, feeling bold and bodiless in the dark, I reach for him. My palm lands on his warm forearm, locking it and squeezing.

"Isadora," he says.

"I'm cold," I say.

He reaches out with that hand, grasping my forearm and moving up, up, up. He stops and squeezes. I let out a breath of air.

Then he, very gently, pulls me.

I turn toward him and prop myself up on my knee and it's something like a psychic intuition, that I know where his body is, exactly, that I know *exactly* how to straddle him in one instant while he sits there cross-legged on the floor. I don't even have to see him. It's better that I don't. We hold each other tightly like this for a moment, my chin in his neck, the bright, salty smell of him. I haven't been this close to someone in well over a year. It comes over me like a fever, this need swelling up in me. And at the same time, another me is saying, *Isadora!?!?!??!?!? What on earth???* But that other me is in the light, and this me is different. She's in the dark. Her eyes are closed, or maybe open, who knows? But her lips? Her lips are on his.

What lips my lips have kissed tonight.

His kiss is kinetic. It starts in our lips, travels through our tongues like a language, and expresses itself all the way through my throat and heart. His hand moves up the back of my shirt, his palm hot on my back. We push together so hard I'm not sure if we're competing or trying to hurt one another or just trying to lose ourselves in the collisions. When we pull back, we pant, our foreheads together, and instead of satisfied, I am wrecked and hungry.

"What is *this*?" he asks, curiously, far too casually considering what just happened.

"I must be losing my mind."

He leans in and puts his lips on my neck. I cry out, bending my neck like Dracula's victim, and then—

Someone is pounding on the door. Oh fuck. What the fuck am I doing. I pull myself off of Chuck and wipe my mouth with my hand. I am washed sickly with adrenaline and regret. In the doorknob, an eye framed with a cat-eye lens peeks through.

"Isadora?"

"Oh my God, Eva," I say, springing to my feet. "Thank God. You need to either get someone to let us out or call a locksmith."

"I wondered where on earth you'd gone!"

"I'm stuck in here." I feel him stand beside me. He slides his arm around my waist, but I swat him away. "With Chuck," I add.

She pauses. "With Chuck," she repeats.

"Yes, and it's been very uncomfortable so please … please let us out."

Chuck and I sit on the other side of the hole as two different buzzed customers come with screwdrivers to try to get us out. Finally, the third—a ninety-pound man with a Dali mustache who calls himself Dragon—unlocks it with ease.

As Chuck and I thank him, squinting like newborn babes, Chuck holds my arm tightly and keeps me from running away. Dragon leaves us here, bathed in the glaring yellow light of the hallway. And now I can see Chuck. Really see him. The soft look in his eyes. The pinkish tinge to his lips, from how hard I kissed him. It seems surreal, it really happened, but now that we see each other, it sinks in.

And my stomach flips.

"That was something," Chuck says.

"Yeah it was." I look past him, at the water heater, because if I lock eyes with him I won't want to stop. And this is a mistake, a bad one. It's the worst idea I've come up with in a while. It could destroy everything to let him in—him, the guy who continually embarrasses and tries to ruin me! Wouldn't that be unhealthy? Some form of abuse? To love someone who tries to tank your business with a childish poem about a man from Nantucket? It would be wrong. I cannot. What happened in the dark was a mistake, was not meant for the light of day. So I lock eyes with the water heater. I steel myself. "I'm sorry I did that. I don't know what I was thinking. I regret it and it will not happen again."

It takes him a moment to respond. I can feel his eyes burning me, looking for direct contact. "You felt something," he says.

Can you imagine if I fell for him, and things went wrong? Can you imagine what power he would hold over me, the weaknesses he would gain insight into, only to ruin my business with that knowledge? Best case scenario, we would have our fun, it wouldn't work out, and then we would avoid each other as we operate parallel businesses next door to one another. There is no way in hell anything could ever really happen between Chuck McCaffrey and me that wouldn't spell disaster. And I did not just work my ass off for years and gain a modest inheritance from tragedy to have it all flushed away because I fell for a charming sportsman who resembles a younger, hotter Prince Harry.

He does. I will give him that.

"I was fucking with you," I say to him, which is mean, I know. Which is very mean. But I feel less awful about it when he cocks his head at me, raises his eyebrows, and grins.

"I was just fucking with you, too," he says.

He dips in for a second like he's going to kiss me, and I am conflicted—wanting to protest but almost kissing him back anyway—when he pulls away again.

"See? Just fucking with you," he says.

Chuck walks out of my office and I watch his back, the world dizzied like after a merry-go-round ride. I don't know if I believe him. I don't know what that was. I don't know if he hurt me, or I him, or if there was no sting at all, only honey.

I don't know.

And I am not used to not knowing.

chuck

SOMETIMES IT TAKES the power of comparison to put a situation in perspective.

I guess that's why writers love their metaphors and similes. Because to set something beside something else, it casts a new light on it, gives it a meaning it didn't have before. Well, that head-exploding kiss in the dark with Isadora the other night made me realize that I need to stop pretending anything could happen between Eva and me.

While Isadora's kiss has played on my mind on repeat to the point of near obsession, every time I remember that car crash of a kiss Eva tried to initiate on our date last month I shudder. Before, I thought it was me. Maybe I was romantically broken or I needed more time to warm up to that kind of affection. But after the absolute electricity Isadora shocked me with, I remember what it feels like to truly want someone. And Eva ain't it.

Rainy days in Santa Caterina are the unicorn of weather events: rare, fleeting, and when they blow into town, they're all anyone talks about for a week straight. I get up early to meet Eva for coffee as the downpour picks up. The gutters along Riviera Avenue are already gushing with muddy rivers, the sidewalks empty. Fallen palm fronds scattered along the streets.

As I get to Jitters, I flash back to the day Sam and I broke up here. Upstairs, near the chess table. What the hell is wrong with me, that I brought Eva here to call it off too? I guess there's no better place to break up than a coffeeshop. A restaurant? You're going to have to suffer through a meal as you do it. A bar? You don't want to mix alcohol and emotional conversations. A coffeeshop just seems like the right place to have this talk. That, and I'm just a guy with no imagination.

Jitters is classy, decorated with paintings that look like a toddler did them yet are apparently abstract expressionist works of art advertised for thousands of dollars. Jazz music plays on the speakers. Students pore over textbooks and groups have intimate conversations. The vibe actually isn't that far off from Gertrude's. I wonder if Isadora's considered opening earlier and getting an espresso machine—there's no good coffeeshop that far up on Riviera and I'm sure she'd get some business. This place is so packed I have a hard time finding a table.

Eva gets here late, her hair wrapped in a plastic babushka, her glasses spotted with raindrops. As she takes off her coat and sits down with a cappuccino in a giant cup, she tells me how great I look, how excited she is to see me. And I feel like the ultimate prick. I can't even bring myself to fake a smile.

"What's wrong?" she asks, leaning in, grabbing my hand in hers. "Are you okay?"

I had envisioned some banter, you know, a small-talk appetizer to cushion the blow of the shitty entrée. But as soon as I see her I feel the overwhelming need to just get this over with.

"Listen, Eva ... I really like you," I say.

Which, fuck, was not the best way to begin, because now her face lights up and she squeezes my hand. "I like you too! So much."

"But I mean, as a friend," I go on. "That's it. I don't feel like we're a fit for anything beyond that."

Her face holds that hopeful expression for a long moment. Then her hand slackens along with her lipsticked smile. She pulls her hand back. "Oh."

"I'm sorry," I say.

She studies the foam on her cappuccino and her eyebrows furrow. Eva's generally a ray of sunshine, bouncy, smiling, exclamation points on the end of every sentence. But right now I'm seeing a shadow in her—the way she purses her lips and her nostrils flare.

"Hey, Eva, I'm sorry," I repeat. "I didn't think you'd be this upset. I mean, we weren't serious or anything. We weren't much of anything."

"We weren't much of anything," she repeats.

"That's not what I meant."

"Listen," she says, leaning back. "Just say it. You have the hots for Isadora. That's what this is about."

"What? No, it's not—"

Her voice climbs. "That's why this conversation is

happening after you came in and read that terrible poem and then she basically jumped your bones onstage, before bringing you back to her office to jump your bones again."

Oh shit, Eva is weeping now. Loudly. Heads are turning.

"Okay, that's not what happened at all," I say lowly. "This has nothing to do with Isadora."

"What about me?" she wails. "You never even gave me a *chance* to jump your bones."

Someone at a nearby table is snickering, and I don't blame them.

"Isadora is grumpy and stuck up and she doesn't even brush her hair," she goes on. "What do you *see* in her?"

"I don't see anything—"

"And she hates your guts. She's like …" Wheels visibly turn in Eva's mind. "Cruella DeVille and you're an adorable little puppy dog."

I'm not going to lie. I'm having a hard time coming up with a response.

"She wants to destroy your business," she says. "You realize that, right? And you still follow her around with that disgusting puppy dog look on your face."

Five seconds ago I was an adorable puppy dog; now I'm a disgusting puppy dog. I'm having a hard time following the metaphorical puppy dog.

"This has nothing to do with Isadora," I say, as slowly as I can in hopes that the words sink in.

Eva stands and puts her coat back on. As she takes the plastic babushka and fastens it around her head, she looks down at me with a glare I didn't know she was capable of until right now.

"I might not be the sharpest Sharpie in the box." (Huh?) "I might not be as booksmart as *Isadora*," she says, with villainous emphasis on Isadora's name, "but I can spot a liar from a mile away. And you're a liar. In fact, you're the worst kind: the kind of liar who lies to himself."

"I thought I was a puppy dog," I can't help myself from saying.

"You deserve each other," she says before flouncing off, first in the wrong direction toward the restrooms, then correcting herself and heading for the front door.

Well, at least that disaster happened fast.

I sit for a couple minutes, rewinding the scene to watch it again in my mind. I'm not sure why it went so horribly wrong or why the guilt all through me. She wasn't even my girlfriend! She never took a hint! And while before I thought she was nice and I legitimately did hope we'd be friends, now I'm seeing she's more unhinged than I realized. Eva seems bitter as hell toward Isadora, which surprises me, because I thought they were friendly. And now I apparently have *two* nemesises—nemisi—nemeses—ugh, you know what I mean—next door.

Since news of the lawsuit spread, Brady's apparently has a new nickname: Shady's. And while it's not exactly the reputation I want for us, I'm beginning to think it's the reputation we deserve. Mom and Dad hired a lawyer to fight our battle for us in court. But look at this place: in the last week alone, we had someone picked up for solicitation outside near closing time, a fight broke out and two people left in an ambulance, and just after I open one night because Chadley is, once again, late to work, some dude in a Hawaiian shirt who looks blitzed out of his mind comes in and asks if I'm Henry and if I know where the ski slopes are.

"Get the hell out of my bar, man," I say. "We don't sell coke."

He leaves with a string of expletives so jam-packed it almost sounds like he's rapping.

This isn't going to be Shady's week. NFL's regular season's coming to a close. College students are on winter break. And Riviera's flooded with holiday shoppers because the two weeks before Christmas, the whole street gets closed off to traffic and street vendors and artists and carolers flock to the area. It seems like every business is booming except mine this week. I even spot Tyrus and Monique toting some shopping bags and checking out a table of homemade jewelry across the street. I go to the door to wave and Tyrus waves at me but doesn't come any closer.

By Friday the weekend before Christmas, the only people flocking to Brady's are a couple fantasy football leagues and a few alcoholics. As soon as Chadley comes behind the counter, two hours late, his chin bleeding and stuck with toilet paper from a shitty shaving job, I chew him out for being late yet again and ditch the counter to head out for a breath of fresh air.

"There's a naked guy next door," Chadley says as I'm about to step out.

"Dude, I saw that," says a bearded guy drinking Jack and watching a hockey game on TV. "What the hell?"

I look back at Chadley, hand on the front door.

"Butt-ass naked," Chadley says. "See for yourself, boss."

Several Brady's customers hear this and come behind me to confirm this is true. Stepping out into the sidewalk, first I take in the holiday scene: the street filled with vendors, the choir singing "O Come All Ye Faithful," a horse-drawn carriage ride. Then I spot Gertrude's window, where, not shitting you, a naked man in a Santa hat stands with his back to us. I stand with arms akimbo and jaw dropped as the Brady's customers snicker and point and take out their phones to snap pictures.

"Nasty," says one guy, with a salacious grin on his face that says very much the opposite. "Why's that dude naked?"

The sandwich board on the sidewalk says *Free Figure Drawing Fridays! Come have a drink and unleash your inner artist.*

"You want to go unleash your inner artist?" one of the Brady's customers chides the other as they head back inside.

I stay out here, shaking my head, amazed that Isadora would do something so bold. Isn't that public nudity or something? Doesn't it scare people away? But as I, curiously, poke my head inside, I see they've pulled quite the crowd. Every table is full, people murmuring quietly to one another over flickering fake candlelight as they sketch and sip glasses of wine. And they're all just calmly studying some dude's junk up there. I see a smiling old lady in a Rudolph sweater carefully drawing his scrotum on her paper. What the actual fuck?

"Is there a problem?" someone whispers in my ear.

That hot breath gives me a shiver. I turn and see Isadora standing next to me in a red velvet dress. Stunning can't even begin to describe how she looks. I have a hard time keeping my eyes on hers because I want to memorize every inch of her in that dress. It's been over a week since we kissed and I haven't seen her since then. Been avoiding Gertrude's like the plague because, well, Eva. But the sight of Isadora infects me with such desire I have to shove my hands in my pockets so I don't reach out and touch her.

I lean over and whisper in her ear. "What the fuck is this?"

"It's called art," she whispers back, her breath giving me tingles. "Ever heard of it?"

"Every heard of public nudity?" I whisper.

"You're just jealous because I've poached your customers," she whispers, and nods toward a table in the back where one of my fantasy football groups is now sitting and giggling while they draw.

"We're still playing games, are we?" I whisper.

My lip brushes against her ear when I say it and I feel her shiver. I, too, have goosebumps, being this near her, breathing in the coconut smell of her skin.

I want her so badly that in one second, an entire scene arises in my mind. We're in her office again. Only this time, the light is on, and she's on the desk, and my hands are up her velvet dress.

"Why are you looking at me like that?" she whispers, her eyes dancing.

"I haven't been able to stop thinking about you," I say.

She shakes her head.

"What?" I whisper. "We have to pretend that didn't happen?"

She nods.

"Come on," I whisper. "You felt it too."

Isadora sighs and yanks me outside. Does she work out? Because this woman's got a grip. She pulls me behind her a few stores down the block, near the entrance to the Chat Auberge. There's a basket of kittens in the window with red and green ribbons on their necks and it's so fucking cute I want to punch something.

"Look, Chuck," she says, shivering a little in the cold. "We have to move on from that. It's creating problems for me."

"Problems? How?"

"Well, for one, Eva's been a real moody pain in the ass since it happened. She says you dumped her because you have feelings for me."

"That is not true at all," I say. "I didn't say anything like that."

"She tells it differently."

"She's lying. You know, she said some pretty rude things about you. I wouldn't trust her."

"Regardless, please don't come into Gertrude's until this blows over, okay? She saw you walk by with a meatball sub the other day and burst into tears behind the counter. Thank God she was too busy making drinks just now to see you or we might have had a nervous breakdown on our hands."

"Fine. I'll steer clear."

"Thank you for understanding."

"But I want you to look me straight in the eye and tell me you haven't thought about what happened."

"Of course I've thought about what happened," she says, looking anywhere but straight in the eye. She turns and looks at the kittens, taps the glass. "I don't know what came over me. I feel like I'm losing my mind." Finally, she meets my gaze. "This can't happen, Chuck. Whatever this is? It can't happen. You and I are completely different people. Not only that, we're competitors. And neighbors. And … there are a million reasons why."

"Those are three reasons, not a million."

She reaches up and places a warm hand on my face. "I can't even fathom the many ways you could destroy me."

"So you're scared," I clarify. "What, like I have nothing to lose, either?"

"Why should either of us run the risk of losing anything?" she asks. "Serious question. You and I both care about our bars so much. We both want to succeed more than anything. Why should either of us let feelings get in the way of that?"

"It's not an either/or," I say.

"Yes, it is. It is for me. I can't be your rival and your lover at the same time."

"So don't be my rival."

"Let it go," she says gently.

"I don't want to play the game anymore," I say. "I forfeit. All right? You win."

"I can't." She shakes her head. "I have to go back to the bar, okay?" She squeezes my arm but doesn't meet my gaze. Off she goes, into the people river of the sidewalk. Leaving me staring at a basket of adorable kittens through the window with an ache in my chest.

Why'd I do that? Whatever happened to playing it cool? And she's right, you idiot, I say silently to my dumb face in the reflection. It's a ridiculous idea to think we could make anything work considering who she is and who I am. We have sparks, but we also have a shit ton of flammable material between the two of us. Eva. Our businesses. The fact we drive each other bananas. But when I'm with her, all that gets washed away and what I'm left with is a pull so simple I can't stay away from her.

I don't go back to Brady's. I'm so frustrated right now, so disappointed, so lonely, that there's only one thing I can do to cheer myself up.

I adopt a fucking kitten.

isadora

THE FOG COMES, but not on little cat feet. It rolls onto Riviera thick as a cloud, obscuring our window view, disappearing the tourists, the carolers, the vendors' tables set up in the street. All I can see are the golden halos of streetlamps through the misty veil. It's Sunday evening and so dead-quiet in Gertrude's that I'm the only person here. Well, except Zofie, who blows inside like a gust of wind in a puffy winter coat and beanie, Gio's bag in hand. She came to spend a night with me since she didn't get a callback for the cat food commercial. Which she will not stop talking about. As she unwraps our sandwich and divvies it up at the bar counter, she brings it up yet again.

"You know, I should file some kind of complaint against Meowies," she says. "For discrimination. Just because I have a cat allergy and had a sneeze attack. I mean, isn't that ableism or something?"

"An allergy is not a disability."

"I was *so* excited. Meowies have legit good commercials. That jingle gets in your head for days."

"Their commercials are awful. Every single one is like a contest to see how many bad cat puns you can fit in. You dodged a bullet."

Zofie shakes her head and bites into her half of the sandwich. I can tell she wanted to continue arguing, but the taste of pastrami appears to have placated her for now.

"So," I say, picking at my sandwich, my stomach a ball of nerves. "It's been a couple weeks since we talked."

"I know. Worst best friend ever."

"Yes, you are."

"I meant you."

"Seriously. I need to tell you something." I lean on the counter and prepare for what's coming by immediately feeling my cheeks flush.

Double-checking no one's entered the bar and it's still just the two of us, I take a deep breath and then, in a trainwreck of an explanation, I catch her up on the mess I've made with Chuck McCaffrey: the kiss in the dark I'm still mortified I initiated; him possibly having feelings for me; Eva, who has turned into a sullen shrew ever since. Zofie sits, her jaw unhinged, her sandwich half-uneaten. Which is how I know I have stunned her—Zofie never stops eating once she's started a beloved sandwich.

"You kissed the ginger asshole?" she asks in disbelief.

I nod and grimace.

"Like, *you* were the one who kissed *him*."

I nod again and grimace again.

"So you like him!?"

"No," I protest. "Not at all."

"But you're attracted to him."

"No."

She studies me unblinkingly. "Something is not adding up."

"I agree," I say. "It makes absolutely no sense. And it's freaking me out. I've never done something so impulsive. Why did I do that?"

"Don't ask me, you weirdo!" she says. "I'm not the one smooching my mortal enemy."

She's still studying me, but takes a tentative bite of her sandwich. I bite my lip, scanning my own mind for a reason. For something I must be missing. It's the most unsettling thing, to be a predictable person, to live life by the book (literally! figuratively!) and to suddenly do something unlike yourself and have no understanding of your own behavior.

"The only other time in life I did something like this was that summer," I say.

"You mean … That Summer?"

I nod.

Zofie chews as she thinks about this, raising her now thinned-out eyebrows. "So you *do* like him. You *are* attracted to him."

That Summer is the time that lives like a secret between Zof and me—the summer that she and I first became close and fell in love with the force and drama of a mad monsoon. We met at Study Hall, we became fast friends, we moved in together, and suddenly I couldn't do without her in this way that was completely unlike me. The rest of the world disappeared and it was just the two of us for a couple of months. But then, internally, I spun out of control. My own jealousy overwhelmed me. I didn't trust it to last, not with Zofie, who never commits to anyone for long. So I saved myself and saved our friendship by ending it. By convincing myself we were better as friends. Which we are. I was right. I've since seen Zofie go through men and women like they're replaceable, and never once have I seen her in anything resembling a relationship.

"Sometimes, babe, I think you hold back too much," Zofie says. "I don't know. You know my feelings on the ginger asshole—I'm still trying to wrap my brain around you doing this with *him* of all people—"

"I know," I moan.

"—but putting my judgment of him aside, it's like, why not? Why not just let yourself have a fling with him and see where it goes?"

This is not at all the advice I expected from my best friend. "Because he is the ginger asshole."

"And?"

"And … and he's right next door, owner of the shittiest bar in town."

"And?"

"And if we end up hating each other when it's done— which we will, there's no way it would last, come on—I have to see him every day until one of us goes out of business."

"And how is that different than what it's been like already?"

"Because I will be *hurt*. Or he'll be hurt. It won't just be a rivalry. It'll be personal."

"I'd wager it's already personal."

I shake my head and open my mouth to attempt a response but am so shocked at her reaction I can't even muster one.

"What?" she asks.

"You give terrible advice," I tell her.

"I do not. I told you to open this bar, didn't I?"

"Yeah, and look," I say, sweeping my hand through the air. "Look at how successful it is."

"It's two days before Christmas. Didn't you say you had a huge turnout yesterday?"

"Yeah, because there was a naked man in here for figure drawing night. Half the people who came in here just gawked and giggled and didn't buy anything. I guess I need a naked person to even draw a crowd."

"I mean, there is a whole business around naked people and drinks, if you want to go that route."

"I do not," I say.

"Are you actually worried about your business?"

"If I hadn't prepaid rent on our apartment for a year, I wouldn't have been able to make rent this month." When I say it out loud, I almost start to cry.

"You're just starting," she says softly. "Be easy on yourself."

"And meanwhile," I say, tearing up, "Chuck's place is raking it in. Did you see how many people were in his bar already when you walked in here?"

"I didn't. But I did see someone smoking out of a four-foot bong right out front. Those folks are *bold*."

Three ladies come through the door and Zofie quickly vacates the bar. I wipe my eyes and arrange my face into a smile. The customers are adorable—three sisters who are in town for the holiday, who heard about Gertrude's from a friend. They linger at the bar and *oooh* over the drink menu, type on the typewriters, ask me if I have any merch for sale. I don't. When they sit down for their drinks at a table, Zofie comes back over with her phone in hand.

"Did you see this?" she asks, pointing to an article on the *Santa Caterina News* website. "Looks like loverboy's got some legal troubles."

CITY LAWSUIT DECLARES DOWNTOWN SPORTS BAR BRADY'S A 'NUISANCE,' THREATENS TO CLOSE

I gasp. I hadn't. And I'm so shocked I don't even tell her not to call him "loverboy." As I read the article by Saturn Martinez, there's a bit of smug satisfaction coursing through me. Because they *are* a nuisance. That's exactly what they are. Having that business gone would inevitably be a boost for Gertrude's, both because it would eliminate competition and because we wouldn't have his asshole clientele, loud music, and Chuck himself driving my customers away.

And, even more importantly, it would insert some much-needed distance between me and Chuck McCaffrey.

～

I close Gertrude's early on Christmas Eve, feeling the opposite of festive: deflated, dejected, and lonely. If there was such a thing as a depressed Ebeneezer Scrooge, I would be it. We had no customers in the two hours I remained open. I gave Eva the night off. The vendors outside packed up early and left when evening hit and Riviera Avenue is still closed to traffic, but dead, nothing but flashing lights reflected on the street.

As I go outside and lock up my doors, though, I see that the flashing lights have nothing to do with the holidays. Next door, in front of Brady's, a man is getting hand-cuffed by two cops.

"My dad's a lawyer!" the man yells. "You can't arrest me! My dad's friends with Cory McCaffrey!"

"Your dad know you're a drug dealer?" one of the cops snickers.

"I gotta call my boss, man!" the man yells as they put him in the back of the cop car.

Wait. Is that one of the losers who works at Brady's? I step out into the sidewalk, trying to get a better view.

"Excuses, excuses," the other cop says, getting into the driver's seat.

The car disappears into the black, dead night, past the barricades closing the streets off.

I peek into Brady's. It's lit up with its ten thousand screens and flashy blue-lit bar and it has an old-beer stink like a recycling bin. There are a couple of despondent-looking patrons sitting apart, drinking and watching TV, apparently completely oblivious to the arrest outside. Did the cops just seriously arrest a bartender here and leave no one in charge?

I hover at the bar counter a moment, stunned. I walk toward the back hallway, just to make sure. There's no one. I peek my head in the bathroom and am relieved to note the urinal no longer has my face on it, but the smell is disgusting. I gag, abandon the room, and head back, trying to open Chuck's office door. It's locked.

Chuck,

I text him,

something's afoot at your bar.

It's Christmas Eve, and who knows what Chuck McCaffrey is doing on Christmas Eve. But the three dots appear and I sigh in relief.

afoot?

I think your bartender was just arrested outside Brady's. There's no one working here.

fuck. you at bradys right now?

Yes. I was seeing if you're here. I saw the arrest outside when I was locking up Gertrude's.

can you stay til i get there? so sorry.

Sure.

I head back out to the front where a couple of middle-aged men in Grizzlies sweatshirts wait at the bar. Certain it's entirely inappropriate but uncertain what other course of action to take in this moment, I slip behind the counter and smile.

"Hey, how can I help you?" I ask.

"Hi there, never seen you before!" the mustached man one. "Nice to see Chuck hiring a lady. This place needs a little more diversity in its hires, if you know what I mean."

"I actually work next door," I explain. "Just covering during an emergency."

"The place with the naked guy?" asks the bearded one.

"Yes, well, we're doing figure drawing on Friday nights."

They snort and snicker like a couple teenage boys.

"You should come by next week," I offer.

"I don't know," mustache says. "I'm pretty hetero."

I love how the use of "pretty" in that sentence actually undermines how hetero he is.

My frozen smile hurts my face. "Well, sexual orientation has nothing to do with being able to draw the human body. But FYI, next month we have a female model," I say.

Both of the men's faces slacken into seriousness. They look at each other, raising their eyebrows.

"You know, I am kinda interested in art," mustache says.

"Me too," beard agrees. "I like art."

God, they are predictable, until they both order pineapple daiquiris. Takes me a minute to find the simple syrup and the limes, but I get to work, and thank God they hand me a credit card because the cash register resembles some futuristic spaceship I wouldn't know how to open.

"Keep a tab open?" I ask.

"Yep."

They retreat to a corner to sip their daiquiris.

Soon after, a few college students come in and order a pitcher. A couple women who seem out of place in expensive clothes come in and order chardonnays. They would have preferred to come to Gertrude's if we were open, I'm sure. By the time Chuck finally arrives, I'm working up a sweat behind the counter.

"Oh shit, I'm so sorry," he says as he comes behind the counter.

He's wearing his Sea Lions sweatshirt, his hair's in his eyes, and he's sporting a five o'clock shadow that makes him look endearingly rough around the edges. But I'm not going to let that soften the fact that I'm here doing him a giant favor holding down the fort of his nuisance of a bar on Christmas Eve and he lollygagged his way over here.

"Took you long enough," I mutter. "Where do you live? The North Pole?"

"I live in your neighborhood, above the Botanical Garden."

"Really?" I ask, surprised. "You didn't tell me that."

"You didn't ask."

"So why'd it take you so long to get here, then?"

"I was with Betty," he says. "She didn't want me to leave."

"Oh," I say, rinsing out the cocktail shaker, trying not to imagine him reluctantly leaving some vixen named Betty with whom he's spending Christmas Eve. Which is fabulous for him, of course. Not sure why the image of his pinup girlfriend bothers me so much. Would it have killed him to mention he was already seeing someone when he claimed he had feelings for me last week? Was he already seeing Betty when I kissed him? When he was flirting with Eva? You know what? I think, my anger picking up steam as I dry the cocktail shaker. Am I *ever* glad I didn't fall for Chuck. Because it turns out he's a giant—

"Want to see her?" he asks, sliding over to me to show me his phone.

"Um, no, I'm fine."

"Seriously?" His facial expression is like I just slapped him. "You don't want to see a picture of the world's cutest kitten?"

The tension releases in me and I turn to a puddle as my eyes fall on his phone where, indeed, the world's cutest kitten sits on a throw pillow, a ribbon around her neck.

"My *God*," I say. "She's adorable. She's like ... like a model kitten. You should get her an agent."

"Do you see why I had a hard time leaving?"

"Yes."

I forgive everything. I hand him his phone back, which he glances at once again with the softest, sweetest smile before he puts it away, sighs, and turns to me, the soft, sweet smile melting.

"Okay, so Chadley got arrested," he says. "Do you know *why* he was arrested?"

"They called him a drug dealer," I say.

"Drugs," he says. "Why am I not in any way shocked."

"I saw him getting escorted into the car and then they drove away. I popped my head in here, saw no one was behind the counter, and I texted you."

"Well, thanks," he says. "Not sure how this would have gone down without you here." He claps. "Hey!" he shouts. "We're closing up now. You got a tab, come up here and let me ring you up."

Groans from the few lackluster patrons. They start shuffling up to the counter.

"Betty calls," Chuck tells me.

"You're very dedicated to this kitten."

"Well, she's new. And I'm new to this being a cat dad thing. So I'm a little nervous leaving her alone."

He starts ringing people up. I realize after a moment that I've been gawking at him, how fast he moves behind the counter and his … swagger. Confidence. It's the first time I've ever seen him *working*, to be honest. Usually he's in the office with his feet kicked up.

"Do you need help closing up?" I ask.

"I'm good," he says. "I'm sure you've got plans."

"Yep, me and a bath bomb and a book. Big plans." I pick up my purse. "Have a good one, Chuck."

"Hey, let me take you home," he says, handing the last customer a credit card receipt and a pen. "Since we're neighbors. I'll put your bike in my trunk again."

My first instinct is to refuse. I don't know why, though.

He's been perfectly polite to me tonight. Grateful for my help, smitten with his kitten, and surprisingly adept at his job, at least in this short time I've watched him. Why am I so resistant to him?

"Okay," I say. "Sure, thanks."

He counts the drawer while whistling a Christmas song and I sit at a table, reading my Kindle. Soon the TVs zap off, the room darkens, and we stride out into the night. I unlock my bike. We're quiet as we walk, the chain clicking, our footsteps the only thing I can hear—that and the intense pounding of my heartbeat in my ears.

"Maybe we could stop by my place first so you could meet Betty," he says.

"Wow, this is getting serious," I say. "First I work a shift at Brady's, now you want me to meet your kitten?"

"It's not like that. I'm not—"

"I know, I know. I'm kidding. Sure, I'd love to meet Betty."

My bike in his trunk, we drive. The streets are empty, near apocalyptic, lit by twinkling Christmas lights. He listens to carols on the radio and hums along. And I don't know why it's now, here—in this understated moment, in the ease and silence in his car, me sitting passenger—that it dawns that I do have feelings for Chuck. And for once in my literary, words-worshiping life, these feelings are so complex, so confounding, so colossal, that I cannot even articulate them.

chuck

"YOU'RE AWFULLY QUIET," I say as I unlock my front door. "I don't think I've ever gone this long without an insult. Should I be worried about you?"

Isadora exhales a foggy breath, hands in the pocket of her fake fur coat. "The rivalry's off. For Christmas."

"How festive." I push open the door. "Disclaimer: I didn't realize I was bringing someone home tonight. My place is a mess." I squat in the foyer and make a kissy noise. "Betty? Where you hiding, girl?"

Betty comes around the corner from my bedroom, small as a fist, white as a cloud, with an amount of cuteness that should be illegal. My heart picks up at the sight of her, relieved she's okay. I scoop her up, giving her a hug she gets lost in.

This two-pound furball is a lifesaver. And I've known her less than a week. After so much frustration with Isadora, with Eva, with the bar, when I took Betty home, it all faded into the background. Now I have this tiny being who is pure sweetness and innocence. Who relies on me. Who's there purring on the pillow next to me in the morning when I wake up.

"She's so delightful," Isadora says, tentatively reaching her hand out to touch Betty's head. "Hi Betty. Hi cutie pie."

Isadora's fingers touch my chest, too, and even through my sweatshirt, I get goosebumps.

"Why'd you name her Betty?" she asks, hands back in her pockets.

"Betty White," I say.

"*Golden Girls* fan?"

"Um, who isn't?"

"You know, Chuck," Isadora says. "You're full of surprises." She steps further into my living room and gives it the once-over. I try to imagine what she's seeing in my drab bachelor pad—the loveseat that sees very little love. The plain blue shag rug that reminds me of muppet skin. The TV mounted on the wall, the remotes lined up in a row on the coffee table next to a copy of *The Midnight Library*.

"You read?" she says skeptically.

"Wow. You really think I'm an idiot," I say, petting Betty's scruff until she purrs. "Then again, I've been working on that book for over a month. So maybe you're right."

"You're not an idiot," Isadora says, which is probably the closest thing to a compliment the woman has ever given me.

Isadora's definitely softened to me, I can tell. There's

almost a tinge of sadness about her since I kind of threw myself at her outside the Chat Auberge. I'm guessing it's pity for me. Pity I deserve for the I-have-feelings-for-you shenanigans the other night. She's not giving me the body language of someone who's looking for more than petting my cat at the moment. In fact, the studious way she's glancing over everything in my house almost makes me feel like she's scoping me out.

"Your place is tidy," Isadora says. "Do you have a house cleaner?"

What is this? An interview?

I scoff. "Um, no. I can clean a six-hundred-square foot apartment on my own."

"I would have imagined you'd have a bigger place, a house cleaner—"

"A nicer car," I finish. "Yes, I know, somehow I keep finding ways to fall short of your expectations."

"It's just … you're rich."

"My dad's rich," I correct her. "I'm a rich guy's son."

"Which makes you rich."

"I guess. Or it makes me a guy on a leash."

"What does that mean?"

"It means I don't actually have anything. I have the *potential* to inherit everything. And behind everything I do I've got the fear of losing that inheritance."

"I feel so sorry for you," she says flatly.

"I know," I say. "I should feel lucky. I'm a jackass to even complain."

Isadora turns and steps closer to me. My pulse speeds up. It's so unexpected, having her in my space. My whole life, my boring existence, is under a microscope. Why'd she agree to come so quickly? Usually I'd think a woman was into me if she accepted an invite to my apartment. But this is Isadora. And I never know what's going on in her head.

"Let me hold her," Isadora says, putting her palms out.

Gently, I remove Betty's claws from my sweatshirt and put her in Isadora's hands.

"She's wily," I say. "Careful not to drop her."

"I'm not going to *drop* her." Isadora folds Betty up in her fuzzy jacket and cuddles her with her cheek. "Oh my God, she's so soft." Isadora gently kisses Betty's head. "She's perfect."

"You see why I was so anxious to get home?"

"Absolutely I do." Betty's purring louder than a motorcycle. The kitten approves. Extra points for Isadora. "Hey Chuck, I saw that article about Brady's."

I sigh. "The lawsuit?"

Isadora nods. "What's going on? Are you really going to close?"

"Maybe. You want a drink?" I ask.

"Sure, a quick one. Then I should probably get going."

"All I have is scotch."

"Scotch it is."

I head back to my kitchen and splash a couple of fingers of Glenmorangie Grand Vintage into a couple water glasses, bring them back to the coffee table with the bottle. Isadora's made herself at home on my loveseat, gazing down into her jacket, where all I see is a tuft of white fuzz.

"She fell asleep," whispers Isadora.

"You can't keep her, all right?" I say, sitting on the floor on the other side of the coffee table. It seems invasive to squeeze onto the loveseat with her. My big ass takes up too much room for two platonic people to comfortably fit. "She's my soulmate."

"But she's *my* soulmate," Isadora says. "So ... the lawsuit."

"Yeah, the city has it out for Brady's. Looks like our time might be up."

"Your parents are countersuing though, according to the article?"

"My parents sue everything with a heartbeat and rarely win."

"Well, aren't you, like ... fighting it?" Isadora sniffs the scotch and makes a face. "Smells like a campfire."

"Funny, I think it smells like the wallet of an old man," I say.

We both take sips. Isadora reaches out and reads the bottle. "Wow, this is ... a ridiculously expensive bottle of scotch."

"Christmas present from Dad," I say. "He gets me the same thing every year since I was eighteen: his favorite brand of scotch."

"Do you like scotch?"

"Not really."

"Have you ever told him you don't like scotch?"

I look at the amber liquid in the glass, twirl it around. "I don't know."

"I mean, that would be a start, right?" She takes a sip, winces. "It's good."

"Yeah, you look like you're loving it with that eating-a-lemon face."

Isadora watches me from the couch. I have no idea what's going on in her head. I never have. Maybe that's what makes me want her so badly—to uncover the mystery of what's inside of her.

"You seem like you don't even care that your bar might close," she says. "I don't understand how you can sit there and be so nonchalant about your business being ruined."

I put the drink on the table and sigh. "You know, it's not my bar. It's not my business. I don't even like Brady's. And as soon as it started sinking in that this might be it, you know what happened?"

Isadora watches me with her bright eyes and faded lipstick, still except for the bouncing leg in her cowgirl boot.

"I felt relief," I say. "I felt like maybe a rope's being cut."

"And so what happens if that rope gets cut?"

"I don't know. Maybe I go back to coaching—I coached pee-wee football before. The Sea Lions."

"Your sweatshirt!" she says, smiling. "That's who the Sea Lions are?"

"Yeah. I love working with kids. Loved that gig. My dad thought it was a joke but it was my favorite thing ever." I smile. "Can't make a real career out of coaching pee-wee, though."

"Why not? People make a living coaching all the time."

I can see my dad shaking his head at me in disappointment. "It's an elevated hobby," he told me once.

"I'm actually more thinking about leaving the area," I say.

Isadora's leg stops bouncing.

"My ex, Sam?" I go on. "She lives in Oxford, you know, and I have an open invitation to go there. I turned her down years ago. But I don't know. Maybe that wasn't the right decision. Maybe I'd have been happier out there, would have found something unexpected waiting for me."

Isadora gives a tight smile. "Sounds like a good opportunity." She downs the rest of the drink and gently removes sleepy-eyed Betty from her jacket, places her on a cushion. "I can't imagine you in Oxford."

"Me neither. Maybe that's why I like trying to."

"Well," she says, with a yawn and a stretch. "Take me home?"

"Sure."

Her apartment is only about five or six blocks away, but when it's this cold—fifty-five, which by Santa Caterina standards, is below freezing—I'm giving her a ride. I blast the heat, the defroster, and the radio. I catch "Santa Baby" and sing the whole thing in a falsetto, which finally cracks the ice of Isadora. She bursts out laughing and keeps it up until we pull in front of her apartment. She wipes her eyes.

"Are you crying?" I ask, so proud to have extracted that level of emotion from the icy goddess she is.

"I cry so easily, Chuck. I'm embarrassing."

"I'm more embarrassing," I say. "My face is splashed

on B1 this week as the poster boy for failed, sketchy businesses."

"Okay, you win."

"Do I, though?" I ask. "*Do I?*"

She laughs again.

I leave the car running and fetch her bike from the trunk. She comes out of the passenger's side and takes the bike from me, offers a smile. Her eyes are still red.

"Have a good night," she says. "Merry Christmas."

The pause makes it so I have to wonder—is she waiting for something? A warm kiss? A long hug? Does she have feelings for me after all? But I'm not about to try anything. Bad idea. She made it clear she has no interest in me like that when I brought it up outside the Chat Auberge. Never want to be one of those pushy guys who won't take no for an answer. Plus, experience proves Isadora will make a move if she wants to. And as this pause goes on and neither of us move, it's obvious she doesn't want to.

"Merry Christmas," I echo.

I watch her walk her bike toward her apartment.

I try to forget the way she makes me ache.

I drive home and dream of Oxford.

A peace has washed over me the last couple of weeks. While Dad barks at our lawyers on the phone and fights the closing of Brady's, I've emotionally detached myself from this bar. Even the small shit that used to annoy me so much—the fact no one knows how to mop this place properly, that Brayden's late all the time, our clients brawling over fantasy football—none of it gets to me anymore. I sit in my office, feet propped up, and read up on Oxford. I message Sam, who sends me short-term apartment listings and pictures of the incredible buildings that make up the city. It's almost like we've picked up where we left off two years ago and we're exploring an alternate ending to our story. The one that ends with me getting on a plane with her and not letting her go.

It hasn't become romantic with Sam but she isn't seeing anyone and neither am I. So of course my mind goes there. It's not that I want to be with her again, exactly. I've grown used to the idea of us being friends. But it's nice to know the possibility's there, that a door's still open. And it's exciting researching a place I've never been and entertaining the idea of the unknown. Because my whole life has been extremely predictable. Not just predictable— hand-selected by my parents. My hobbies. My job. Even a girlfriend. I'm ready to do something that has none of their fingerprints on it.

So I wouldn't just say that I'm apathetic about Brady's at this point. I would say I'm actually, privately, rooting for its failure. And my spirit's never felt freer.

"Charles," Dad says, putting his cell phone on my desk with a smack. "What the hell's going on in your head? I'm here bleeding cash to our lawyers, taking time out of my day to deal with the shitshow *you've* made of this place and what are you doing? Hiding in your office playing games on your phone."

I put my phone down.

"You do realize this isn't a game?" he asks. "This is your future at stake? It's not a joke. They're going to shut you down unless we turn this thing around."

"I don't have a lot of hope we can do much here."

"Well, when you sit on your ass all day, no, there's not much hope."

"What do you expect me to do?"

"Anything!" he yells, exasperated. "This is your fucking mess!"

Usually when my dad gets pissed at me, I shrink. I go blank. But right now, seeing him red-faced in front of me, spitting with anger, something new builds inside me. I stand up. I meet his gaze over the desk.

"Let's get one thing straight," I say. "This is *your* fucking mess. The idiots you hired, because you're chummy with their dads—they set us up to fail from the get-go. And one of them was a drug dealer."

"Don't play the victim here. You had the power to fire them," he says. "You manage the goddamn place!"

"I manage a business you picked out, you designed, you renovated, you staffed, you set up."

"Because if I hadn't done it, you would never have done any of those things on your own." He puts his sunglasses on his face and points a finger at me. "Sometimes I think I've spoiled you with how much I've done for you your whole life. Maybe you'd have been better if I'd given you nothing and pushed you out on your own and said, figure it out yourself."

"I don't disagree with you there," I say.

He huffs and shakes his head at the damn shame I am and leaves the room.

Clearly following up on this scene, Mom swings by the office less than two hours later. I'm sure Dad went straight to her and complained about what a lazy good-for-nothing loser I am and asked Mom to talk some sense into me. So now she's here on cleanup duty, bringing me a meatball sub right around dinnertime. She's wearing her favorite Grizzlies shirt with Dad's face on it and yoga pants, like she was called in from home.

"Hi hon," she says cheerfully, putting the meatball sub on my desk. "Thought you might be hungry."

"Thanks. But you don't have to pretend like Dad didn't send you here."

"He didn't *send* me. I have a mind of my own."

I would be inclined to disagree—it's like the two of them have one mind at this point. But I don't mention this.

"I don't think you realize how serious this is," she says, sitting on the edge of the desk. "The bar could be shut down in a matter of weeks if we don't turn this around."

Reading from the same script, I swear.

"We don't have control over what the court decides," I say.

"No, but we can fight." She emphasizes this with her fist, the diamonds on her fingers catching the light. "And I'm not seeing any fight in you."

"That's because there is none."

"Why are you going to fold like this, Chucky?" she asks, her voice climbing. "You do this and I don't under-stand why you do this."

"I do this? What do you mean I do this?"

"Well, like your knee injury in high school. *One* doctor tells you not to play and you listen to him and refuse to get a second opinion."

"He's the best orthopedic surgeon in the state."

"Or like your relationship with Tatum."

"Oh my God," I groan. "We're dredging *her* up now?"

"You were so good together and you didn't even fight for her."

"I didn't have feelings for her!" I start to open the sub in front of me, but, you know what? I'm not even hungry for it. Which says a lot about my emotional state, because I'm a human garbage disposal. "What about Sam? You mad I didn't fight harder for Sam?"

"That's a very different situation," Mom says, folding her arms.

"Because you didn't like her."

"No, I liked her fine. I just didn't think you were a fit like you and Tatum were. And I didn't see the use in you following her halfway around the world to move to a town in England where she'd be going to school. I didn't see a future for you there."

"You saw a future for me here."

"There are so many opportunities for you here."

"Like opening a failing bar?"

"It doesn't have to fail," she says.

I look up at her and lean back in my chair. I wonder what it's like being Isadora, being a poet, a person who loves words so much you open a whole business around it. Does she have the right words to say to people all the time? Would she know what I'm supposed to say right now? Because if you open up my mind, I'm a blank book. I don't know how to express the way I feel to my parents at this point. I feel like I've been trying for years and it never comes out right.

"You know what might help you," Mom says, snapping her fingers. "I'll set you up with my life coach."

"Oh, for the love of—"

"I'm serious, Chucky. Alejandro is helping me home in on my true desires through aroma-hypnotherapy. We had a major breakthrough last week when I remembered my childhood love of crystals and came up with this idea for a crystal-of-the-month club—"

"That is a terrible idea."

Mom sucks in a breath. "Excuse me?"

"I'm sorry, that came out wrong. I'm just trying to be real with you. No one is going to want to join a crystal-of-the-month club."

"Your problem," she says, pointing with a long fake fingernail, voice trembling with emotion. "Is you've never had the courage to dream."

"Oh, I've had dreams. You've just never liked them."

"Like what? I've *always* supported you. Who was in the first row screaming your name at every football game?"

"You don't get it," I say. "Why weren't you supporting me like that when I wanted to run track?"

"In junior *high*? Oh, brother."

"Or when I decided to drop out of football senior year? You were so bitter, even though I was following doctor's orders."

"We didn't even get a second *opinion*—"

"Or Sam. Or coaching football. Or the car I ended up buying. Or the clothes I wear. I could go on and on and on."

It hurts to say those things out loud—the litany of disappointments I've been. But she looks more hurt than I am. Her eyes water and she stands up.

"I've only tried to help you," she says. "And obviously you don't want my help. Fine. I'll let you do your thing. But what's going to happen if Brady's closes, huh? What's next?"

"I'm going to Oxford," I say.

Her mouth drops open. "You're kidding me. To get back together with *Sam*?"

"To go somewhere else and do something else and maybe figure myself out."

"You know, you think that's what you're doing," she says. "But it sounds to me like you're just running away from your problems. And you really think that's so much better than accepting help from your parents? Moving to a city because your ex-girlfriend lives there? If what you want is a life of your own, without other people's influence—which is what it sounds like—why is that the answer?"

"To what?"

"To you."

"I'm not a question, Mom. I'm a person."

When Mom gets upset, you see it in her complexion: red, blotchy. I'm seeing it now.

"I wasn't saying you weren't. Geez, hon," she says.

"Enjoy your dinner, I've got a hot stone massage appointment."

Watching her leave, her back reminding me my dad is #1 G.O.A.T. GRIZZLES QB, what bothers me most about the conversation isn't that we fought, or that she still doesn't seem to see how much the heavy hand of my parents' wishes has burdened me. It's that there's a kernel of truth in what she said there at the end about Sam, about just running away from a life they set up for me to a life Sam sets up for me. I still want to go to Oxford, but the city I've imagined has a black cloud over it now.

How can I become a person who writes their own life story?

ONCE UPON A MIDNIGHT DREARY, I wander back to Gertrude's to lend Eva my key so she can close later, since she left hers at home. Weary, freezing from the January bike ride, I'm shocked to see how busy Gertrude's is. Yes, it's Figure Drawing Friday, and yes, there is a naked woman inside. That must be the explanation? I lock up my bike, go inside, and slip behind the counter. Eva's sweating as she makes a cocktail.

"It's been like this all night!" she says.

"Wow, you should have called me in."

"I wanted you to enjoy your night off."

I pour someone a glass of pinot grigio and scan the crowd. Every table is packed. The demographics are different, skewing much more male than usual. Many more baseball caps. Multiple men in Grizzlies jerseys. A copious amount of beer rather than craft cocktails. A lot more guffawing and loud conversation. Brady's customers—I could spot them from a mile away. I smile. So our Figure

Drawing Friday poached Brady's customers, all because of a female nude model. Well, that was easy. I should have thought of this months ago.

After attending the bar for a few minutes to help Eva, mixing two Sextons and pouring many more pints, I head back outside with a smug expression on my face, ready to go next door to rub it in Chuck's face if he's around. It's hilarious to see all these Brady's customers' loyalty so easily tested. But as I step out the door into the chilly air, I notice Brady's shut doors for the first time, the CLOSED PERMENANTLY sign, butcher paper over the windows.

I gasp, clamping a hand over my mouth.

It wasn't like this yesterday.

For a minute, I am frozen here, a woman made of ice, feet glued to the sidewalk, pedestrians weaving around me. What shocks me more, I'm not sure. Is it the sight of Brady's closing after all? Because I never somehow believed it would happen, considering the power and access the McCaffreys have. Or is it the fact I feel like someone plunged an invisible dagger into my gut, like I'm staring at a loss that's mine too?

Why the hell am I standing on Riviera Avenue gazing upon my supposed enemy's closed business with what feels like a bomb in my chest?

It's going to be such a boost for Gertrude's, my brain whispers as I pedal my bicycle through the streetlamp-lit back streets, past the majestic courthouse surrounded by palm trees, up the hill along the long park with wooden castle-like structures and a duck pond, toward my apartment. It's going to make Gertrude's the only bar within a four-block radius. It's going to mean we don't have to worry about loud music thundering through the walls, or shirtless drunk dudes congregating outside on the sidewalk, or tourists wandering in asking if this is Cory McCaffrey's bar. And maybe Eva will stop pouting every time Brady's gets mentioned. Staff morale boost! Those are all positives. Those are all benefits.

I don't understand this melancholy pit in my stomach, then.

Pedaling faster, uphill, I break a sweat, trying to outpace this ineffable disappointment. I'm inside-out—something's not computing within me. I'm never like this. I can always articulate my feelings with precision. I can speak them aloud in varied turns of phrase, I can offer a list of multisyllabic vocabulary words as descriptors, I can write my feelings in iambic pentameter if need be. But right now, I'm a bundle of nerves, nausea, and a nameless, shapeless ache.

It's only when I reach the corner of Flora and Fauna that I realize I passed my own apartment minutes ago and have arrived on the corner outside of Chuck's apartment. As I make a sudden stop, inertia lurches. Here I am, inexplicably staring up at the faint golden light of Chuck's apartment window.

"Go home, Isadora," I whisper to myself.

But my body remains stubborn and clenched, unwilling to move.

Look at what you've done to me, Chuck. You've split me into two people. You've literally created a schism of a woman. Here I am, trying to get my body to listen to me—to turn around, to go home—and instead, I am disobediently locking my bike to the street sign and then tiptoeing up his stairs. Expecting what? Why? Because I'm a fool. Because Chuck and the whirlwind shitshow of Brady's has turned me into a person who makes no sense.

And now I'm knocking. On his door! At nearly one AM!

Isadora! I scream inside myself.

"Isadora?" Chuck says simultaneously, opening the door, remote in hand. He's in his Sea Lions sweatshirt and Betty's sweet dandelion fluff of a head pokes out of the pocket.

"I think," I say, "I may perhaps be experiencing a mental breakdown."

"Okay," he says slowly. "You want to come inside?"

I nod.

His apartment is warm and the first thing I notice this time is not the shocking cleanliness or the fact his décor is drably well put together, more like an Ikea floor model than a home. It's the cardboard boxes stacked in the corner.

"What's going on?" he asks.

"You're closed," I say, the tears welling, stinging, burning as they become more than a feeling, become a wet, salty river heading for my cheeks. "Brady's is closed."

He watches me with something between suspicion and amusement. "Are those tears of joy?"

"No," I say, wiping my cheeks on my sleeves. "I don't think so. I told you, I'm losing my mind."

"You need a hug?" he asks.

I shake my head, only because I can't trust myself in his arms right now. "I'm okay, thanks."

"So … yeah. Brady's is done," he says. "Judge ordered us closed."

"Just like that, they can shut you down?"

He shrugs. "Dad wanted to keep fighting, but I told him I was out."

"Because you're going to Oxford."

"For now." He rakes a hand through his hair. "I'm so confused right now, I'm sorry—why are you here, exactly?"

"I couldn't believe the sign when I saw it. I had to verify it."

"It's true. Verified. It's got the Chuck McCaffrey stamp of approval." He backs toward his kitchen, where his sliding glass door is open. "You want to sit outside? I was looking at the stars. You want to look at them with me?"

"Sure," I say, and follow him.

His kitchen, like the living room, is simple and devoid of personality. But his balcony is another story. He's transformed this cramped patio space into a secret paradise. Framed with bamboo plants, lit with gold hanging lights, an angel fountain spitting water and a wrought iron bench, this spot immediately sucks the exhalation from my lungs. I sink into the bench and breathe in the scent of jasmine. So many potted plants, hanging, or on shelves, or sitting in corners out here. He sinks into the seat beside me with a yawn. But I continue to stare at him, baffled. Because Chuck McCaffrey has more layers than an onion. It seems every time I think I know who he is, I peel back another layer and there's more there. And of course, right when I realized this, his business gets ruined and he's makes plans to leave the country.

"How are you?" I ask. "God. *You* doing okay?"

"I mean, I feel like a piece of shit failure, but what else is new?" he grins at me, petting Betty, who's still there in his pocket.

"Don't say that."

"Honestly, part of me's relieved. Can I tell you now how much I hated that fucking bar?"

"What?"

"I hated it," he confirms, not even blinking his flame-blue eyes. "I don't even like bars. *Especially* sports bars."

"Well then why—"

"Because my dad." He leans down, fussing with a potted plant, gently tugging off the brown leaves. "That's why. That's why I've done everything I've ever done." He sits back up. "And I'm kind of over it now."

"So you're going to Oxford."

He doesn't answer for a second. "How'd you know?"

"I saw boxes. And you said, last time."

"Just for a bit," he says. "To clear my head."

"Betty coming with you?" I ask, looking down at his giant, gentle freckled hand petting her snowflake of a head.

"Of course."

"You can't just leave like that, Chuck," I say, the words

sticking in my throat. I shake my head—it's not coming out right. That is not what I meant at all. That is not, it at all.

"You can't just run away," I try again.

"Run away from what?" he asks, with a bewildered grin on his face. "And Isadora, with all due respect, why the fuck do you care what I run away from?"

The man has a point. Why do I care? In fact, I ask myself—trying to observe myself in third person instead of first—why am I here? Why did I come here? What is it that binds me to this man in such a way that I felt the need to pedal through the January midnight air to find him when I saw his windows papered over? What is it I want from him? To stay? Why do I feel so entitled to make such demands of a man I hardly know? What is it about him that does this to me, that wrenches my insides and dries my throat out and makes me want to cry and smash my lips upon his all at once? What is this feeling with no word?

I cannot stand the inability to understand myself.

And that's what Chuck brings out in me. A rift. A rift inside me between the woman I thought I was and the woman I maybe am or could be.

"It was like—" I swallow and a shiver snakes up my spine. "It was like we were accidentally in it together. You know? As if some odd twist of fate put Gertrude's right next to Brady's. And yes, you were my nemesis, my rival, but also … you and I were in the same place. We shared something."

"Well, lucky for you we're not in the same place anymore. Because you're open and I'm not."

"I'm sure I'll be next," I say with a heavy sigh. "Business hasn't been great."

"Aww, cheer up. It'll be better with Brady's gone."

I shake my head. "I don't want you to be gone."

He studies me, his hands a tent in front of his mouth. "Are you high right now? You hated my bar. You hated our customers. You hate sports. You hate everything about that bar."

"I don't hate *you*," I say softly.

"You had me fooled."

"I kissed you," I say, sitting up straighter. "*I kissed you.*"

"A momentary lapse of sanity, clearly. Because when I tried to bring it up again, you shot me down," he says, a flicker of hurt in his eyes.

"I'm sorry I did that," I say, reaching out and putting my hand on his, his warmth traveling from my fingertips up to my lips within a single second.

"Isadora, don't do this." He pulls his hand away, puts it back in his pocket with Betty. "You know what I think? I think you only like me when there are obstacles in the way. And when those obstacles are removed, you have no fucking interest in me."

"That's cold," I say, blinking to stop the sting in my eyes.

"How have you shown me otherwise?" he asks. "Come on. You kissed me one night when the lights were out and other than that, you've given me nothing. You've never even said one nice thing about me to my face."

"I've said lots of nice things."

"Name one."

"You give good hugs!" I almost shout, with the fervor of a game show contestant. Okay, Isadora. Dial it back. "And you're actually adept at running a bar. Sometimes."

"'Sometimes,'" he scoffs.

"You're effortlessly, maddeningly attractive," I go on. "Annoyingly so."

"See, this isn't sounding like a compliment."

I survey the different plants in pots, little lives he's kept thriving back here in secret. What will happen to them when he flies to the other side of the world?

"My favorite thing about you," I say, "is your constant ability to surprise me."

He snickers.

"I mean it," I say. "I never see what's coming with you."

Without moving any other muscle in his body, he, at an excruciatingly slow-motion pace, keeps his eyes steady on me, but moves his hand to the back of my skull and runs his fingers through my hair, gently pulling it in a way that thrills me, that piques every nerve upon my skin.

"Have I told you I how much I love your hair?" he asks.

"No," I whisper.

Chuck uses his hand to pull my head toward his and though I expect a kiss, and my lips are parted and primed and ready for it, instead he puts his forehead to mine.

"I have wanted you so bad," he says. "Or badly. Shit. Which is it?"

"Badly," I whisper.

"But it makes no sense," he says. "Do you see that? This makes no sense."

"I agree completely."

"Finally, we agree on something."

"Just kiss me."

"And now we agree on something else."

His lips land on mine, soft, magnetic, everything; I can feel his entire being pulling mine, from our mouths to his fingers through my hair to my fingers in his hair and the sweet hot taste of him oh my God what is happening, suddenly I'm straddling him again on this bench, me on my knees on the seat over him, my skin absolutely screaming for him, me feeling the shape of him underneath me, it's like I can't get close enough to him, the more we push together, the more I want him, fuck it, fuck everything, I would—

"Shit!" he says, pushing me away. "Betty!"

I lose balance and fall backward on the patio, my ass and lower back immediately in pain from the impact. As I lay here groaning and gaping at the stars, the last of the tingly, amatory, spontaneous moment evaporating into the thin winter air, I admonish myself internally. What did you expect, Isadora, pouncing on Chuck like a cheetah in heat? Now here you are on the ground with a possibly fractured coccyx.

"You okay?" he asks.

"I think so. My butt hurts." I sit up and do a sitting cat-cow. "Yeah, I think I'll be all right. How's Betty?"

"She's okay," he says, holding out a hand. "Sorry I reacted that way. I was afraid she'd get crushed."

"No, I get it. I'm sorry."

He lends a hand down to me, but I get up myself. I'm almost grateful for the physical pain to outshine the embarrassment I feel right now. Chuck and I have kissed twice now, and it was all my doing. I can't even blame him for it. I follow him inside, where the light seems almost painfully bright.

"I'm so sorry I made you fall like that," he says, pulling my sleeve.

"No, totally fine." I smile at him. "I should go."

He's still pulling my sleeve. "Okay."

When he lets go, it's like I'm falling for a split second.

Reluctantly, wishing he would have made me stay and realizing how ludicrous and disgusting that is, I head to the door. As I step through his living room, I'm internally arrested once more by the sight of the cardboard boxes. By the realization that this isn't some beginning—this is the end of me and Chuck. This is when the fork in the road goes the other way.

"When are you going?" I ask.

"Ticket's for January 31," he says. "I'm subletting starting February 1."

"Wow," I say. "So a week."

"It wouldn't work," he says quickly. "Right, Isadora? It wouldn't work with us."

"It wouldn't," I agree, though I don't know if I do

anymore. I bite a nail and then stop myself, because I haven't bitten my nails since eighth grade. "Unless…"

"Unless what?" he asks.

Here, in the pale living room light, I lose myself a moment in his freckles. I could stare at them for hours and never memorize them.

"Unless you stayed," I say in a quiet voice. "Stayed and, I don't know, found a new purpose. Coached pee-wee football maybe and found some new things to pursue for you, for just you and … were with me."

I don't understand myself. I don't understand how I don't understand myself. Why am I saying these things? But worse, who is Chuck McCaffrey to hear these things come from my mouth and say, "I'm sorry, I just … I can't say I see that right now."

My eyes fill with tears. An invisible boot has kicked me in the chest. This is like every teenage rejection balled together and multiplied. I have practically groveled for this man—a man I detested, who was my enemy, who was my rival—opened my heart to him, said *here's a fork, bon appetit*—and I don't even have a good reason why. And he's telling me no. I have laid myself bare for a man all wrong for me and who, worse, doesn't even want me.

"Hurt" is not strong enough a word.

"I hope you surprise me," I say, eyes blurring, and open the door.

My cheeks welcome the cool night. Welcome the chill of the air and the way it freezes the tears to my cheeks, freezes and dries them so when I get home, I can lock my bike up, head up the stairs into my dark apartment, and pretend they never happened.

And pretend I never met him.

Because that's what I have to do: erase him. Edit him out like a storyline that didn't work, an unnecessary character who didn't fill my life's plot. In a matter of weeks, he will be in another country. In a matter of months, a new business will spring up next door where Brady's used to be.

Such sweet sorrow. Farewell, Chuck.

A week goes by. Each afternoon, the sight of Brady's covered windows and the chain securing its front doors shocks me a little less. But replaying in my mind in an infinite loop is the last scene at his apartment, me begging him to stay like a fool, me kissing him on his balcony and landing on my ass. The sheer humiliation repeats each time I go over it, my cheeks blazing at the horrible memory.

"It's okay," Zofie says to me. "Babe, you've got to let it go."

She's caught me standing in the doorway of my office in consternation. I came back here to put my sweater away and found myself gazing at the spot on the floor where Chuck and I spent over an hour in the dark together, when I first felt that unstoppable force that's so turned me upside down. I hate that even in here, my own damn bar, he's ruined the place with memories. Out there, Callista is setting up for open mic night and guess what? He's ruined that too because now I'm remembering the man from Nantucket incident with *fondness*. Chuckling a little bit at his endearing idiocy. What has happened to me?!

"Wow, you have it so much worse than I thought," Zofie the Clairvoyant says, coming up behind me and giving me a hug, resting her head on my back.

"I know. It all really snuck up on me." I toss my sweater on my desk and turn around. "He's leaving this weekend. He might already be gone."

"You could call him, you know," she says.

Zofie drove here straight from an audition for a true crime show about an unsolved murder that happened in the 1980s, so she's got hair sprayed high as a drag queen and formidable shoulder pads.

"I practically groveled," I say. "It was up to him. If he'd wanted to see me, he knows where I am." I lean against the wall outside my office. "I threw myself at a guy who wasn't even worth it. I must have worse self-esteem than I thought."

"Pffft. Want to talk about dating lows?" Zofie asks. "Listen to this: I went out with a guy I met on an app last night. I show up to this *crazy* expensive place and meet this pouty goth guy who looks like he crawled straight out of a Tim Burton movie. He says his name is—I am not joking—'Bowie Zanzibar.'"

Zofie's story is improving my mood, I will admit. "Go on."

"Okay, so there I am, trying to be polite. I ask him if he's an actor and if that's a stage name. The guy asks me if

I've been locked in a basement for the last ten years. I'm like ... *what*?"

"Yeah, what?"

"And he looks me in the eyes and says, 'You're messing with me. You're trying to mess with me and I don't play games like that.'"

"What games??"

"Exactly! What? So I say, I honestly don't understand what's the matter, and he says, it's a fake name he uses on first dates so he doesn't have to out himself on the app. Because he's a well-known musician. And I'm like ... um, not well-known to me. He gets up to use the bathroom and never comes back."

"You got ghosted by Bowie Zanzibar," I say, covering my mouth to hide my smile.

"Go ahead, laugh. That's what I get for using a dating app in West Hollywood."

"So who was he?"

"Fuck if I know," Zofie says.

"Thanks, Zof," I say, squeezing her arm. "That did make me feel better."

"I still don't get what you see in the ginger asshole, but he still beats out Bowie Zanzibar."

I sigh. Zofie and I head back out to the bar, which is getting busier as the open mic night crowd rolls in. Callista's performing the mic check, repeating "Asparagus despair! Asparagus despair!" The guy with the self-published autobiography has set up his usual table with printed copies and a jar for donations that always just has his single dollar in it. There's a new guy with curly hair and an accordion. I slip behind the counter and help Eva make some drinks, and right as I'm starting to get into the groove of it, some dudes with backwards baseball caps come in asking if we know anything about Cory McCaffrey's bar closing down and when I tell them no, they say "What a fucking bummer, man. We drove all the way from Fresno." Then they take a look at the menu, exchange a look of mutual disappointment, and leave the bar.

Ugh. And it hits me that Chuck probably *is* gone by now. His place packed up, subletted, Betty in a cat carrier; I can imagine how sweet he probably was with her the whole flight, talking softly to her while she sat on his lap. I can imagine him contemplating clouds out his window and all I can do is hope he at least thought of me for a minute and felt a pinch of regret. To really drive matters home, a woman in a shirt covered with middle fingers goes up onstage and shouts a bitter confessional called "To the Man Who Chewed Up My Already Mangled Heart and Then Spit It Out Like the Rancid Meat It Is." It says a lot about my mood that I find myself snapping my fingers with the audience for that one.

This is what I do, it seems: go for strange choices in men and women, and then, when they leave or it doesn't work out, it's almost predictable. *Of course* the obnoxious philosophy major and I weren't meant to be. *Obviously* the instantaneous passion that erupted between Zofie and me couldn't sustain itself. *Clearly* Chuck was the worst choice I'd made in men in a long time, and on top of that, he wanted to move about as far away from me as he physically could. I have some sort of nameless disease when it comes to picking lovers, or maybe a secret desire for self-sabotage, I don't know.

I'm contemplating whether I might need therapy when Eva comes up behind me and says, "Look out, boss! You think he came back to ruin another open mic night?"

Onstage, the philosophical rapper is rhyming "freaky" with "Nietzsche" and "Hegel" with "bagel." My heart forgets how to beat as I turn and see, close to the entrance, Chuck standing and chatting with Callista. No—can't be. Impossible. But after a half a minute of gawking, I accept it *is* him. It's his Sea Lions sweatshirt he always wears, his Converse shoes.

Why is Chuck here?

Did he not leave quite yet?

Is he here to say goodbye?

My heart remembers how to beat again, but now goes into overdrive.

I try to catch his eye but he slips into a seat at a table with his back to me as if he never saw me. Suddenly, I grow angry staring at the hood of his sweatshirt. How dare he not call me and then come back here like this, to my bar, with no explanation. Maybe Eva's right—maybe he came to humiliate me one last time, to get the final word in on our feud. As I consider this, sending invisible fireballs to the back of his head with my eyes—he didn't even buy a drink!—Callista comes up and says, "Hey eloquent denizens, next up we have Chuck who you might remember as the man from Nantucket guy."

A swell of boos erupts in the room, which raises my soul up like a boat on the water. They hate him. Whatever it is he's trying to come in here and pull, this whole room has got my back. I cross my arms and give a sideways glance to Eva, whose pose is identical to mine as we both watch Chuck jump up on stage and take the mic from Callista.

"Yeah, I wanted to apologize about that," Chuck says. "That was tasteless of me."

Boos erupt again, but they're weaker this time. Folks are listening. Chuck tries to adjust the mic stand to his height but can't so he takes the mic out of it and holds it like a lounge singer, muttering, "Christ on a mic stand." Then he scans the room and rests his eyes on me and grins.

I stand, my entire body clenched, not knowing what he's going to do.

"I wrote a poem," he says, "for real this time." And at the sound of those eight words, I soften, I melt, and it's just him and me and the whole room around us disappears.

A poem. Chuck wrote a poem. I can hardly breathe, can't look away, can't move a muscle as he speaks.

> *I won't compare you to a summer's day —*
> *you're more like autumn, fire-colored,*
> *with the star-stung depth of cool nights*
> *and surprisingly warm afternoons.*
> *I won't say your eyes are nothing like the sun,*
> *because they are, and so much more —*
> *the sun, the earth, the ocean are all there*
> *in the mixed-up color of your stare.*
> *I'm no bard. But you make me want to pretend*
> *To be one, so I can light you up.*

I'm just the idiot next door
Who's not so great with metaphors.
But I'm not the man I was before
I met you, Isadora.

My hands settle on my cheeks as the room swells with applause. I'm burning with a gleeful embarrassment to unexpectedly be the center of attention as people who know me turn to watch me from the audience, including Zofie, whose hand is on her heart and whose eyes are shining. I cover my face with my hands. And I'm sobbing. I'm gutted and shocked he's here, that he found a way to surprise me yet again before he leaves. I don't ever want to take my hands off my face. I want to stay here in the dark, wet warmth of my palms so I never have to say goodbye to him.

Eventually, though, fingers encircle my wrists and gently pull my hands away.

"Hey," Chuck says. "Can we talk a minute?"

And even though I don't, I don't want to, I don't want this ending, I nod and take his hand. Onstage, Callista is saying, in a flat voice, "Well, I'm asexual, but I believe most people would call that romantic."

I pull Chuck through the crowd and walk him to my back office, where I shut the door behind me.

"I made you cry," he says, much too cheerfully. "My poem made you cry."

"Don't flatter yourself. I think I got salt in my eye from a Hemingway," I say.

"*You liked my poem,*" he says in a singsongy voice.

And I want to banter with him, want to volley a playful insult back at him, but there's no time for that. Instead, I put my arms around his neck and my cheek on his shoulder and I hold him tight. He wraps his arms around me and squeezes back, running a hand through the back of my hair. I get a rush from head to toes back to head again and beg this moment not to end.

"I loved it, Chuck," I say. "It was probably the sweetest thing anyone has ever done for me in my entire life. God, I hate you."

He relaxes his embrace to pull back and study me inquisitively. "Come again?"

"I hate you," I say weakly, pushing him away and taking a moment to wipe underneath my eyes, where I'm sure my mascara has run rampant. "I like you so much I hate you."

"For a person who claims to be a poet, you have an odd way of describing things sometimes."

"I don't want last-minute romantic gestures or grand goodbyes. I want you to just *go* already so I can get over you."

"That's what you want?"

"Yes."

"So ..." His unblinking, azure stare severs me. And those obnoxiously long eyelashes. "I canceled my trip for nothing?"

Those six words aren't anything special, if you break them apart: a pronoun, verb, possessive adjective, noun, preposition, and another common noun. Just an ordinary, unpoetic sentence spoken in the English language. But at the sound of those words, I swell like a symphony. I stand stunned a moment in disbelief, thinking he must be screwing with me. This is Chuck's last sadistic prank.

"You canceled your trip," I repeat.

He steps forward and puts his hand under my chin. "Sold my ticket. Backed out of the sublet deal. Oxford isn't going anywhere. I couldn't leave without finding out what kind of a story you and I have together." He strokes my skin. "If I had to, I'd swim across the ocean and hitchhike all the way back to the west coast for just one chance with you."

Lord. Did he really say that?

I might swoon.

Our lips don't merely meet—they meet again. The reunite with a new, sacred mutual knowing, because now I remember the taste of him, I know this familiar pull of his body to mine, I know this is not just a meeting of mouths but a beginning, ripe with potential, hot with promise, his hands in my hair and then traveling, slowly, up my arms, then down my back, exploring all my unmapped nerves.

"You stayed for me," I say out loud, to make sure it's true.

"For you," he confirms.

And I'm jelly.

Gently, one being now, we slide onto the chair. I straddle him as he slowly unzips the back of my dress and touches each vertebrae on my spine with a fingertip, one by one, beginning on my neck and ending on my tailbone. Goosebumps prickle my skin, all over, all the way over, in places I didn't even know goosebumps were possible. I pull his sweatshirt and shirt off, throw them in a corner. My palm rests on his chest. I trace the constellations of freckles there, over the muscles on his stomach, and bury my mouth in his neck, releasing a shiver in him.

He unhooks my bra and guides my dress down my shoulders. When I pull them both all the way off, he inhales sharply, beholding my naked body for the first time.

"Good Lord, Isadora," he says, his hand running up my curves. "How can anyone be this perfect?"

He kisses my throat as he runs his fingers through the back in my hair. His kisses travel down, to my clavicle, to my breasts, his tongue exploring every inch at an agonizingly patient pace.

I fight the urge to scream as desire pulsates through me. It's as if the closer the two of us get, the more our skin connects, the more excruciating it becomes. I am high with the want right now, my body feeling like it's going to burst.

"Do you want this?" I ask.

"You really need to ask me?"

"In my office? Is this wrong?"

"Doesn't your door have a lock?"

"You think I'd be doing this if the door wasn't locked?"

"Can we stop asking so many questions, then?"

We don't say another word, leaving communication now to the undoing of buttons and unzipping of zippers and tearing of wrappers. And *wow*. I'll just say, once his pants and boxers go down, I'm in for yet another very pleasant—very *big*—surprise. I mount him and descend slowly, slowly, drawing this moment out so long we shiver in unison. We try to be as quiet as we can, moaning into each other's mouths as I take him all the way in.

"You fit me perfectly," he whispers.

I might explode. He's touching me as I rock on him, touching me like he knows me, like our bodies aren't strangers.

"What have you *done* to me?" I say.

"I was about to ask you the same thing."

He thrusts in a gentle rhythm, closing his eyes in ecstasy. "How have I ever lived without this?"

We pick up speed, a sizzling, wet momentum, and I dig my nails into his back as it builds, as if I need to hang onto him or I might fly away from the rapture of it. He pulls my hair in response, not too hard, just enough, and I cry out, loving it. We're picking up speed now and I ask him if he's close.

"I've been close since the second we started," he says breathlessly.

It's one thing, one thing—the physical euphoria we're nearing together. I can hardly hold it back any longer.

"Take me there," I murmur in his ear.

"I'll take you anywhere you want, Isadora."

"Now."

"You got it."

In these urgent final moments, we soar. We ascend. I can't stop it from happening. Our bodies have a language all their own until finally, we both quake in perfect time, pulsing, moaning, holding onto one another as tightly as we can and then slowing to a stop. It's over. I hold him here, both of us panting, and then pull my head back to gaze at him.

"Well, shit," he says.

"That's all you have to say?"

"*You're* the poet."

"I know," I say, laying my head on his shoulder. A world awaits us out that door. This is ridiculous, what we've done in this room. And yet I want to pause this moment I can't comprehend. I feel more myself in this uncharacteristic moment than I have ever felt before. What does that say?

"But right now," I admit for the first time in my life, "I'm speechless."

chuck

WELL, *that* was unexpected.

Obviously I hoped she'd like the poem. Took me hours and a lot of help from Thesaurus.com and the online archive of Shakespeare's sonnets to write, so I hoped she'd respond positively. But I never even bothered to hope that we would get to know each other in the biblical sense in her office. Not that I'm complaining. Her soft, olive skin, the magnetic pull of her kiss, her maddening coconut scent … I'll be replaying it for months to come. But it was a bit of a sexy little whirlwind. I'm shaken off my course a bit. I've got pudding legs.

Isadora's zipping up the back of her dress and as I pull my shirt back on, I'm still buzzing with her, dizzy from what just happened. She fixes her hair with half a smile.

"Um," she says. "Hi."

"Hey." I pull my sweatshirt on. "Does this mean you're my girlfriend now?"

"What are you, in junior high?" She shoots me that

good old *you're an idiot* look, which I am learning doesn't go away once she actually likes me. "Sure. Fine."

"Wow, don't get too excited. Calm down now."

"I would love nothing more," she says, mock dramatically, "than to be your girlfriend."

"Okay, that's more like it."

I grin and she plants a kiss on my cheek. We exchange a look, the wild shudder in her eyes matching the one in my chest. I squeeze her hand, hoping that says what my lips are too kiss-stung and tired to say. That I adore her. That this isn't some joke. I've never canceled a non-refundable ticket, never revoked a lease agreement for someone. I'd be lying if I didn't say there was a slithering sense of fear beneath the passion.

Then someone starts pounding on the door.

"Um, hope I'm not interrupting anything," says Zofie loudly.

"Shit," Isadora murmurs, pulling out a mirror from her handbag to check her already perfect face. "We were … talking. What is it, Zof?"

I open the door. Zofie's there, arms akimbo. "Talking, huh?"

"Hello," I say.

Zofie's eyes float to the condom wrapper on the floor, which I do a waltz-like step to gracefully cover with my checkered Van.

"Classy, McCaffrey. *Reeeeeal* classy," Zofie says, and then shifts her attention back to me as if she has no time for the nonsense under the sole of my shoe (phew). "Listen, we've got a situation," she tells Isadora. "Eva stormed out of here after Chuck's Romeo performance. I can't find her anywhere and I'm out there bartending solo. Little help?"

"Oh no," Isadora says. "She's probably blowing off steam."

"Um, babe, I don't think she's coming back," Zofie says, with a grimacing smile. "She took all the money in the drawer with her."

"What?" Isadora and I say in unison.

"Yeah and … the safe's open and looks empty, too."

"Shit," I say, at the same time that Isadora says, "No shit."

Isadora and I follow Zofie out to the hallway, who turns around to shout-whisper, "I can't believe you two boned in your office."

"Shhhhzzzofie," Isadora says. Her cheeks are flushed redder than I've ever seen them. I'm not normally easily embarrassed but I'm sure mine are too.

Back in the main room, a woman is onstage reading a story about, I kid you not, a vision of Jesus she saw in her quesadilla. Christ on a tortilla. I'm not sure if it's supposed to be funny or not, and the audience seems to agree. A few stifled awkward laughs, a couple forced fake ones. Moving through the crowd toward the bar, I follow Zofie and Isadora as they slip behind the counter. They debate and hunt around for the drawer that disappeared, and then I disappear, too. Into my own head. I take a seat on a barstool. While, in the background, the words *with eyes of dusted flour and a beard of melted cheese/ I met my Lord and savior in a Chili's* drone on.

Everything that happened in the office right now becomes real. This spontaneous decision I made yesterday to cancel the lease and the ticket because I couldn't think of anything except Isadora. I had to know what would happen if I stayed. And that poem I spent so much time on, it seemed like such a gamble, impossible I could win her over with it. But I did. And then we banged in her office. And now in under an hour it's over, and we're, what, together? With the snap of some fingers?

Unreal. Something's not right.

This isn't how I pictured it. I didn't think it would be this easy. I certainly didn't think that our first time would be an explosion of horniness in her closet-sized office while shitty poets performed an open mic night in the other room. As reality sinks in, it also just sinks. I threw Oxford out the window for this, disappointing Sam, forfeiting a deposit on the Airbnb, screwing over the tenant who was supposed to sublet my apartment. And now what? Now Isadora and I are going to be together? I can't see the next step. Can't see how I fit into this scene right now at Gertrude's. Can't see where this goes from here. Who Isadora and I are if we're in love and not enemies.

What if I made a huge mistake?

"Hey," I say, leaning over the bar, where Isadora is anxiously eyeing her phone. "You calling Eva?"

"I did, twice. Nothing."

"I know where she lives," I say.

Isadora raises one perfect eyebrow. I love that move of hers. But no time for that. Focus.

"You want me to go see if I can find her?" I ask.

"Would you?" she asks. "Zofie needs to run and get some change so I can keep tending bar. If you don't find Eva, I'll call the police."

"How much did she get away with?" I ask.

Isadora comes over to me. That flushed color from a few minutes ago? Washed out completely. She's pale as a statue. "At least twenty thousand. I hadn't made a deposit in weeks."

"You're joking."

"I wish."

I am stunned. "You don't … make nightly deposits?"

"I usually do it weekly. But I skipped last week."

"Isadora," I say lowly. "You need to do it *every night*."

"I had a safe," she says, her eyes watering.

"A safe is not the bank." My shock has a gravity to it, making it hard to stop my jaw from dropping. "Even at shady-ass Brady's, we knew that."

"Well, for all your business smarts, look where you are now," Isadora snaps.

Ouch. She clamps a hand over her mouth and shuts her watering eyes. Then she opens them again, wipes them with her fingertips, and reaches out for my hands. She squeezes. "I'm sorry. That was callous."

"Not untrue, though."

"No, but rude. It's just—if I can't find that money Eva took, I'm going to end up out of business too."

Her hand is delicate, a wiry ring with a star in it on her right pinky finger. There seems to be so much of her that is still mysterious, so much left to explore. My heart pounds at the thought, at how much I've risked and derailed everything just to know. At how scary badly I want to know.

"I'll find her," I say, standing up.

"Thanks, Chuck," she says.

She's still holding on to my hands. Her eyes shine. A couple at the end of the bar is waiting to make an order.

"You should get back to making drinks," I say.

"I know, but …" She swallows. "In spite of this mess, I'm—I'm happy you're here. I hope you're happy too. To have stayed."

"Of course I'm happy," I say. "*Obviously* I'm happy."

The way I say *obviously* though seems to give it away. Make it obvious, so to speak.

"I'll find her," I say, backing away from the bar. "Be back soon."

Out of Gertrude's, the night air fills my lungs. I catch my breath as if I'm finally slowing down after running a marathon. When I hold my palm up in the air, it's shaking. I shove it in my hoodie pocket and head down Riviera. My car's in the opposite direction; I know I should be getting into it and driving toward Eva's place. But I need a few minutes to get my head together.

In January, the tourists have cleared out of Santa Caterina. The fog clings to the streets in the mornings and evenings, the restaurants have empty patios. People say California has no seasons, but we do—they're just subtle is all. I like winters when the city gets quieter and the beaches empty. I walk a few blocks, the brisk night air waking me up, and at the end of Riviera, make my way across the crosswalk toward the tumbling waves. The moon lights up the sand and I'm the only person around.

I plop in the sand and start a staring contest with the ocean. The moonlight dances on the black water, the waves spray and recede. Up above my head, a mess of stars. I feel so small. Smaller than I've ever felt before. Tonight I took a bold step in a new direction and frankly, I'm terrified in a way that evokes some déjà vu. This sick-excited, can't-see-ahead-of-me feeling is one I've experienced only twice before in my life.

The first time I felt this way, as if I had crossed a threshold into a new world, was when I first told my parents I was following doctor's orders and quitting football. I forged that decision alone. Mom and Dad spent days haranguing me, saying I was making a mistake, that I would ruin my future. Hearing that over and over again worried me. I questioned if they were right and I was wrong. But there was something inside me—a compass, pointing to the right direction—that I followed. For once, I stuck to my guns and didn't cave to my parents. And you know what? My instincts were right. I never regretted that decision. As meandering as my life has been since then, I've never stopped and wished I'd played college football. It wasn't for me. I knew that.

The second time I felt that way was when I first met Sam. Yeah, she and I were different in so many ways. She taught herself foreign languages in her spare time, preferred the symphony to rock concerts. She thought soccer was far superior to football. She was clever and driven, curious about everything around her. She was nothing like any girl I had dated before. But immediately when she plopped down next to me in that English prerequisite class and laughed at my dumb joke about Gatsby's car being "a real hit with the ladies," I knew she was it. The fact we had little in common on paper, the fact I couldn't imagine us together at first, didn't matter. My compass was right to point straight at her. Sam was the best relationship I ever had, someone who stretched me, who made me reach to be a more curious person, a better man.

I trace the name *Isadora* in the sand. Look up at the sky and make up some constellations: Picasso's banjo, intergalactic banana. And all at once I get this flash of the future, imagining Isadora here next to me, her head on my shoulder. Imagining that this is just the first page of the first chapter of our story, and that there's so much more to come. That I have a place here with her. That there are things I can offer her—some business help, for one. Christ, I can't believe she doesn't even make nightly deposits. And now that her one employee has run off with twenty thousand dollars … I could fill in. Bartend with her. Help her figure out how to save the place, blow off the cobwebs, bring it a little twenty-first century flair. And then suddenly it's been fifteen, twenty minutes of me sitting here in the shivering cold against the backdrop of rolling, raging waves, and I realize that I'm dreaming up a future with Isadora. I'm not a man with a broken imagination. I know just what it will look like to be with her, to reach out and wrap my arms around her whenever I want. To keep finding ways to surprise her and light her face up in the way I lit it up tonight with the poem. To help her. To support her and her big dreams and her hard work. I want to be that person and I am that person.

So why the fuck am I shivering here alone on the beach at almost midnight?

I get up, recharged. Give the ocean one last long look. Then I turn around and power walk up Riviera, back to my car, so I can go find Eva and get that money back.

I haven't been to Eva's since the Great Tofu Disaster, but I can remember exactly where it is. After parking in front of the Spanish-style mansion, I use my phone as a flashlight and head up the long set of steps, tripping a set of automatic flood lights, and almost stumble when a male voice yells, "You! What are you doing in my yard?"

"Hey," I say, hands in the air, squinting around me to locate the voice. Up in the window, I see the dim shape of an older man. "Mr. Harrow?"

"Who the hell are you?"

"Eva's friend—son of Cory McCaffrey?"

"The politician?"

"Former quarterback. For the Grizzlies."

"Didn't they play the Superbowl last year?"

"Three years ago," I say.

Déjà vu, man.

"I'm looking for Eva," I shout.

"You can try her up there. But I saw her a few minutes ago and she said she was leaving town to visit a friend."

"Did she."

"Seemed in a rush. Some kind of family emergency."

"I'll bet," I say between my teeth.

But we're interrupted by the sound of a door slamming shut. At the top of the stairs, Eva is carrying a large suitcase in one hand and a mannequin under her other arm. Seeing me, she stops short and freezes.

"There she is," I say. "Thanks, Mr. Harrow."

Mr. Harrow slams the window shut.

"Where do you think you're going?" I ask.

Eva's clearly feeling cornered. She cautiously steps down the stairs, arms full, and flashes me a weak smile.

"Oh hi, Chuck," she says. "That was a real nice poem you read earlier."

"Cut the crap," I say as she nears me. "You need to return that money right now."

"Money?"

"Don't do that."

Eva stops in front of me. Her pink hair's a mess, her face is red and sweaty. She's clearly been hustling to get out of here. "Listen, I … I'm in some trouble. It's complicated. Family emergency."

"More like grand theft."

"No, it's not like that, I swear." Her eyes quiver from behind her glasses. "Please, you've got to trust me."

"Actually, I don't. That's Isadora's money. You're going to put her out of business."

"So cute you care about that, considering what she did to Brady's."

"That wasn't her. That was my own dumbass fault."

Eva huffs and pushes past me, making her way down the stairs.

"Eva," I call, following her. "You're going to ruin your life."

"I don't care," she calls over her shoulder. "I'm like a cat, Chuck. I'll destroy this life and then I'll just start another."

At the bottom of the stairs, Eva hurries across the street to a blue van and opens the driver's car door with the window rolled down, gets in, heaves her suitcase and mannequin in the passenger seat. I watch her in disbelief, get my phone out.

"I'm calling the cops," I say.

Eva waves a hand as she puts her seatbelt on. "Go ahead."

Plugging her keys in, she revs the engine. She takes her glasses off, throws them behind her, and turns to look at me. Her voice drops in pitch and she sounds completely different. "You know, at first I pegged you as being pretty stupid. A real easy chunk of change. But I have to say, you've surprised me, Chuck. You're a genius parading as a fool. Whereas Isadora? She's a fool parading as a genius. You're perfect for each other."

And with that, Eva burns rubber and zooms away on the street. I push 9-1-1 and run after the car in a puff of nasty smoke, and when it clears, I realize not only is she too far away for me to make out her license plate—she doesn't even have one. When I talk to the dispatcher I can't even tell them what make or model her van was.

Dispatcher tells me they'll send an officer out to Gertrude's right away to take a report.

Back in my car, I revisit the interaction with Eva. The way her voice changed at the end, how she tossed her glasses over her shoulder like she didn't even need them. The dig at both Isadora and me there at the end. She isn't who we thought she was and it's possible we might not ever find her or recover the money she stole. And that would be awful. What if Isadora *does* go out of business? Twenty thousand dollars is a lot of money to lose. I know she's struggling. God, what a depressing ending that would be here—for both Brady's and Gertrude's to fold.

I can't let that happen.

As I drive back to Gertrude's, I come up with a plan. I think it's a good one. Risky emotionally? Maybe. But solid financially. It'll pay off in the end. And it'll save Gertrude's for the time being. Isadora's not going to like it. My dad probably won't either, at first. But he's a man who can't turn down a business opportunity, and that's what I'm going to pitch this as: a business opportunity.

At the bar, open mic night is over and Isadora's talking to a cop as Zofie cleans the place up. I help wipe off tables, stack chairs, wash dishes. When Isadora's done, she slips into the back where I've got my hands in a sink full of suds. She puts her arms around me from behind, lays her head on my back.

"Chuck," she says.

"Isadora," I answer.

"I don't know what I'm going to do if they can't find the money."

I turn, wrap my arms around her. Gaze into her dark eyes full of color. You can see blue in their centers, hints of green, all surrounded by a swirl of amber. She's everything. "We'll figure it out."

We stay there a long time. Longer than I've ever held her before, longer than I've ever seen the hummingbird she is go still. Long enough for the two of us to feel like one being, for our breath to fall into the same rhythm. I could stay like this all night and tomorrow, through next week and next month, through a year and more.

And still, still, it wouldn't be long enough.

Yeah. No question, just an answer.

I love this girl.

PERHAPS GERTRUDE STEIN'S most famous line is "a rose is a rose is a rose," a gorgeous, poetic repetition that swells in the mouth like an undulating wave. And while I love Gertrude Stein's writing—enough to name a bar after her—those are not the lines of hers that tend to stick in my mind. The lines of hers I most vividly and often recall are those she spoke on her deathbed, when she turned to her partner and asked, "What is the question?" and then replied to herself by saying, "If there is no question, then there is no answer."

I like to imagine a life free of questions and answers, a life unconstrained. A life where we splash cream in our coffee and pursue dreams with a blazing heart because there's no reason not to. A life where we run headfirst into the fire of a daring and wild love.

Gertrude was right. There is no answer. No perfect career path nor perfect person. There are no soulmates, and fate is but a dream. What there is instead is serendipity—a poetic juxtaposition of circumstances. If you remain open and attuned to it, you just may find a piece of harmony in the universe there in those magic spaces. And that is exactly where I met Chuck McCaffrey and why I trusted that, despite our differences, we rhymed.

Nine months after we opened Gertrude's and Brady's, six months after Brady's closed, Gertrude's is enjoying its GRAND RE-OPENING as advertised on the banner outside beneath our new sign with a glowing red rose you can spot from blocks away. Tonight we've attracted quite the eclectic crowd. All of Gertrude's diehards are here, from Callista to the guy in the zebra coat and I might have even spotted Guy somewhere sipping a glass of bubbly water. My dad's here from Ohio, seated in a corner reading a book. Which normally would be a social faux pas. But at Gertrude's? We live for it.

Then we have the other side of the social coin—Aislin Gray and Cory McCaffrey and their paparazzi photographer trailing behind them. A gang of men in football jerseys drinking beer up on the balcony, appearing out of place against the backdrop of bookshelves. But since we expanded the place, built the spiral staircase leading up to the second bar and moved the stage upstairs, it leaves room for a bit more division at times. Now we have a full coffee counter downstairs on the opposite end of the room as the original bar. Now we've got nearly twice the seating since we expanded upstairs. It was an investment, and I was uncertain at first, but the coffee business we now get in the early mornings and afternoons has been a game changer. We attracted loyal clientele who work or study in the coffee bar and return for cocktails in the evenings, author events, and open mic nights on Saturdays.

"How are we?" Chuck whispers in my ear, reaching down to weave his fingers in mine.

"I think we're doing rather well," I whisper back. "What do you think?"

"I'd say it's a success."

He bends in to plant a deep kiss on my lips. Doesn't matter how many people surround us or where we are: Chuck knows how to stop time and the earth on his axis when our lips meet.

"Saturn corner you yet?" he asks.

"I spotted her earlier but didn't talk to her."

"She wants to sit down with the two of us and do a profile."

"Oooh, the coveted B1 spot."

"I'll tell her we'll catch up with her later," he says. "We should probably wrap up the schmoozefest and one of us should go relieve poor Zofie."

"I volunteer," I say. "My face needs a break from this fake smile."

"I love your fake smile."

I make crazy eyes at him and shift my smile to a grimace.

"Shit, never mind. Go make some drinks."

We part with a quick squeeze of hands and I watch him travel through the crowd, grinning and clapping people on the back, going in to hug a buff man with long locs. Chuck's so adept at this game. I get exhausted by this kind of attention and bustle, but Chuck thrives on it. It's one of the many ways I've discovered, over the past few months, that our ostensible differences perfectly complement each other.

"Hey," I say as I slip behind the bar counter, where Zofie's garnishing a Faulkner with a sprig of mint. "What do you need?"

"A dirty Sexton, an Angelou, and a glass of house white."

"You got it."

Zofie and I have this special rhythm, the two of us; get us behind a bar and we know exactly how to maneuver around each other, how to hand the other what the other just realized she needed, how to exchange a glance that conveys an entire paragraph. As the two of us pour, stir, shake, splash, dash, garnish, and serve, it's a comfort to have her here. To know that even though she's officially gone, she's never really. She might have landed a gig in some reality show she's been cagey about, but she's still the same old Zof, ready to come back on Saturday nights and play the role of understudy bartender whenever she's available.

"Thanks again for coming," I tell her once the two of us have a lull in orders. I wipe the sweat from my brow and Zofie comes over and wipes underneath my eye.

"Runaway eyeliner," she says, then steps back to show off her outfit. "How do I look?"

"Perfect, as always."

"This turnout's pretty phenomenal," she says, sweeping a hand through the air at the sight of the packed house.

I glance over at a corner where the flash bulb's flickering on Cory McCaffrey's big bald head. "Amazing what happens when you get Cory McCaffrey involved in your business."

"You regretting that at all?" she asks.

"I mean, it was that or go under." I take a sip of water from a glass. "And, I don't know, I'm kind of fond of that guy's son."

"I was skeptical, I admit," she says, slicing a few limes on a cutting board. "But the whole coffeeshop expansion's undeniably brilliant. And you've got some big names doing book signings here this month. That rom-com writer who hit the bestseller list … you know that's going to draw some heads."

"I sure hope so."

"So cute your dad flew out for this."

"Yeah, I think he mainly came to meet Chuck."

"And?"

I glance over to the corner where my dad's been seated all night. Now Chuck is seated next to him, reading the back of my dad's book, nodding as my dad talks to him. Chuck's made such an effort with my dad all night, introducing his parents to him, checking in periodically, bringing him sodas with no ice just like he likes them. "I think he passes the test."

"The ginger gentleman," Zofie says.

"Nice revision there." I lean across the bar to take a

customer's order and shovel some ice in a glass, fill it two-thirds full of margarita mix and the rest full of tequila, salt the rim, slide it across to the customer in exchange for their card. "So when does the job start?" I ask Zofie.

"We start shooting in six weeks," she says, putting away a few pint glasses.

I wipe the countertop off. "And what is it, exactly?"

"I signed an NDA," she says, straightening the menus and napkins along the counter. "So … you're just going to have to wait and see."

"You're really not going to tell me?"

"Okay, no dirty details, but … it's a reality dating show." She puts a finger up to my lips. "Don't laugh."

"I wasn't!"

(I very much was.)

I'm collecting my thoughts, trying to shape them into something inoffensive. Because it is utterly cringeworthy. The idea of Zofie going on one of those brainless reality dating shows where you're put on an island drinking an endless stream of liquor and stumbling around in a bikini, stirring up drama … I am experiencing vicarious embarrassment at the mere thought.

"Listen, I of all people know what a judgmental bitch you can be about trashy reality shows," Zofie says.

"I'm not judging you. It's just a show, just a gig, I get it."

"A stepping stone, you know?"

"Right."

Though I can't think of one successful actor who ever

started on a reality dating show. But I'm rooting for Zofie to be the first.

"You know what? This is exciting," I say. "Zof! You got a part on a show. You're going to be on TV."

She nods, grinning, and I can see the thrill of it beaming in her eyes. "It's one of the big ones. A careermaker."

"This is huge." The shock blooms—this isn't some part as a sitcom extra or a one-liner in a toothpaste commercial. I open the fridge. "Should we be busting out the bubbly right now?"

"Hey, I won't argue," she says, coming behind me and slinging an arm around my back. "I mean, it's your grand re-opening, after all."

I pour us a couple of glasses and Zofie and I toast with an unquivering stare, one that holds so much: a friendship, a long working relationship, a secret summer fling. My inexplicable love for her swells up in my chest.

"This probably means you won't be coming up to bartend on weekends as much," I say as we drink. "I'll miss this."

"I know," she says. "But who knows. We thought I wouldn't before, and look, here I am."

Chuck comes behind the bar and joins us.

"Plus you have this guy now," Zofie says, giving him a sideways glance.

"What are we toasting to?" Chuck asks. "Am I invited to this toast?"

"Of course," I say, pouring him a glass and handing it to him. I'm not sure how to phrase what it is that I want to say. Chuck, of all people, does this to me more than anyone else. I want to toast to this buzzing night of such an unexpected mix of people. To toast to new business opportunities and romantic serendipity. To Zofie and the gleaming potential of this role she's landed. To Chuck and me, to this life we've been bold enough to run headfirst into together like a couple of free spirits cannonballing into the sea.

"To transformation," I say to him. "To surprises."

His kiss holds the power of elimination. In his kiss, there's something transcendent, something that wipes the world around us away and centers me solely in the place our lips meet and the stir it creates in my soul. I cannot be anywhere right now but his kiss. This kiss is all we are. A kiss is a kiss is a kiss.

The best part is, when it ends, when the colorless, boundless feeling of it is done, he's always still standing there with arms around me, those whirlpool eyes and crooked grin. Chuck. My sweet Chuck.

"Hate to kill the moment," he says. "But you might want to take your dad home."

Chuck points to a corner, where my dad is leaning back in his chair amidst the celebration, asleep with his mouth wide open.

"Oh God," I say.

"I'll stay back here," Chuck says, giving me his keys. "Go ahead."

I plant a kiss on his cheek. "Thanks."

Outside, the night's dry and warm, not a sweater or a coat in sight. The sidewalks are thick with tourists, the restaurants packed and open late, a club buzzing with salsa music. I walk with Dad arm-in-arm up to where Chuck's car is parked.

"I like him," Dad says.

"Oh yeah?" I ask.

"Not sure about his parents, but I like him."

"I feel the same. His parents mean well. They're just … a different breed than us."

"You think he's the one?"

"If there's such a thing as 'the one,' then yes, I think Chuck might be it."

Dad and I stand on a streetcorner waiting for the light to change. A double decker filled with inebriated individuals zips by and a chorus of screams rises and fades into the night. I'm afraid my dad's getting frazzled—this is a far, far cry from the sleepy streets of Brockman—but he just gazes at me with pure love and says, "Your mother would be so happy to see that you found a man who's a partner to you the way Chuck is."

I roll my eyes. "Yeah, I know, easy to love that I'm with a son of a millionaire."

"Not the money," he says. "Not what I mean. He's a nurturer. You know?"

I smile. "I do."

"That's what I'm talking about," he says as the light turns green. "Your mother would have loved him."

We cross the street and I exchange a meaningful look with the stars.

～

Betty's growing up to be a wily teen cat these days, and she's taken to nestling herself right between Chuck and me when we sleep at night. She's become our feline alarm clock, waking us up by batting our noses with her soft paw and jumping all over us until we get up. Usually it's adorable. Today though, the morning after the grand re-opening, before the fog's even had a chance to peel away from the windows and hint at a promise of sunlight, is another story. Chuck and I groan in unison. He gets up to feed the cat her wet food and then comes back to get in bed, but I'm already up, slipping my robe on.

"Come on, you," he says, gently tackling me onto the mattress. "You can't get up yet."

I giggle as he rubs his stubble all over my neck.

"I have to pee!" I squeal. "You want me to wet your bed?"

He lets go and stands up. With mock seriousness, there in his boxers and socks, he says, "*Our* bed. I want you to wet *our* bed."

When I come out of the bathroom, Chuck's in the kitchen making our drinks. He's quite the barista, turns out. He's the one who did all the research into the coffee shop business, the buying of the espresso machine, picking the roastery we work with. He hands me a cup and saucer with a cappuccino in it with a heart in the foam. He never ceases to surprise me.

"Pretty heart," I say.

"It was supposed to be a cat," he says.

"Well, valiant effort."

"Story of my life."

He and I go out to the balcony, where Chuck recently replaced the bench with a table and two chairs so we can eat breakfast and lunch out here. The sun is just starting to shine through the fog. Over the tips of the bamboo along the edge, I spy the explosive heads of faraway palm trees. We sit at the table, sip our coffees, and listen to the cheerful twitter of birds. Chuck's put his Sea Lions sweatshirt on and his hood up. His eyes are bright behind those impossibly long lashes.

"I think it was a success," Chuck says. "You?"

"Yeah, it went well. It was a bizarre blending of our worlds." I sip my cappuccino. "But … it seemed to fit, right?"

"Fit just fine," he says, putting a hand on my knee and squeezing.

"You're going to make me spill this gorgeous coffee you made."

He grins. "Sorry."

I put the cup down on the table and reach under the table, find his hand in mine. "I still don't think your parents like me."

"My parents don't like anything in my life they haven't designed themselves." He traces a finger along my wrist. "But I think they do like you. I think they believe in you and your business, or else they wouldn't have invested."

"It still makes me sick to my stomach when I think about how someone else other than me has a share of Gertrude's."

"Look, they don't want in this for long. You and I are

going to turn it around, make a profit, and buy them back out again."

"I know," I say softly. "But if it doesn't work out, then what?"

Chuck watches me a long time, beaming. Sometimes he reminds me of a blue lagoon—that shining, mesmerizing stare, with so much unknown beneath it. He's deeper than I could have imagined. And I've learned there are levels to Chuck's smiles. The one he's giving me now, that tiny one that just barely cracked his lips, is one that means he's feeling joy he's working to contain. There's a straight smile he gives people when he doesn't know them well but wants to make a positive first impression, like the one he has on when my dad's around. There's his wide mischievous grin he has when he gets a wild idea—that grin was one that used to make me want to slap him before we were together.

"I met this really smart woman once," Chuck says. "I mean, *brilliant*. And hot. Smoking hot. Couldn't take my eyes off her for a second."

"And you're telling me this because ..."

"Because this brilliant, gorgeous woman taught me that life's too short to worry about *what if*s." Chuck reaches out and puts a warm palm to my face. "We're going to figure it out. That's what we've done so far, right?"

I kiss his hand.

"We never know what could happen," he goes on. "I mean, for all we know, Eva could show up with the twenty grand—"

"Stop. Give it up. And according to the cops, her name isn't even Eva."

In the week after the investigation, we discovered that the social security number, the driver's license I had on file for Eva were fakes. I was duped.

"All right," he goes on. "Hortense, or whatever her real name is. Hortense will show up—"

"*Hortense*?"

"—and she'll return the money and you can pay my dad back and we'll be all straight." He shrugs with a wide grimace. "Just trying to be optimistic."

"That's not optimism. That's idiocy."

"Awww, I love it when you call me an idiot, honey. Reminds me of old times."

I give him a playful push.

"Hey, know who I saw last night?" Chuck asks. "Tyrus. He's the head coach for the Sea Lions."

"That's sweet he came out."

"His wife Monique's pregnant and he's going to have to take leave later this year … so I'm thinking of going back to help with the team again."

"Really?" I say, sitting up. "That's great."

"Nothing's set in stone yet and I know we're still working out our hiring, so—"

"Do it," I tell him. "Don't worry about the schedule when the time comes. I love this for you."

He smiles and squints, because the sun's suddenly peeked out of the clouds above us. "You don't think it's dumb to show a bunch of tweens how to throw a ball around?"

"Chuck, my parents were educators. I think teaching children anything is about the most noble thing a person can do. You'd be a wonderful teacher if you wanted to."

His mouth is open to respond, but instead he glances past me and points a finger. "Do you see that?"

I turn my head. On the balcony, perched on the head of the angel on the fountain, is a crimson bird with a delicate edging of black around its beak. It twitches its head a moment and I hold a breath.

"I've never seen a bird like that here," Chuck whispers.

"It's a cardinal," I tell him. "I've never seen one on the west coast."

It seems like its beady eyes are on me. And I can't help, of course, but think of my mother—of the fact my dad thinks the cardinal who comes and visits him every morning is the spirit of my mother. That, by all counts of logic, makes zero sense. But how peculiar and divine it is that this bird appeared now, while Chuck and I discuss the future—while I just told him he should teach, and spoke of my parents—how touching it is to have this miraculous coincidence at this moment.

My mother was the first person in the world who told me hope was the thing with feathers.

My hand is on my heart and when the bird flies away, I let out a small cry, because I don't want it to go. While I well up and Chuck asks me what's wrong, I shake my head and sit a moment with the sting. Because life is like this. It makes no sense, and yet it means everything. It hurts. It's beautiful. Sometimes it's so beautiful it hurts.

Chuck doesn't ask me to explain myself, and I love him

for that, because I'm beginning to learn there are many, many times in my life when I don't have the words. Instead, we stand and come together, our arms wrapped around each other, the sun radiating us with its warmth as it burns through the fog, and we don't say anything, just listen to the old brag of our hearts: we are, we are, we are.

a note from the author

If you got this far, I just want to thank you for being here! I can't tell you what it means to have *Make Me a Double* out in the world. After years of trying to get this book traditionally published and being turned down by agents, I decided that I wanted to get Chuck and Isadora's story out there. So I took matters into my own hands and went indie.

Being an indie author isn't easy. This was a ton of work, but I had fun and learned a lot in the process. If you enjoyed the book, please consider leaving a review. I can't stress enough how important reviews are for writers. They make our world go round! And if you're interested in keeping up with book news, please join my newsletter or follow me on social media. And I love to hear from readers anytime at raina@rainajoywilder.com.

As always, I tried my damndest to fix every typo, but I'm only human. If you spot an error, please let me know! I appreciate every reader who makes me look smarter.

about the author

Raina Joy Wilder writes romantic comedies. When she's not writing, you can bet she's either reading, cooking, playing music, or watching trashy yet deeply satisfying reality dating shows. She lives in the Bay Area with her family and can be found at rainajoywilder.com.